A *LESS THAN ZERO* ROCKSTAR ROMANCE

TIMELESS

ENCORE

KAYLENE WINTER

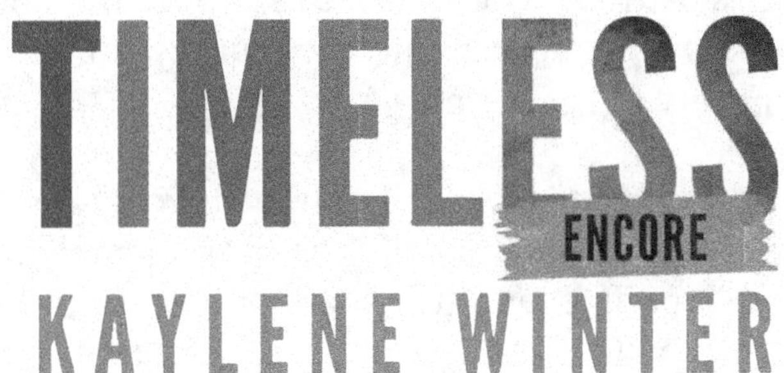

A LESS THAN ZERO ROCKSTAR ROMANCE
TIMELESS
ENCORE
KAYLENE WINTER

Sensitivity Statement

READERS,

THE LESS THAN ZERO series dives into the highs and lows of rockstar life, inspired by the raw and real experiences of many in the music world. Across these stories, some characters face challenging themes, including abuse, sexual assault, mental health, fertility, and struggles with addiction. These topics are not universal to every character but are woven into the journeys of a few, which impact the entirety of the series.

At its heart, though, this series is about love—how it grows, heals, and transforms. Each couple's story ultimately leads to a well-deserved happily ever after, filled with passion, hope, and redemption. The band's journey supporting each other as "band brothers" also is a predominant theme throughout.

Please take a moment to reflect on your comfort with these themes before reading, and know that these stories are told with care and respect, sensitivity readers have vetted each one. Thank you for joining me on this emotional journey through love, life, and music.

With all my love,

Kaylene

Prologue - Here We Go Again

TRYING TO QUIET MY mind is fucking useless.

Nothing works right now. Not music. Not Krav Maga. Not therapy. Not even hot, dirty, fuck-until-my-dick-falls-off marathon sex.

Not that you have much sex anymore, son.

"Twenty minutes to landing, Mr. Rocks." Evvie, the tall, angular flight attendant with unusual golden eyes brushes her fingers across my bicep like feathers. "Would you like a refill? Or, if you're done, I can take your glass."

Christ.

I can't remember what life was like before my group, Less Than Zero, became the most successful band of the past decade. Sadly, I've grown used to being recognized. Coveted. People are not subtle. The "accidental" touches. The breathy laughs. Flirty winks. Suggestive comments. Outright attempts at seduction.

Case in point? When we reached altitude, Evvie set up our catering while yammering on about the "phenomenal" oversized bedroom in the back with "fresh sheets." Jesus, she even twirled a lock of her hair around her finger as she spoke.

As if.

I mean, my daughter, Mia, is right next to me. Thank God she's oblivious—buried in a game on her iPad. The new Miley Cyrus is likely blaring away in her headphones. Still.

Rude. Rude. Rude.

God, it fucking bugs me. Who does she think she is? So fucking inappropriate.

Clearly, Evvie didn't pay attention to my preference sheet. Otherwise, she'd know propositioning me is a guaranteed way to never be in my presence again. It's the one thing I've made abundantly clear to anyone who provides services to me or my band.

When it comes to interacting with me, no one is to ever disrespect—or give the appearance of disrespecting—my wife Fiona.

Fee and I are each other's destiny. Our other halves. She is and has always been the single most important person in my life. Our relationship is precious. Sacred. Our love is so deep, she's embedded in every cell of my body. Last year, we got married for real. It was, hands down, the best day of my entire damn life.

A wonderful, magical ritual where, in addition to all of the usual marital vows, we promised to leave our past mistakes behind us. To forgive, forget, and move on together. When I put the ring on Fee's finger, I felt it cleansed us of nearly three decades of family drama. Free of the shackles of addiction. Separation. Mental abuse. Custody wars. Death.

Free of the Godforsaken love hack that nearly drove us apart forever.

I looked into Fiona's sapphire eyes and knew we were both finally where we belonged. Together. With our daughter, Mia. Forever. Never to be separated again.

It was as true a moment as I've ever had.

Will ever have.

Mia's the reason I don't say something mean or snarky to Evvie. Being touched by strangers will never be normal, but I'm well capable of deftly evading advances of women like her. Or men. Non-gender-conforming people too.

The thing is, I'm not a cruel person. It's not in my nature. There's no reason for me to be an asshole in my daughter's presence. I'll handle the Evvie situation with my travel concierge after the jet lands.

I reach for my glass and set it on her tray, deftly avoiding her wandering fingers. "No, I'm fine. Take it. It's yours."

"Of course." She winks before sauntering off, swaying her hips as she disappears behind the curtain into the service area.

I glance down at Mia, who wears a green Pat's Pub sweatshirt over black leggings. She's oblivious. Absolutely entranced with *Animal Jam*, her latest game obsession. I lean over and kiss the top of her head to get her attention. Her blue eyes blink up at me and she flashes me a gap-toothed grin. I can't believe she lost her first tooth on our short trip to Baltimore. She's growing up so fast.

Needing to snuggle my precious little girl, I tap my knee. She climbs over the seat, nestles into my lap. I wrap my arm around her and she's back to ignoring me in favor of her game. I can't help but chuckle to myself. Kids. They push the envelope when you let them. At least this little girl does—she's as sassy as her mom was at this age.

I don't bother taking the device away. Ordinarily, Fee's fairly strict about limiting Mia's screen time. I can admit it though, a lot of parenting practice has gone out the window. Well, at least since our lives exploded in spectacular fashion a couple of months ago.

Our lives changed in the blink of an eye. Fee and I are trying to pick up the pieces. Neither of us is doing a great job. At least she's focused on reopening her restaurant. I'm flailing. If I thought a year of hiatus nearly killed me, nothing could have prepared me for the night when my band imploded.

Without LTZ, I feel untethered. Useless. The deep sorrow I've held in my heart since Ty's meltdown never quite subsides. It takes every ounce of my inner strength to snap myself out of it, though. Now that Mia's legally my child, it's my honor and duty to be a better father to her than my dad, Carter Pope, was to me.

I'm not going to let her down.

So, when a friend of mine, Hunter Maxwell, a singer-songwriter who got his break on a reality show called February Stars, invited me to play a set at his wife's family pub in Baltimore, I decided to bring Mia. It was a great distraction. I actually forgot about my personal turmoil and had some normal and enlightening moments.

I didn't realize Hunter's in-laws were Sky Mitchell and Teagan Collins of The Universe, a band my dad's band, Limelight, used to open for when they were a baby band. Hunter's wife and manager, Ailis, grew up touring with her parents and her sister. The Collins clan, an incredibly tightknit and welcoming group, made Mia and I feel like family.

While Mia was surrounded by dozens of kids her own age, I jammed with Hunter, Sky, and Teagan and a bunch of other local musicians to celebrate the anniversary of the reopening of the pub, which had been destroyed by a fire. I was blown away by how many shared experiences I had with the Collins family. Particularly with Ailis. Not many people grew up with parents as famous as ours are.

"Will we be home soon, Daddy?" Mia squiggles around in my lap and leans her cheek against my chest. "I miss Mommy."

I take her iPad and set it on the seat beside me and point out the small window. "Well, what do you see?"

Our native city of Seattle is just coming into view. The Space Needle stands proudly against the backdrop of gleaming glass buildings and the Cascade mountain range. Puget Sound sparkles in the sunlight. A ferry chugs from the city over to Bainbridge Island, where

LTZ's drummer Jace lives. It's a beautiful late-summer day.

I've traveled the entire world more than once, and my native Seattle is still the most beautiful city I've ever been to. Mia's little hand is pressed against the glass. She points excitedly. "I see our house."

"Oh yeah? Show me." I peer out. My smart girl spotted our huge West Seattle mansion amongst the trees.

"Mr. Rocks, it's time to buckle up." Evvie reappears and gestures for us to prepare for landing.

Mia climbs back into her own seat. I click her belt and then my own. "We'll be home before you know it, Meems."

God, I wish I felt some sense of joy at returning home. I should be psyched about reuniting with my wife. My heart yearns for Fiona. My Fee. The most beautiful woman who has ever walked the planet. The smartest. The sharpest. The person who knows me better than anyone else.

She's tried her best to help me navigate my personal shitstorm, but Fee's in the middle of her own crisis. After what happened, I don't expect her to drop what she's doing to help me get my head straight. Not when everything is so fucked up.

God dammit. I want to be a better husband. I want to be the perfect man. The kind of guy who can put my own needs aside to help her pick up the pieces.

I'm trying. I am. God, the guilt I have. I'm actually fantasizing about telling the pilot to turn the jet around. So I can bury myself in music and enmesh myself into someone else's family.

You're letting the love of your life down. Just admit it.

I push the thought out of my mind when I hear the landing gear lock in place. I wind my long, unruly hair into a knot at the base of my neck. Pack up Mia's backpack. By the time the plane touches down, I've taken a million cleansing breaths. Focused my mind.

I'm ready. I can do this. I can be a strong, supportive husband and father.

The second the door opens, I'm out of my seat and, with Mia in my arms, I whoosh past Evvie and into the waiting car. The ground crew loads our bags into the trunk. I slide into the backseat and relax against the soft, buttery leather with Mia tucked next to me. Text Fee. She doesn't text back, but that's not unusual when she's cooking.

I focus on my breathing exercises.

Prepare myself.

Not fifteen minutes later, the car drops us off at the house. Fee's car is out front, so she's working from home.

Mia runs ahead and uses her key code to unlock the front door.

By the time I enter the house, Mia's yelling, "Mommy! Mommy! Daddy and me are home. Where are you?"

I shut the door behind me. Something about the air in the house feels strange. All the hairs on my arms stand up. A long-buried but familiar slither of panic works its way through my guts. "Fee?" I call out as I cross the living room into the kitchen.

No answer.

Oddly, I'm comforted by the state of our kitchen, which is in its usual state of organized disaster. Fee's new seasonal recipes, which are in various degrees of preparation, cover all seven countertops and all three islands. Sheet pans, a steak, trays of pastry, ramekins, jars and squeeze bottles filled with sauces, clear containers of garnish.

It smells fucking amazing. Something's in the oven. The stove is also loaded with several pots of simmering yumminess.

I shake my head, grinning. Blow out a sigh of relief. Fee's workspace mirrors her soul. Even though every surface in this giant kitchen is being used, the pans, jars, squeeze bottles and plates are neat and spotlessly clean.

"Fee?" I call out as I flip through mail I found on the edge of the counter. Junk. No answer. I notice the sliding door to the garden is open. Aha!

Mia bounds down the stairs. "I can't find Mommy."

"I think she's out in the garden." In addition to flowers, veggies, and a small orchard, Fee has an impressive greenhouse filled with unusual herbs and other produce native to the northwest. "Let's go check. As you can see, she must be expecting us to test some new dishes for *Gus*."

Mia dashes to the sliding glass door. "Awesome, I'm so hungry."

I follow her out, and the slithery feeling returns. I'm a couple paces behind as she skips toward the greenhouse through rows of sunflowers, which have bloomed early this year.

We're almost there when my heart stops beating. "Mia come back here. Right now," I choke out.

But it's too late.

"Mommy!" she shrieks and shifts into turbocharge. As do I.

Fee is slumped against the door, half-unconscious.

History never repeats itself. It's a motherfucking lie. It's also the motherfucking truth. Carter's ominous words fill my head as I text "Code 2" to Zeke, the head of my personal security.

Because this is motherfucking déjà vu. The one thing that neither Fee nor I would have ever wished for Mia. A repeat of a trauma we both survived but has haunted both of us our entire lives.

You have to do better.

Attempting to remain calm and not scare our daughter, I crouch next to my precious wife. "Zaaanne," she slurs.

"It's okay, baby." I kiss her forehead. "Mia's with me."

Fee's eyes open slightly, but enough for me to see her fear. With a slight nod, I silently reassure her. I know what to do.

"Mia?" I turn to my left and loosely encircle her wrist and look into her eyes. "Can you please help me with something very, very important?"

She nods, her little face pinched with worry. "Is Mommy sick?"

"Yes, Meems. She's sick and I've arranged to take her to the doctor. It's too cold outside for you to wait without your coat. Would you please go in? Olga will make you some hot cocoa. I promise everything is going to be fine. I'll be right there. Okay?" I hope that I'm keeping my shit together for Mia, because alarm bells, sirens, and panic whistles are simultaneously going off in my head.

Mia gazes deep into my soul. Makes her decision. "Okay, Daddy. I'll go inside."

"Thank you, sweetheart." She turns and trots back to the house, allowing me to return my attention to my wife. "Fee, what happened?"

"Zannnie. Passsssed owwwt." Her words are craggy. Drawn out. Her eyes shut. It's definitely not warm out here but sweat beads on her eyebrow and upper lip.

Fuck.

"Baby, I'm taking you to the hospital." I sit next to my wife. Her head slumps against my shoulder. I didn't think things could get any worse, but I guess I was wrong...

Trying not to lose my shit completely, I pull out my phone and tap our nanny Olga's number. "Olga, I have a Code 2. Zeke is on it. Fee is very ill, we're going to the hospital. Mia is on her way to the house." I suck in a breath. "Can you take over for a bit? Fee left some stuff on the stove and in the oven. Oh, and get Meems some hot chocolate, maybe an art project to distract her?"

Olga gives me assurances and we hang up. Thank Christ we have her. As I listen for a siren which should be approaching any second now, I wrap my arms around my wife and force myself to stay positive. At least my fame and money allows a level of privilege most people don't get to experience. None of this will be public.

It rarely is in my family. It's perhaps the one light at the end of the seemingly never-ending tunnel.

I kiss Fee's face over and over. Whisper to her how much I love her. Tell her she's my other half. Assure her that we've been through so much shit and we'll get through this too.

She's limp in my arms. Breathing shallowly. I smooth the magenta hair from her perfect face. Considering our history, to know she's done something so stupid—so out of character—is devastating. Incomprehensible.

Inevitable?

No. It doesn't do any good to think that way. It doesn't matter one way or the other.

I'm not going anywhere.

I'll never leave her. Not in a billion years.

I know she'd never risk leaving Mia. Or me.

All of this is a terrible dream.

I hope I wake up soon.

Chapter One

Nearly Two Years Prior

IT'S KIND OF LIKE being suspended in time when you drown.

Slowly you slip down, sinking farther and farther into a vast, aqua-blue ocean. At first, the sun flitters at the surface, making the sea look like glittery, blue diamonds. It's like heaven. Dreamlike. Floaty. Beautiful.

Once the light begins to dissipate, suddenly your surroundings feel ominous. The water feels heavy, not light. Stifling. Claustrophobic. The sea turns midnight blue.

Then it is so dark you can't even see your hand inches from your face.

That's when survival instinct kicks in. Arms sluice upward. Your legs scissor and kick in attempt to reach the surface. All you want is to find the light again. Just one more time.

All of this happens in a minute, though it feels like hours. Days. Weeks. Years.

But it's too late. Your lungs fill. When you try to breathe, all you do is suck water into your windpipe. You panic. Flail. Gasp. Scream. Fight with everything you have, because if you don't reach the surface ...

I shoot up in bed, clutching my chest. Gulping in air. Tears stream down my face. I can't catch my breath. My heart pounds.

Goddammit.

This sucks so bad. I can't keep having these drowning dreams. They're freaking me the fuck out.

I'm pulled from behind into a full-body hug.

"Your doctor said this would pass in another week or two. Stick with it, Fee. Subconsciously you know I'd never let you drown." He nuzzles my neck with his scruffy face, tickling me a bit.

I lean back against Zane. My best friend. My lover. My everything from the day I was born. "I know you wouldn't. It's just a lot freakier than they said it would be.

If I'd known it was this hard to wean myself off Xanax, I'd never have started taking it in the first place."

"You've been under tremendous amounts of stress with Mia's custody stuff for so long, babe." Zane eases me down so he's spooning me. "It was either that or not sleeping. Now that Corey-fucking-Johnson is firmly in the rearview mirror, you just need a little recoup time and you'll be as good as new. The world is ours for the taking. At-fucking-last."

My entire body relaxes against him. "Yeah, I knew I had to stop when I realized I was taking double my dose. There's no way I'm going down that path. *Obviously.*"

Addiction has taken so much away from my man, there's no way I'd ever do that to him. Not after we've overcome so much to have our happily ever after.

"Obviously." Zane skims his hand under my tank top down my belly. I stiffen...then relax when he continues lower and cups my mound, his finger circling my clit. "How does a nice, relaxing fuck sound right about now? Will that take the edge off? I'll make you come. Put that beautiful smile back on your lips."

I twist around to face him. Grab his cheeks with both my hands and pull him toward me. Hungrily, I mash my lips against his. "I'd rather tie you up and tease you. Then I want you to fuck me so hard you split me in two."

"Hell to the yeah." Zane rolls over to grab a silk scarf from the nightstand and holds it up. *"Blindfold?"*

"Sure." I take it from him and he scoots up the bed and lies back against the headboard.

I reach behind the headboard and flip over the restraints we keep hidden from Mia. Zane watches with amusement when I buckle one wrist and then the other to the bedposts. He looks like a hot, heathen Jesus with the beginnings of a boner.

No, screw the blasphemy. He's a Goddamn Adonis. Long, curly black hair flows past his shoulders. Deep. soulful brown eyes bore into me. Chiseled jaw with a smattering of whiskers. Bare chest with defined abs. Cut hipbones. Lean but muscled legs. Long, thick cock at half-mast against his belly.

Mine.

"Take your shirt off, Fee. Let me see your tits," Zane growls.

I wag my finger at him and flutter the scarf in the air. "You're going to be blindfolded, remember?"

"I admit, I didn't think this through." He purses his lips then grins.

I straddle him and leisurely kiss his entire face. Forehead. Temples. Eyelids. Nose. Cheekbones. Chin. I avoid his lips. For now. When he relaxes against the pillows, I smooth his hair and tie the blindfold around his eyes. "I'm going to make you come so hard."

"God, yeah." He tilts his hips, showing me his cock is fully erect now because it nudges my ass.

I climb off him and rest my cheek against his hard stomach, high enough so that the tip of his shaft reaches my mouth. I stroke his thighs with my fingers and guide them apart so I have access to everything I want to play with. "Whatever you do, don't come. Save it for later. Okay?"

"Mmm-hmmm." He smiles. His dick twitches, which makes me incredibly happy. And horny. I love giving Zane pleasure.

"I'm going to focus on my prize for a while. Just concentrate on everything I do to you." I kiss his belly button.

Zane's reply comes out breathy. Eager. "Yeah. Yeah."

Using the tips of my fingers, I stroke the underside of his cock at a snail's pace from root to tip, using a hint of pressure. Just enough to tease, not tickle. On the eighth or ninth pass, he's lulled into a bit of a trance. Puffing out little "ohhs" and "ahhhs."

Now, I concentrate strictly on his balls. Fondle. Stroke. Cup. Repeat. From my vantage point, I watch in fascination as Zane's cock jerks and bobs, depending on my cadence and force. He grows harder. Like steel. The tip turns dark red. Zane's moaning now. His hips buck like he's trying to find a warm, wet vessel for his cock to fuck.

So I shift back to gentle stroking to bring him back down.

Zane is so blissed out by the time I repeat the sequence several times, I decide it's time to add in the trifecta. This time, after I'm done playing with his balls, I press my fingertips against his gooch and stroke firmly in a circular motion, just the way he likes it. With my other hand, I rim his anus. Dipping the tip in just a bit.

"Ahhhhhh. Holy fucking hell, Fee," Zane moans. His dick strains so hard, it's nearly pointing at the ceiling.

I press my finger in up to the knuckle and press harder against his prostate. "Do. Not. Come." I kiss his belly again.

Zane's moans are desperate now. He chants. "Oh God. Oh God. Oh God." His hips swivel. The tip of his cock weeps. My pussy is soaking.

It's time. It's easily been twenty minutes and I don't want his arms to go numb.

Abruptly I stop what I'm doing, unbuckle the restraints and untie the blindfold. In seconds, Zane grabs my hips and pulls me on top of him. "Take off your top."

"I'm fine." I smile down at him, not wanting to let him know I feel self-conscious, but he pulls it up anyway so I let him strip it off.

He slaps my asscheeks with his hand. "Sit on my face."

"Zane, I'm too heavy. Stop asking me to do that. Let's not waste this mega-boner." I scoot down his body, thinking I'll just impale myself on him.

Instead, he palms my butt and actually lifts me up so my pussy hovers over his lips. "I want to eat you out like this. You have no idea how much I fantasize about it."

His tongue darts out and licks my seam. My knees dig into the mattress and my thighs strain to avoid actually sitting on his face. He nibbles and kisses my clit. Sips my juices and then buries his entire face into me. Savoring. Sucking. Feasting.

His arms support my back, so I can't help but get lost in all that he's doing to me. I pluck at my nipples and grind against his mouth. My first orgasm hits me like a tsunami. I cry out, undulating. Chasing. Seeking an even higher nirvana.

Zane sucks my clit into his mouth and savors it. His fingers spread my ass cheeks. He pulls me all the way down against him. Suckling. Flicking. Swirling. I come again all over his face, gushing my release, and nearly pass out from the indulgence of it all.

In an instant, I'm flipped over on my stomach and Zane rams himself inside me. His cock tunnels so deep I feel him in my throat. "Fuck yeah, Fee. You're so wet. God, you feel like heaven."

"Give it to me hard, Zaney," I croak, overcome by how well he fills me.

Zane pummels me vigorously. Slams his hips into me. His balls slap against my pussy. Gives me a little spank now and then. One hand circles my throat as he eases my chest off the bed. Once I'm where he wants me, he squeezes just a bit to cut off a little bit of air when he picks up the pace.

I'm so close to detonating again, and when Zane's other hand pinches my clit I go into the stratosphere. My pussy clenches his cock so tightly he grunts, "Christ. Oh fucking Christ."

His hot release fills me and spills over. He's coming and coming. We both cry out. Keening through our exquisite carnality. The kind only the two of us can create. Definitively.

We are magical orgasmic creatures.

Zane eases us down, careful to stay firmly rooted inside me. He hates pulling out. As do I. When Zane's inside me, it's the only time I feel whole.

"I love you, Fee. I love you so much." His arms are wound tightly around my middle. My back to his front.

His cock twitches so I squeeze him. "I love you too. Stay in me. *Please.*"

"Yes." He bites my shoulder. One hand sneaks up and cups my breast. He rolls my nipple between his thumb and forefinger. I feel his cock stiffen inside me again.

It's always like this with us. Ever since we first had sex at eighteen. We can go for hours. And usually do.

This time it's lazy. Zane thrusts into me from behind and plays with my tits. He kisses my nape, then the sensitive spot behind my ear. One hand snakes down and rubs my oversensitive clit. I reach back and grip his ass cheek. Our rolling orgasms are gentle but satisfying.

Eventually, Zane softens and slips out. His breathing evens out and his grip around my body relaxes as he falls asleep.

I glance at the clock. It's three a.m. Jesus.

Tomorrow we leave for Maui. To the new, seven-bedroom oceanfront home we purchased sight unseen with the settlement money I received from Corey's family. Our friends and family will join us in a couple of weeks when we get married.

By then, I'll be weaned off my anxiety medicine, thank God.

I've waited my entire life for a future with this man. We've survived, against all odds. We're free of our family shit. Free from the shit of our own making. Mia's free too, her asshole biological father is out of her life forever.

We're truly happy. Together. Our own family with our own future and our own rules.

I nestle back against my love and shut my eyes. Make a definitive decision.

Zane and I have suffered enough. I'm done with these fucking drowning dreams. Done with the stress. Done with obstacles.

I'm taking control.

The past will *not* invade our future.

Ever. Again.

Chapter Two

A Month or So Later

FEE AND I HAVE dreamed about this day for such a long time.

Our wedding in Maui was fucking amazing. The new house is spectacular and was the perfect place to hold a sunset ceremony. Our band family was there. My mom and dad came—together, for fuck's sake. Fee's mom, Faye even managed to hold her snarky comments to a minimum during the trip. All in all, we celebrated. Had an epic party.

I think everyone was relieved the two of us managed to pull the trigger.

But...as fantastic as Maui was, today is going to be even better.

"Mia?" I bellow to a group of giggly girls standing in the pick-up zone at the elementary school. "Let's go, your mom and I have a surprise for you."

She tosses her long, black hair over her shoulder and struts over to my car, a tricked-out black Bentley Bentayga SUV. Stops to look back over her shoulder and flash a peace sign to her friends. Opens the door, tosses her backpack onto the seat next to her and climbs into her booster seat. "What's the hurry, Daddy?"

God, she's too cool for school. Just like her mom was at her age. I love her so much.

"We're having some people over for a party." I'm at a stoplight so I crane my neck around and wink at her.

She squinches her nose. "For what? It's not my birthday."

"Uh, *duh*. I said it's a surprise, goofball." The car behind us beeps at me. I whirl around to find the light is green and accelerate through the intersection.

Mia's way smarter than me. "When you're surprising someone, you don't tell them there's going to be a surprise. That's just a mean thing to do."

I roll my eyes, making certain she can see me in the rearview mirror. "Yeah. I know. I'm a big, huge meanie."

"True that." She blinks her lids rapidly and purses her lips.

Holy hell, my kid is something else. I never want her to lose that fire. That sass. Neither does Fee. She should know. Her own mother isolated her, berated her and nearly put out her flame. We'd never do that to our child.

Our child. Wow.

Today's the day. It's official.

"Da-deeeeee." Mia pouts and crosses her arms defiantly across her chest. "Tell me about the par-teeeeeee."

I sigh dramatically. "Fine. Your Uncle Ty is getting an award for his charity. We're throwing him a surprise party."

"Well, that's stupid," she scoffs.

I can't help but laugh, but it's time to be a parent. "Really? You think Ty getting an award is stupid? He's helping hundreds of kids who can't afford to get music lessons."

"Oh, well, I guess that's cool." She purses her lips, considering. "I thought it was for me, though."

"I never said that. I told you we're having a party, Meems. You're adorable. Beautiful. Smart and wicked funny. Please try not to be selfish. It's okay to celebrate someone else. In fact, it's better." I keep my voice stern. Dad-like.

Her blue eyes grow wide. Like she gets it. "Okay. I'm sorry."

"You're fine, baby girl." I turn up the Sirius station because its playing *Down* from our Z album.

So rip the scales from my in-
nocent eyes.

My love for you has fucked
me up so deep inside.

You turned your back on me,
how could you cast me out?

Down. Down. Down.

We sing at the top of our lungs all the way home. Neither Fee nor I care if Mia curses, the two of us swore like sailors at her age. Her teacher isn't too impressed, though.

By the time we pull into the gate, Mia seems to have forgotten all about the party. We just moved into this house in West Seattle, several blocks away from Ty. It's new construction and perfect, except we're adding an extension so Fee can have her dream supersized chef's kitchen.

I've gone from owning no homes to two giant mansions in the span of two months.

Man, I love being rich. And, surprisingly, I also love adulting.

"Wait for me, Meems." I slide out of the driver seat and open her door, turning away and crouching down a bit. "Piggyback?"

Mia throws her arms around my neck and I make stirrups out of my hands for her feet. She grips my hair like a horse's mane and kicks my hips. "Take me inside to the party."

I guess she didn't forget.

As I gallop up the walkway to the house, Fee flings open the front door wearing black jeans and my favorite magenta sweater, which makes her tits look massive. "There you two are. We couldn't start without you."

"We're here now." I give her a little smooch and sneak in a quick grope when we cross the threshold into the foyer.

I'm so proud of her for getting off the Xanax. That shit's no joke.

With Mia's father threatening to take her away, Fiona's stress level was dangerous. She'd actually hallucinate from lack of sleep. A condition she developed when she was pregnant means she's predisposed to high blood pressure. Anti-anxiety medicine—in this case Xanax—was the prescribed solution.

Knowing she was on such a strong dose stressed both of us out. Carter's addiction fucked up our childhood. Drove our families apart. Neither of us will ever allow ourselves to go down that path.

We're fucking survivors.

Fee plucks Mia off my back and sets her down. "Meems, do you know what today is?"

Confused, my daughter looks at me, then her mother. "Uh, yeah. We're having a party for Uncle Ty."

"Uh, no." Fee rubs her temples and shoots me an exasperated look.

"I lied, Meems. The party is totally for you." I laugh, wrapping my arm around Fiona.

Mia's not mad at all. She jumps up and down and claps her hands. "What did I do? Why do I get a party?"

"Well, let's find out," Fiona coos. "Close your eyes, baby girl. Squeeze them shut real tight."

She squishes her eyelids together and scrunches her entire face inward. Fee guides her by the shoulders through the kitchen construction zone, down the steps into the conservatory, where a crowd awaits.

My smile is so fucking big. This house is the bomb. I can't fucking believe I have a conservatory. We're so posh.

"Okay. One. Two. Three ... *Open!*" Fee's just as excited as I am.

When she opens her eyes, our entire LTZ family cheers for her. Mia is startled, but also happy to see people she loves.

I kneel down to her level. "So you *really* don't know what today is?"

"Nuh-uh." She shakes her head vigorously.

"Well, today is the day I'm officially your daddy!" I kiss her little cheeks. "It's the happiest day of my life."

Mia screams, flinging herself into my arms. "I'm 'dopted?"

Fee crouches beside us. "Yep. Zane officially adopted you because you're the best girl in the whole world. We signed the paperwork and now he's your real daddy. We'll celebrate today every year for the rest of our lives. What do you think?"

"This is the *best* day, *EVER!*" Mia twirls around, causing the entire room to burst into happy laughter.

My dad, Carter joins us. "Your adoption also makes me your bonafide grandpapa, Meems. And Lianne's your LeeLee. What do you say you help me get some cake?"

"We have cake?" Mia shrieks before spotting the three-tier hot-pink confection, which is set up on a table by the floor-to-ceiling windows leading to the backyard. Carter chuckles and follows her. My dad definitely has a sweet tooth.

It warms my heart that Carter is so present for his granddaughter. She's going to have the best version of him, which makes me so happy.

"Congratulations." Ty wraps an arm around my shoulder. "I know how long you've waited for this day to come."

"Thanks, my brother." I thunk his upper back, bro-style. Ty's been my best friend and pseudo-brother since the tenth grade when Carter essentially took him under his wing. Our relationship has deepened over the years being on tour together. He's been through many ups and downs, but he's the best man I know.

Zoey wraps her arms around my waist. "I'm so happy for you both."

"Bring on the babies!" Ronni rests her hand on top of her belly. She's pregnant with twins, God help her. "Mia is going to be the best cousin ever to these little guys."

Alex and Jace walk up, holding hands. Jace drawls, "Well, we might have some news of our own."

"OMG, are you *pregnant?*" Zoey claps her hand over her mouth.

Alex shakes her head vigorously. "God no, Z. We've decided to adopt Helena, Cassie's daughter. Jace's dad referred us to a family lawyer and we have some hoops to jump through, but it's pretty much a done deal."

"Dude, that's so cool." I fist pump Jace.

"Before you know it, we'll have a dozen wee ones running around." Connor loops his arm around Ronni's shoulder. He gazes at her lovingly. "When are you two going to give Mia a sister or brother?"

Fee wags her finger. "Uh, not for a while. We still have a couple months of construction on The Mission. I'm finalizing the drawings for Gus any day now."

"Gus?" Ronni cocks her head.

"Fee's naming her restaurant after her dad." I take her hand and squeeze.

Her eyes mist just slightly. Gus died just over a year after Mia was born. She misses her dad so much. "Zane's helping me achieve a dream I've had for so many years. Back when I was finishing culinary school and worked at La Bernardin, I knew I wanted to own the first Michelin-Starred restaurant in Seattle. Life's taken a couple of twists and turns, but now's my time."

"Don't open until we get back," Ty admonishes. "LTZ should play the first show."

Fiona points between Ty and Zoey. "When do you leave and when are you coming back?"

"Who knows? We're winging it." Zoey giggles up at Ty, who bends down to kiss her.

The two of them never stop with the PDA, but I'm glad they don't. Ty spent years being heartbroken over her. All because my dad came up with some hair-brained scheme to keep them apart so Ty could focus on the band when we were going out on our first tour.

Shit, the apple doesn't fall far from the tree. Fee and I stupidly split ourselves up for no good reason too. Huh. Never made *that* connection before.

"When are you two leaving for Ireland?" Jace cocks an eyebrow at Connor. "You're still going, right?"

Connor rests his big palm on Ronni's belly. "Oh, aye. We're flying out day after tomorrow. My Aunt Saoirse is getting the house ready. All of yous are welcome to visit. Anytime. Our plan is to just hole up there until hiatus is over."

"Or until my show gets picked up." Ronni nudges him.

Ty holds his hand up. "We're planning to be in Europe in a couple months. After the awards thing and an extended tropical beach vacation."

"We won't be able to make the awards show, Ty. I'm sorry, so I am." Connor doesn't actually look that sorry. He looks content. Maybe for the first time ever.

Zoey rubs her temples with her thumbs. "Maybe we can visit this spring. I've never been to Europe. We're hoping to spend at least two months exploring."

"Another headache? You should get that checked out." Alex peers at her BFF.

"I know." Zoey sighs heavily. "I'll do my best. I just realized I may not be there when you bring Helena home. Please give me dates so we can try to fly back."

Fiona slips under my arm. I bend down to kiss her. Hearing about everyone's plans for the next year bums me out a bit. She knows how much I'm going to miss my bandmates when they're off on their own adventures. I never wanted to take a hiatus. I'm terrible at sitting still. Building out The Mission and Gus isn't going to be enough for me.

My soul needs to create. Music is my therapy. My passion. My soul.

For now, though, I try to be present. Enjoy the time we all have together. Participate in the many conversations we're having. I love these guys. So much. I love their women too. Every single one of them. Stellar, stellar humans.

The truth is, life's going to change for all of us over this next year.

Excellent changes. Engagements. Weddings. Babies. Adoptions.

Expanding the LTZ family means we're enriching our lives with new adventures. It will make the band better. The only problem is, I have no clue what the hell I'm going to do with myself.

I better figure it out.

I've never done well when I have too much time on my hands.

Chapter Three

A Month Later

A YEAR.

An entire fucking year.

That's how long it's going to take to complete the build-out of the restaurant of my dreams. I wouldn't say I'm devastated, per se. It's just that I hoped for a longer runway before Zane's band gets back together and they head back out on the road.

The timing is tricky. Unlike LTZ's last tour, Mia's in school now. I'll be busy doing everything it takes to earn a Michelin Star. I was counting on having Zane home during the band's hiatus to help me. Now, I'll have to come up with a new plan.

My face must show my extraordinary disappointment. Zane, who's sitting with me at the architect's office, grips my hand tightly in his. "Seriously, Fee. Don't sweat this shit. Everything will work out. I can bring Mia out with me on the road, we can hire a tutor. Lots of bands bring their families with them."

Not helping.

"Uh, I appreciate it, babe, but I wouldn't be all that psyched about being away from Mia. Or coming home to an empty house for months on end." I can't help but stick out my lower lip.

Zane looks over at Peter Vander, our architect and designer, whom we chose because he's unconventional. "Can you pull some magic out of your ass to speed this up?"

"It's the permits. You're doing so much custom stuff. I'm trying to give you worst-case scenario." Peter shoves the sleeves of his hoodie up to his elbows, revealing full ink on both arms. He's an interesting character. His shoulder-length blond hair is neat. He wears nondescript clothes. He gives off biker vibes, you can sense he's not a dude who belongs in an office.

In any case, he's not a bullshitter. It certainly looks like Gus isn't going to open this year. The news is crushing.

I try not to cry. Or feel sorry for myself. I'm so ready to make my own contribution in the world. All the other LTZ women have killer careers. I did too until my dad died. It's been over a decade since I made a promise to myself to follow my dream of being a Michelin Star chef. This seems like such a setback.

"If we can do anything—and I mean anything—to help move the timeline." Zane clutches my hand, rubbing his thumb across my knuckles. "I'm off all year, we want to open as soon as possible."

Peter sighs and leans back in his chair. "Look, now that we're done with the kitchen remodel at your house, I'll do my best to make it happen. No promises, though. Most of this shit is out of my control. I'm not a restauranteur, but have you considered shifting menu development to your house?

A lightbulb goes off. "Are you certain you're not in the business? I mean, that's fucking brilliant." I get up and hug the poor man, who seems very uncomfortable with my proximity. Maybe because my unexpected show of affection caused him to flinch and now his chin is essentially nestled between my ample boobs.

Gah. I back off and sit, smoothing my palms against my jeans.

Zane cocks an eyebrow and just shakes his head. "Awwwwkward."

"Well, um." Peter covers his jaw with his hand. "It's just an idea."

I stand and motion for Zane to join me. "It's brilliant. I'll noodle on it, but that could actually work."

We're not two steps into the elevator when Zane cages me into the corner with his arms. "If you thought I'd be jealous when you shoved your tits in Peter's face, you'd be sadly mistaken." He leans down, kisses me, then smirks at my boobs.

"Ah, you weren't wishing my tits were in your face?" I wind my arms around his neck and pull his hair at the nape so he's looking into my eyes. Then I flick my gaze down to his mouth. I lean in and gently nibble his bottom lip.

The elevator opens. Zane grabs my hand and looks around wildly when we step out. He spots a support pillar behind the elevator bank and drags me over. "Lift up your shirt."

"Fuck no." I look around. "Someone will see."

"So what?" He reaches for the hem of my sweater.

I grab his wrists. "Zane, c'mon."

"I want to lick your nipples. Chew on them a little. Lick them into hard little points while you hump my leg until you come." He tugs me farther into the shadows where we're shielded from view. "Then, if I'm a good boy and get you off, maybe you'll suck *me* off." He waggles his eyebrows, then looks at the floor and up at me from under his hair.

This man. He's irresistible. And, ever since our first time in the park, he loves public sex. I actually do too, so even though I'm feeling a bit pudgier than normal, I still pull up my shirt. "Yes. Do it."

Like lightning, he presses me against the pillar and shoves his knee in between my legs. I feel his boner against my hip. He drags my shirt up over my head and twists the fabric in his fist before it's all the way off. Essentially, he's got my hands immobilized.

With his other hand, he flicks open my front-clasp bra, freeing my breasts. "Christ, Fee," Zane moans. You'd think he'd be used to my tits after all these years, but no. He loves a big reveal and reacts *every* time like it's the first time he's seen a bare boob in real life.

He leans down and softly blows on my nipples in succession. They pucker immediately. Zane's tongue darts out. He traces circles around my areolas. Back and forth. Leisurely. Flicks my nipples with the tip of his tongue and then flattens it to vary the sensation. Back and forth he worships both of my boobs.

I'll confess, nipple play has become my jam. Zane's so talented at it, soon I'm squirming and undulating against his thigh, which he shoves against my pussy. He continues to alternate back and forth, drawing my nipples into his mouth. Sucking, nibbling. Blowing. God.

It goes on and on as people get on and off the elevator behind us. I'm so turned on it's unbelievable. Heightened by the possibility someone could see us—if they looked hard enough.

The zings in my pussy build gradually, so gradually until—BAM—I explode out of nowhere.

My breath comes in bursts. Zane is still nibbling on my nipple when he releases the grip on my sweater and grabs my ass with both hands to yank me harder against his thigh. "Give it to me, Fee."

Like a wild sex beast, I cling to his shoulders and hump his leg while he bites each nipple. Careful not to break skin. Blows air to sooth. Repeats. A couple of repetitions later, white sparks flicker behind my eyes. My back arches when my second orgasm hits and I scream, "Zannnnnne."

Then I remember where we are and pull away.

Zane doesn't let me. "No one heard you," he whispers. "Now, suck me off. Please, babe. I'm dying here."

We switch places so Zane's leaning against the pillar. I unbuckle his studded belt and unzip his black jeans. Of course he's commando, I'd expect nothing less from my husband. I pull out his long, thick, beautiful cock and wrap my hand firmly around the base. Covering my teeth with my lips, I suck the tip of his dick into my mouth.

My tongue swoops and swirls around his crown where I flick it along his banjo string. Add hand strokes and twists with just enough tension that his hips buck rapidly. I let him fuck my face and go deep enough to swallow his tip. He grips the sides of my cheeks and takes over. Thrusts. Retreats. Hard enough to make saliva pool in my mouth but not enough so I choke.

"Your mouth is so wet, babe. You feel amazing. I'm so close." His thumbs stroke my lips as he watches himself pump in and out.

I reach up and gently cup his balls with one hand, rolling them with my fingertips. His cock thickens and Zane's breathing becomes erratic. "Fuck. Fuck. Fuck," he chants in cadence with his bucking hips.

My strokes are faster. I lick his shaft with the flat part of my tongue. Suck him. Worship him. I'm rewarded by streams of hot release, which I swallow gladly.

When I've cleaned him up thoroughly with my tongue, he helps me to standing. I kiss him deeply, allowing him to savor himself. Zane eats so many strawberries, his come is my favorite dessert. "You taste so delicious, Zaney." I can't help but giggle a bit. We're so brazen together. He eggs me on. I egg him on.

It *works*.

"That was fun." He laughs and hands me my shirt, which I put on after refastening my bra.

"Don't think I didn't know what you were doing." I hip check him. "You're always there to make me feel better. To cheer me up."

"Nah, I'm just here to distract you until you figure it out for yourself." His grin stretches from ear to ear.

"God, I love you, Zaney." I cup his cheek.

He places his hand over mine. "I love you. Thanks for indulging me. That was incredibly fucking hot, don't you think?"

"Uh, yeah." On the way to his Bentley, a ridiculous car that only someone like Zane could make seem cool, he grabs my hand. There's something I've been reluctant to talk to him about, but it's been weighing on my mind. Our little sexcapade makes it timely. "Does public sex turn you on the most?"

Zane looks genuinely confused. "Sex with you turns me on, wherever we do it."

We get into the car. I turn in my seat toward him before he turns on the engine. " I'm asking because you've been a little obsessed with fucking me in public lately." I think about the Mission construction site, where we've done it on sawhorses, stacks of wood, up against walls, the list goes on and on. Then there's the beach in Maui. In Ty and Zoey's bathroom. Backstage at the Grammys. In the locker room at the Seahawks game when Zane raised the 12th-man flag.

Oh, I'm into it. Hell, I initiate it half the time.

For me, there's never been anyone but Zane. If he wants to bang me in a parking lot, I'm all in. We've always been that annoying couple who gets each other off, whenever—and wherever—the mood strikes.

Admittedly, lately I've been more self-conscious about my weight than normal. I'm heavier now than I've ever been. Stress eating for months will do that to you. Now that I'm free of the constant worry of losing Mia, I'm struggling with adopting better habits.

A vicious cycle, but I'm nervous that one of our public romps will be caught on camera. I'd be humiliated.

Especially because ...

I felt so beautiful on my wedding day. I loved my dress, my shoes, my makeup—I thought I looked hot. So did Zane. Let's just say a vocal contingent of the LTZ fandom disagreed. I want to ignore them, but the band's blogs and socials were brutal.

Zane's hot but who's the fat chick?

LOL who knew ZR wuz a Fatty chaser?

She's pretty for a plus-sized girl.

Here's what I'd say to her- stop eating burgers.

He settled for that?

On and on.

I can't believe the comments bother me so much. Before I had Mia, I was genuinely sassy and strong-willed. Super comfortable and secure with myself—and with Zane. I never worried about how much I weighed. Or how I looked. Or what anyone thought. I knew Zane loved me unconditionally so I didn't care what anyone thought.

It's infuriating that I'm letting people I don't know make me feel less-than.

But I *do*. Feel less than, that is.

More and more each day, unfortunately.

I might project a certain don't-fuck-with-me attitude, but most days there's a constant inner nagging voice that spurs anxiety beyond anything I've ever known.

Am I enough?

Zane's at the top of his game. He's seen and experienced the world. Earned the right to take a year off. He's had a ton of sexual experience outside of our relationship.

I mean, what do I have to offer, really? I'm not bringing anything new or exciting to him, I'm the same old Fee. Mia's the best thing about me, truth be told.

"Huh. I haven't thought much about it." Zane shrugs. "I'd fuck you all day if you'd let me."

"So why sex clubs when we broke up?" I pinch my nose between my fingers. It's a little painful to talk about the past, but I need to know what he wants. Because, I'll give it to him.

Zane pulls my hand away from my face and places it on his thigh. "Uh, well, it's hard to explain. The thing is, I was ruined without you, Fee. When we split, I couldn't get it up. My dick wasn't functioning. Not for a long time. I tried the clubs to find out if I was broken. If I'd ever want sex again. This is so fucking embarrassing. Christ—I thought you'd moved on with someone else and were having a baby with him. It destroyed me."

"But you enjoyed it? Public sex?" I tilt my head, deliberately ignoring the substance of what he's trying to tell me.

He squints, thinking. "Uh…yeah, I won't lie but um … what does that have to do with garage blowjobs?"

Huh. Not what I wanted to hear but hell, I'm not going to shame him for it. Not if he likes that kind of thing. I should keep quiet, but my mouth keeps talking. "Do you want to bring me to a club?"

He's genuinely shocked. "What?"

Shit. I don't want him to know there's a part of me that still harbors insecurities about sexual experiences he had without me. And who they were with. We've talked about it before, I *should* let this go.

I know the past is firmly behind us. He loves *me*. Wants *me*. He couldn't tell me—or show me—any more than he does. It's just … we have gaps.

Our connection was always so strong, we had an un-spoken promise to discover and explore our sexuality together. Circumstances intervened.

Our first gap happened when my mom kept us apart during high school. We barely spoke, I was essentially locked up. With no contact from me for over a year, Zane lost his virginity in the band room. I was devastated.

Until he came for me on my graduation day. Time stood still. I gave him my virginity that day and we promised each other all the rest of our firsts. And we followed through. Every chance we got. Even when we lived on opposite coasts.

It all changed again when he went on the road with LTZ.

Stupid me, I sanctioned the whole goddamn thing.

My stupid "love hack" allowed both of us to fuck other people so long as we kept our conquests secret. I thought I was being so clever. Figured we'd avoid all the mistakes our parents made—and talked about all the fucking time.

I was young. Immature. I failed to comprehended the fragileness of relationships.

It was a devious trust test, though, wasn't it? Oh, I talked a big game about wanting to spread my wings and blah, blah, blah. But, I never used the love hack. Never intended to. The thought of anyone else touching me made my skin crawl.

I sincerely believed Zane would feel the same way.

But, no. Zane fucked hundreds of women over a two-year period while I pined for him at home. Technically, he didn't do anything wrong. It was my idea, after all. I was still furious. Hurt. Betrayed. I knew I wasn't being fair. That didn't stop me from gaslighting him. Making him feel like shit. Shaming him.

My reaction cut him to the core. It drove Zane away.

Losing him utterly destroyed me, but I was still mad. That's how I succumbed to Corey Johnson's flirtations, not realizing he'd targeted me. Not realizing my fate had been sealed in the band room back at Zane's high school.

Zane and I ran into Corey, a fellow student at Garfield High, at dinner when we were vacationing on Lummi Island. Later that night, I learned about the other women and Zane and I split. Corey showed up at The Mission weeks later knowing I had been Zane's girlfriend. He seduced me, the condom broke and I got pregnant with Mia.

He made my life miserable. My dad lost everything trying to protect me. The excruciating fight for my daughter lasted six long years. During Mia's custody proceedings, we learned Corey hated Zane because his ex was the girl who took Zane's V-card.

My errors in judgment nearly cost me everything. First Zane. Then my daughter. I can't afford any more mistakes. The price is too high. I've got to make sure Zane and I have open communication. Even about this.

"Earth to Fee." Zane waves his hand in front of my face. "Where did you go? I don't like the look on your face."

I puff out my breath. "I'm sorry. Started going down the rabbit hole."

He caresses the side of my face. His thumb brushes my cheek. "Fee, please don't look backward. You're the only woman I've ever wanted or needed. Stay present with me. We're in love. Mia's our child. You're going to open the best damn Michelin Star restaurant the world has ever seen. The Mission is going to be the most kick-ass venue. LTZ will be back better than ever. We're golden, babe. I don't even think about those clubs."

God. This man. With his family history he could—justifiably—be the most bitter guy around.

He's not, though.

He's adorable. Sexy. Fascinating. Supportive. Kind. He's mine.

I'm never going to do anything to jeopardize our relationship.

Ever again.

Chapter Four

A Few Weeks Later

I'VE SPENT A BORING morning researching new customized tour buses so the band can bring our families on the road next year. Ty and Zoey are visiting Connor and Ronni in Ireland. Jace and Alex are bringing home their new adopted daughter today. I just sent my bandmates an email with links and my list of pros and cons, which will likely go unopened and unanswered.

Now I have nothing to do.

The smells coming from the kitchen make my stomach growl. One of my favorite things to do is watch Fee when she's cooking. It's when she's the most relaxed. And damn, she's so fucking talented. I'm in awe of her ability to make literally any type of food delicious.

"Whatcha cooking?" I lean against the pantry door across from where Fee is meticulously forming tiny pastries into the shape of stars.

Fee looks up, startled. Her magenta hair is pulled back in two braids. She wears a black bandana over her head. A black apron over a gray tank top that her tits are spilling out of. "I'm working on a savory puff pastry topper for a rabbit dish I want to put on a spring menu."

I slide in behind her and cup her boobs. "You're so sexy when you make pastry."

"Hey ... let me at least finish. I'm about ready to pop these in the oven." She cranes her neck up. I kiss her pouty pink lips.

"Promises. Promises." I feather kisses along her jaw and thumb her nipples, which harden into tight peaks. My hands wander down her sides, under her apron across her soft belly...

Fiona slaps my hand away, giggling. "Zane. I said give me a minute."

"But I want to get lost in your body *noowwwww*. I'm so horny," I whisper in her ear. Grip her hips. She makes me so fucking hot. With so much time on my hands, I've been making a serious effort to be inside her as much as possible, and she's thwarted my advances for days. I'm determined to have a better outcome today.

She relaxes back against me when I dip my fingers under the waistband of her leggings but continues to work on her pastry stars. I need her full attention so I inch lower and dive into her panties.

Ahhh, yeah. I home in on her clit, which is already a bit swollen. I roll it. Rub it. Tap it. Suck on her earlobe. *Finally*, she stops what she's doing and slaps her palms on the marble countertop. I thrust my hard cock against her ass. Band my arm around her collarbone to hold her in position. Thrust my fingers inside her.

She's dripping. *Always* dripping for me.

"Let me help you up." I pat the counter.

A look of trepidation flits across her face. "Uh ... not here. Um. Just a sec ..."

She doesn't have a chance to finish before I reach around, palm the backs of her thighs, lift and plunk her down. "Now, we're talking." I kiss the surprise off her face and get to work peeling her leggings and panties off in one fell swoop.

"Zane ..." Fee looks down at me, her face is a mixture of desire and— embarrassment? Shame? I don't know exactly, but it's an expression I've seen on and off over the past couple months.

It guts me. I never want my girl to feel anything but awesome. I have no discernible job for the foreseeable future, so I decide making Fee come every single day is now *my profession* until LTZ reunites later this year.

I stand and take her face in my hands. "Mia won't be home from school for hours. Let's fool around. My cock misses you."

She casts her eyes downward. "I ... um."

"You can't tell me you don't want me to fuck you. Your pussy wants me." I move my face lower so she has to look into my eyes. *"Fee? ..."*

She squinches her eyes shut. Slurps some air through pursed lips. Sighs. "I ... I, uh. I weighed myself today. I've gained nearly twenty pounds since our wedding when I already needed to lose ten. I'm fat. I'm embarrassed for you to see me naked." Fiona tugs the hem of her tank top down and stretches it to mid-thigh.

Ahh. That explains why we've been having sex in the dark the past couple weeks. "No. No. No. I won't hear you say that. You're fucking gorgeous. I *love* your body." I pull the fabric from her fists and yank the tank over her head, revealing her heavy breasts and her belly, which has an adorable, soft pooch.

She tries to cover it with her hands and wrists. "I'm serious, Zaney. Please don't look ..." Her voice catches.

Fee's always been semi-self-conscious about her size. I've deduced this from her snarky self-depreciating comments. Chatter about diets she thinks she should try. Complaints about clothes that don't fit her. Stuff like that.

I've rarely paid too much attention to it because she's my dream girl. I fucking worship her. Our sex life is out of this world. Uninhibited. Raunchy. Playful. Fiona and I can't keep our body parts apart. They gravitate toward each other like magnets.

So, no. Just no. Her request of me not to look at her is unacceptable. I will never let her ever feel bad about herself with me.

I deliberately scan her up and down. Creamy, milky skin. Sad, blue eyes. Bee-stung lips. Curves to get lost in. She's so fucking beautiful. Inside and out.

I grab her wrists, bend down and kiss her stomach. "Fee, you're stunning. You make me so fucking hard." I lick her belly button. Nuzzle her pillowy softness. God, I love her body. No one else does it for me. I look up at her. "Get it through your stubborn skull. You're the only one I'll ever want to fuck whether you're ninety or nine hundred pounds, What is going on with you these past weeks? Why are you apprehensive around me? We don't do insecure. That's not us."

"I don't know." She winces.

I smooth my hands over her thighs. Press them apart. Step between her legs and cup her tits. Roll her nipples with my thumb and forefingers. *"Ahhhh."* She wriggles and moans, clinging to my shoulders.

"Now lean back and open your legs wider for me."

Slowly, Fiona lies back on her elbows. Spreads her legs, which dangle over the edge of the island. Holy hell, the sweet scent of her pussy is intoxicating. My dick lurches in my jeans.

Fee keeps her eyes squeezed shut. Her teeth are nearly, but not quite, clenched.

I kiss the insides of her knees while I kick off my boots and shed my jeans and T-shirt. "You're an absolute goddess."

"Shut up, Zane. I'm not " She keeps her eyes squeezed closed.

I take her hands in mine and together we stroke her chest. Fee's breath hitches. "Shh, Fee. Don't snark at me, just see yourself like I see you." I move our hands over her breasts. Her nipples. Her belly. Her thighs. "Your body is incredible. It gave us Mia. You nourish it with the most amazing food you create. It's a temple. My temple. When you don't love yourself, then it hurts me. Because I love every single millimeter of this body."

"I know you do, babe." Her voice softens. "I hate feeling this way. It makes me so angry with myself. Sometimes I hear the things I say and I'd swear it's my mom talking."

I bury my face in her pussy. Roll her clit between my lips, nibble and lick it. Drive my tongue into her opening and devour her.

I'm lost in a Fee frenzy. I lave and worship. Caress and suckle. I work my finger deep inside her and press and flick the magic little spongy bit just below her G-spot. When she's on the brink of detonation, I press her soft thighs apart and guide myself inside her.

Fiona grips the edge of the counter as I tunnel in and out of her, caressing each part of her body I can reach. Gone are the frown lines. Worry lines—erased. Fee's expression is blissful. Ecstatic. She's lost in the sensation of me making love to her. Worshipping her. Her pussy milks my cock. Squeezing. Releasing. "Ohhhh. Ohhhh," she chants in breathy little mewls.

I slide my hands under her back and lift her so she's sitting on the edge. "Do you feel it?" I slide back in to the hilt.

"Your cock?" She drapes her arms across my shoulders and nuzzles my neck.

I lean back a bit so I can keep a visual of where she's impaled. "No. The magic. Look at us."

She looks down. Her eyes flutter when I swivel my hips to corkscrew my dick against her G-spot. "*Mmmm.* Yeah ..."

"No, Fee. Watch." I press my forehead to hers. We both cast our eyes to where we're joined. "Together we're magic. Look at you gushing all around me. My cock wants to be where it is right now."

"Mm. Hmm." She licks her lips. Almost in slow motion. Fascinated by our interlocked bodies.

I can't help but pick up the pace until the sounds of us slapping together fill the room. I spread her pussy lips apart and thumb her hard clit. "Come, Fee. Come all over me."

As if on command, Fiona clamps down on my shaft so hard my eyes roll back in my head. "Ohmyfuckinggod," she wails through her release.

"I love you so fucking much," I cry out when I explode a second later.

We stay entwined for a while. Her legs locked around the backs of my thighs. My hands running up and down her back.

"Thank you for putting up with me, Zaney." Fiona's blue eyes blink up at me. "I'm a lot."

I kiss her forehead. "No. You're perfect. It kills me when you cut yourself down."

She sighs. "I wish I could be as perfect as you make me feel."

I squeeze her tightly. We stay wrapped together for a long stretch. I'm still buried inside her. "I've brought this up before, but have you ever considered talking to someone?"

Fiona stiffens.

"Look, babe. I know you're not into it." I keep her pressed tightly against me. "I also know you don't want to go back on the anti-anxiety meds. Truth be told, they scared the shit out of me, so I'm glad you decided to get them out of your system. The thing is, if you need some support—therapist, anti-depressants—there's no stigma. There's lots of ways to deal with insecurity. Anxiety."

She wriggles free from my grasp. "I'm fucking fine. Just because I'm getting fat doesn't mean I'm broken, Zane." She reaches for her top and leggings and begins to get dressed.

"You know I didn't mean that as a dig." I watch her put her clothes on but make no move to put on mine.

"Ah, but you meant something." She squints at me. "I'll be fine. I'll go keto and drop the weight."

I'm so frustrated. She still doesn't get it. And she's not fine. I'm also not her father. I'm her husband. Lover. There's a thin line between being there for her and telling her what to do. My mind drifts to Ty, randomly. How he denied. Denied. Denied. Then got addicted to coke.

Fuck. I wonder if that's how it started for my dad. I've never asked him too much about his own demons.

Fee walks back to her pastries. Grabs the trash can. Before I can stop her, all of her hard work is tossed into the garbage.

I pull on my jeans. Walk to her and put my arms around her. "I love you. I'm sorry if I said the wrong thing. I just want to make you happy."

"No, *I'm* sorry. I overreacted." She breathes out heavily. "I'm just hormonal."

I don't want to hurt her, so I accept her explanation. Decide to let it go—for now.

I thought once Gus was back on track, Fee would bounce back to her old self.

Instead, it seems like her negative self-talk is ramping up.

I'm at a loss.

What happens if I can't make things better?

Chapter Five

One Month Later

LATE LAST FALL, A doctor prescribed Xanax for depression and anxiety.

The stress of Mia's custody. My fear of losing Zane. My mother's constant criticism. It all became too much.

I needed help. It wasn't the first time, but it had been a long time.

In the past, short stints on Xanax helped me get through particularly stressful times. Zane and I breaking up. My encounter with Corey at The Mission. Dad's death. The custody battles after Mia was born.

It didn't take much convincing to procure a prescription. My doctor and I had a frank conversation about the traumas I'd been through. She took a detailed history of my stress. It wasn't fun to relive the worst times of my life, but we were able to pinpoint several instances that, essentially, broke my spirit as a kid.

My decision to go to culinary school, against my parents' wishes, helped break me free from my family's destructive patterns. With school to look forward to and a long-distance romance with Zane, I regained my independence. I found confidence in my chosen profession. Rose to the top of the most esteemed kitchen in New York. Then moved back to Seattle and rose to the top of my career here.

It was the best feeling in the world. Zane and I were on track. My career was on track. I was so happy. I'd found myself again. I was me. Through and through.

Then it all came crashing down. Zane was gone. I was a single mother. My dad died.

I was sad. Depressed, even. But I persevered. With the help of an occasional Xanax. Knowing I had to set a better example for Mia than my mom set for me, I was extraordinarily careful. I didn't abuse it and slowly I built up my self-worth again. Zane and I reunited. I felt like all my suffering had been worth it. I was going to be happy.

Live life on my own terms with the man I was destined to be with.

Like the evil villain he is, Corey wouldn't allow us to be happy. He renewed the custody battle, determined to use his wealth and power to destroy me. For years, I lived in fear if I died, the only parent Mia would ever know is a father who had zero interest in his biological daughter.

I knew what that felt like. I'd never let that happen to Meems.

It kept me up at night. I couldn't sleep. My stress level was through the roof. At risk for high blood pressure, I needed help. Real, immediate help. I asked my new doctor for a prescription for Xanax.

She prescribed it as a short-term solution. Insisted I needed to get into therapy and find an antidepressant that worked for me. I didn't want to do either of those things. I mean, why? Xanax did the trick. It made me feel relaxed. Focused. Determined. Confident.

It was like a magic elixir—instant relief. I finished the bottle. When I ran out, I was seriously worried about my own sanity. I was the most stressed I'd ever been. The idea I'd lose Mia...

So, I renewed the prescription Just until I got through the custody situation. I promised myself I'd stop taking it before I got addicted.

Earlier this year, that's just what I did. I followed her instructions. Weaned myself off the dose under her supervision. It took weeks, but honestly wasn't that hard.

Until it was.

Things are settled down, but I realize all of my past trauma is still with me. I've never actually dealt with it. Now, I have new stress. The restaurant. Hiring staff. Menu prep. It's exciting, but I feel like I'm under so much stress. Self-induced stress, truth be told. Zane certainly couldn't be more supportive.

To cope, I'm falling back on an old habit—overeating. A lot. I've gained a ton of weight. I'm the heaviest I've ever been. I'm so disgusted with myself. I know it can't continue, but I can't seem to stop. Each day I swear I'll get myself under control.

Then I find myself stuffing samples of the food I make into my mouth.

All. Day. Long.

God. Zane could have his pick of women. He'll be back out on the road next year. I've got to get a handle on the situation before he goes.

I'm not proud, but I've dipped into my not-quite-empty bottle of Xanax. I take half of a 2mg pill in the morning. The second half early evening. It's better than the alternative. Because I feel calm again. I've dropped a few pounds too.

I'm so fucking thankful I never flushed the extra twenty pills.

"Fee! Fee! Connor and Ronni are parents. They named the boys Torin and Tristan." Zane bounds into the bathroom after I swallow my dose. I must look sketchy because he stops in his tracks. "What's going on?"

I splash some cold water on my face. "Uh, nothing. Why?"

"You look weird." He cocks his head.

He's so fucking intuitive. Especially with me. I can't lie to him. Can I? He'd be devastated if I wasn't honest.

Shit. I've got to confess. "Okay. Fine. I've been feeling stressed."

"Yeah." He crosses his arms, waiting.

"I took Xanax again ..." I hold out my palm. "Before you say anything, I know. I know. I'll make an appointment. Do the things. I just couldn't take how anxious I felt. It was too much."

He's hard to read. His expression isn't, well, supportive. But, he isn't angry either. "Okay."

"Just okay?" I stare him down.

"Thanks for telling me?" He says this like a question.

"Zane." I now plead with my voice.

He sighs. Toes the floor. "It scares me, Fee."

"I promise. I'll go this week. Get on a plan. You can come with me. Please. I just want to feel normal," I beg him. I need him.

We're interrupted by Mia, who shoves a form at me. "Mommy, can you sign this?"

"Okay, are you ready for school?" I look down to see if it's a field trip signup for later in the week. The kids are going to MoPOP, the pop culture museum that just so happens to be curating an exhibit on northwest music featuring Limelight and Less Than Zero, which will open in the fall. I show it to Zane.

He grins. "Did you know my band's going to be featured there soon, Meems?"

"No way!" Her mouth is a little "o."

"Yes way." He ruffles her hair. "Maybe I should be a chaperone. Should I call your teacher?"

Mia twirls around then looks at him from under her bangs. I love that she's copying his signature move and using it against him. "Yes, Daddy."

"Okay, go finish getting ready. We need to leave in about ten minutes." He kisses her head and shoos her back to her room.

When she's gone, I go to him. Press my lips to his. "I'm sorry."

"I'm trying not to lecture. I'm trying to be supportive. You know I don't want you to live with anxiety, Fee." He wraps his arms around me. "I do want to go with you. I want us to do it together because you being on these meds affects both me and Mia."

"I said I'm okay with it." I don't mean to sound irritated, but I know it comes out snarky.

He winces. "Uh, good? I'll go get Mia off to school." He turns to leave.

"Zane ..." I call after him.

He stops. "It's fine, Fee. If it means you won't snap at me, I'm all for it."

I don't know what to say. So, I say nothing. Let him go.

A couple hours later, I'm online pouring over various menus of Michelin-Starred restaurants around the world. A couple of months ago, I created a spreadsheet, where I have dishes cataloged by course and main ingredient. My intention is to keep track of what customers love and narrow my menus to dishes that are creative for me to make, but also not so far out of bounds they put people off.

My business degree in restaurant management is *not* going to waste. Not for my restaurant.

Gus.

My dad's name. I intend to make him proud. If he were alive, he'd be so supportive of me. I know it. I'm feeling psyched. Excited. Which, despite Zane's misgivings, makes me even less regretful of my decision to take Xanax. It's helping me. This is proof.

I'm going to be respectful of his opinion on it though. Ultimately, I can't continue living with a pharmaceutical crutch. I'll have to find another way.

"You look happy." Zane smiles at me. I didn't hear him come in, which isn't uncommon. I glance at the clock and realize it's been a while since he took Mia to school.

I walk over to him. Cup his face. "You make me happy, Zaney. I don't ever want you to think otherwise."

"Can I say something?" He casts his eyes down. "I mean. Can I get something off my chest?" He looks back up at me.

I stare deeply into his brown, soulful eyes, which are filled with so much love I can hardly stand it. "Of course."

"I don't want to waste this time off. The guys are all off doing their thing. Jace and Connor are figuring out being parents. Ty and Zoey are fucking each other all around the world. It would have been fine if we were opening up The Mission and Gus. I guess...um. Well, I guess I don't want to look back on this year and have nothing to show for it." He sighs. "I'm bored, Fee. Really fucking bored."

To say I'm shocked is an understatement. I've been so focused on my own issues, I haven't even thought to ask Zane how he's doing with the LTZ hiatus. Of course he's bored. He's a man who needs to be moving. Doing something. The construction delays aren't just affecting me.

"What do you have in mind?" I stroke his cheeks with my thumbs.

He covers my hands with his. "I want to travel around the country a bit. See some sights. Jam with some musician friends. I've never had much time to spare when we've toured the US. Would you and Mia want to come with me?"

"Like where?" The thought of the three of us going on vacation excites me. We had the best time last year traveling with LTZ throughout Asia. At least until Corey renewed the custody shit and we had to cut the trip short.

He pulls away and paces. "Well. New York, of course. But, I was thinking. If we plan ahead enough, we can go to the cities with Michelin Star restaurants and you can eat the menus instead of reading about them."

"Wow." Now, I'm intrigued. "That would be incredible. Most of them book out months in advance, though."

He cocks a brow. It takes me a minute and then I clue in. I sometimes still forget that my Zane is also famous guitar player Zane Rocks, who can get into any place, anywhere, at any time.

"When would we leave?" I shut my laptop and focus on the conversation at hand.

He walks over to the fridge where Mia's school schedule is posted. He taps the calendar. "Maybe aim for the weekend after school ends?"

"I promised Alex I'd bring Mia over to meet Lena this summer." I join him and peer at the dates. "I was also planning on hiring some staff in a month or two, now that I have a handle on the food vibe I want. Once they're on board, I'll be buried in training, menu development. Hiring a PR firm. All the things I'll need to do to get open and then provide the type of service that will get Gus noticed."

His arm loops around my neck. "You can do all that stuff and we'd still have time to take a few weeks off to just chill. Wouldn't it be fun to have some adventure time with our daughter?"

"Yeah. It would." I press my lips to his. "OMG. This is so exciting."

"Should we take Olga?" He's giddy. Olga is our new nanny. A fifty-something badass whose kids are all grown. We hired her thinking I'd be at the restaurant this summer. When the construction delays overwhelmed us, she agreed to be on call. I get where he's going with this. It could be the perfect opportunity to integrate her into our routine.

I nod vigorously. "That's a great idea. Hell yeah."

"Good. I'll get it all arranged." He kisses me. Savors my lips. Nuzzles my neck.

I pull up his shirt. "Take this off, I want to show my appreciation."

"I don't have a problem with that." He grins and flings his tee to the floor.

"I made the appointment." I lick his neck and suck on his earlobe. "We'll go in next week, okay?"

His relief is palpable. Zane grips my shoulders and touches his forehead to mine. "Thank you, Fee."

"I'll never do anything to hurt you, babe. To hurt us." I hope he can see how sincere I am.

He nods. Breathes out a final sigh he'd obviously been holding in. "I know."

"I want to figure it all out. Having your support is everything." I close my eyes and breathe in deeply as we melt into each other.

Zane rests his hands on my waist, which is thicker than I want it to be, but I don't flinch. He strokes around to my round ass and grips. I allow myself to enjoy his touch. Push thoughts of my weight and size out of my mind. Zane loves me as I am. With the help of Xanax quelling my negative thoughts, I settle into the feeling. Accept it. Enjoy it.

He takes my hand and leads me upstairs to our bedroom where he strips me naked.

When we make love, it feels incredible.
Transcendent.
Like we're back on track.
I'm going to make certain it stays this way.

Chapter Six

A Few Weeks Later

NEARLY THIRTY THOUSAND FANS at Leader Bank Pavilion in Boston chant and scream for an encore. I'm standing stage left, waiting for my queue. I glance over at Knox Gallagher, the guitarist for Wycked Obsession. He tips his chin at me. I nod back.

Adrenaline courses through my body. It's been months since I've been on stage and I'm so fucking stoked. I glance behind me where Fee stands with the significant others of the band. Her arms are wrapped protectively around Mia, who wears full rock-chick regalia including an LTZ T-shirt. Hot-pink headphones. Both waive and smile. I make a kissy face back to them and then turn back toward the stage.

Singer Ajia Stone blows past us and runs on stage. The crowd loses its ever-loving mind.

God I miss this. I miss Ty. I miss my band.

"Are you ready for a couple more?" Ajia throws his fist in the air and holds his mic out to the audience. The stadium goes wild.

The rest of Wycked Obsession take their places and Knox jumps into the opening riff of their hit song, Run.

Ajia shakes out his hair, looks over at me and waves me onstage. "Tonight, we have a special guest. A friend of the band's. Please welcome Zane Rocks of Less than Zero."

I strut onstage with my Gibson to the roar of nearly thirty thousand fans. When I strum the counter-melody to what Knox is playing, the crowd goes dead quiet. Fully entranced. Then they go absolutely fucking wild. As the song progresses, he and I are back to back jamming. Dueling solos. Drawing out the song into a full-blown audience participation masterpiece. When it ends, I'm so fucking energized.

Being onstage is like fuel. I need it. Maybe I underestimated how much.

After two songs, I leave the stage to thunderous applause and head straight over to Fiona and kiss her like I haven't seen her in weeks.

"Gross. Daddy!" Mia tugs at my jeans. "Everyone can see you."

I lean down. Pull one of her ear coverings out a bit. "Sweetheart, I will kiss your mom wherever I want because I love her. Kissing is not gross. Trust me on this."

She doesn't look convinced.

I pick her up and put her on my shoulders. Grab Fee's hand and watch the final song of the show. Afterward, we hang out backstage. While I catch up with the band, who have had their own fair share of drama, Bree, Ajai's girlfriend, braids Mia's hair. Wicked Obsession's bassist, also named Zayne with a "y," and I bicker over which spelling is correct. His girlfriend, Grace, is deep in conversation with Fiona, like long-lost sisters. I have to pull her away when I notice the crew's loaded out all the gear and the place is empty.

On the way back to the hotel, Mia's sound asleep between us and Fee's in a great mood. "That was so fun. Mia loved it. You did amazing, babe."

"It's always such a rush." I'm still wound up. Generally it takes hours before I come down after a show. The best natural high there is.

She reaches around our daughter to stroke my hair. "You miss it." A statement, not a question.

"So much." I close my eyes and lean back against the soft leather. Just a few more months. I'm calling a band meeting at the end of this year to get the guys back on track. We need to write. Record. Tour. I realize working together will be different now that we all have kids. Well, all but Ty and Zoey.

I think about touring with our families on customized buses. We can truly have it all. Each of us can have our own space. The kids will all have tutors. It will be like a traveling family.

Then I remember. Fiona will be opening Gus. She won't want to go anywhere. Rightfully, it's her turn to shine in her own profession. The thought does douse a bit of water on my flame, though.

We arrive at the hotel. I pick Mia up. Fee grabs her purse. Hand-in-hand we walk through the ornate front entrance. Olga had the night off, so Zeke, my bodyguard is with us tonight. He's a couple paces ahead with my guitar and backpack. All is quiet until a woman sitting in the lobby jumps up and runs over to us before Zeke can intervene.

"Zane. I'm Tawnee. Customer Experience Manager at the Luxe? Max told me you were in town. He wanted me to stop by and give you this." She hands me a card with a phone number and password on it. "Please let us know if we can accommodate you during your stay."

I glance over at Fiona, who openly stares at Tawnee, an extremely tall woman wearing a black leather corset and some flowy purplish pants. Her brown hair is pulled back tightly into a ponytail. I can tell my wife isn't psyched about this interaction.

"Not this time. Thank you for stopping by." I smile and keep moving, tugging Fee with me. Zeke seamlessly moves to block Tawnee, allowing us to pass without further conversation.

We get into the elevator leaving Zeke behind. "Who was that?" Fee asks the expected question the second the doors close behind us.

"Let's get Mia into bed." I shoot her a look. Fee catches my meaning: adult conversation. She's decidedly not impressed.

Once inside our suite, Fiona changes Mia into her pajamas and puts her to bed in the adjoining room where Olga is staying. I'm already washing the night off in the big walk-in shower by the time she returns. Instead of joining me, Fee sits on the edge of the tub. Rubs her temples with her fingers. "So, are you going to tell me what that shit was down there?"

"Join me." I hold my hand out to her.

She shakes her head. Sticks her lip out.

I wiggle my fingers and gesture for her to get in the shower.

She just stares. Mouths, "No."

I decide to take matters into my own hands. Literally. I step out onto the mat and yank Fiona into the shower with me fully clothed.

"What the fuck, Zane?" she sputters and tries to get away.

I hug her tightly to me until she's soaked. I hold out the little scrunchy thing to her. "Wash my back?"

"You're such a shit." She sits on the bench to pull her leggings off. They splat at the bottom of the shower stall. Next, she peels her wet T-shirt off. Then her bra. *Splat. Splat.*

I stand between her knees. Guide her mouth to my cock. Fuck her face a bit until her eye makeup runs down her cheeks. She clings to my hips and gags when my crown hits the back of her throat. She's so fucking beautiful with her lips stretched around my girth. She hums and swallows. My dick erupts.

All I want is her. All the fucking time.

I pull out of her mouth and kneel on the tile in between her knees. "Shoving your cock in my mouth is a far cry from washing your back," she grumbles, licking her lips.

"Oh yeah? Do you like this better?" I stroke her pussy then insert two fingers inside her velvet awesomeness.

Move them in and out. Thumb her clit a little. Then lean over and lap at her little nub in time to my thrusts.

"Yessssss..." She leans back against the wall and gets lost in the pleasure I'm trying to give her. It makes me so happy. She seems to have gotten over any self-consciousness about her weight gain. Maybe I've convinced her I truly love the way she looks. I keep telling her she's like my own personal Renaissance painting, except with jet-black hair that's dyed magenta.

Her lips, still puffy from my cock stretching them, are parted in ecstasy. Her thighs quiver when I hit the magic spot inside her. I suck harder on her clit. Rub like a madman. I want to get her there so bad. Seconds later, Fee's entire torso is heaving. Seizing. Her mouth opens and closes as she cries out, keening. She's pinching her nipples so hard they're nearly purple.

I try to hold her still but she lets out a wail and thrusts her pussy against my mouth, gushing all over my face.

Needless to say, it surprises us both.

"Holy shit, Fee. I made you squirt." I feel like a sexual emperor because it's been *years* since she's been able to let go like this.

Before Mia, I realize.

She's slumped against the tile, shuddering through an aftershock. Nearly incoherent. "Wow. I forgot how much...wow."

I withdraw my fingers and hold them up to her lips. With hooded eyes, she sucks herself off me. My dick twitches. I want to be inside her, but Fee's a noodle. We both had awesome orgasms tonight. Fucking her can wait until morning.

"Let's go to bed." I stand, shut off the water and hold my hands out to her. She takes them. I pull her up into my arms and carefully dry her off and wipe myself down too.

Fee's alert now and like a dog looking for her bone. "Are you going to tell me who that woman in the lobby was?"

Fuck.

"She's the VIP host for a sex club in town," I say as I'm toweling off Fee's hair. "If I remember correctly, it's a house in the woods an hour or so away. The owners have converted it into multiple themed rooms. There's a public viewing area where people go at it and you can watch them. Participate. Whatever."

Her eyes open a little wider. She's curious, that much is clear. I'd love to be able to tell Fee everything she wants to know, but I'm reluctant to talk about that period in my life with her. We were split up. Both heartbroken. She got herself pregnant with someone else.

Fuck it. I should just be honest. We're way past letting that shit fuck with our relationship. Even if one of our rules was never to talk about the sex we had.

I guess those rules are obsolete, though?

"Could you take me there?" Her words come out meek. She looks so vulnerable. Unsure.

I gather her against my chest. Wrap my arms around her. "I *could*. But, is that something we want to bring into our lives?"

"I ... I, uh ..." Her blue eyes shimmer with uncertainty.

Our gazes lock. "I'll take you wherever you want to go, Fee. Because I want to make you happy. The thing is, I don't want to have sex with *anyone* but you ever again. And, just so you know, I think it would kill me to watch you have sex with someone else."

"Wait, so if we went to this place, we'd be *expected* to have sex with people?" She tilts her head. Questioning.

I move toward the bed and motion for her to follow. When we're snuggled up under the covers facing each other it reminds me of how we grew up. Sleeping in the same bed. Taking comfort from our closeness. It's where I always feel safest, in bed with Fiona.

"In answer to your question, no. Not expected. But, it's tricky. The environment is, well ... a whole scene. You find yourself doing things you didn't plan on. Not that there is anything to be ashamed of if it floats your boat."

I unscrunch my face, which I realize is clenched. "Why are you so curious about the sex clubs? I promise I won't be upset. I just feel super weird talking about a time in my life I don't particularly have fond memories of." I take her hand and put it on my heart. Cover it with mine.

She lifts her shoulder slightly. "When we talked about it before, you said you enjoyed it. I'll always feel responsible for driving you away. Into that life. I'm not judging. Or even jealous. Though, maybe I am a little. I never imagined you'd find yourself exploring your own sexuality that way. Fucking men. Women."

"Yeah, well, after you showed up at my house, told me you were pregnant and walked away, sex was the last thing on my mind. I was shattered. I didn't want anyone but you and ... well, you weren't ... Um ... Anyway, I thought watching people have sex would wake up my defective cock." I shake my head, thinking back at the worst time in my whole life.

"And?" she whispers, fascinated but, true to her word, not judgmental.

"Then, I tried things from time to time, but ... meh. A crew member from a band we toured with invited me to a private mansion when we were in Berlin. Guests were required to be naked and wear a full masquerade mask. The entire club was, essentially, one giant orgy.

"Before I knew what was happening, some chick was sucking me off while getting fucked by two guys. I glanced away for a second, when I looked back she had a third man's dick in her ass and some random guy had my cock in his mouth. Some dude rubbed lube on my asshole. It was a flurry of random fucking. I was in over my head, truth be told."

I shudder a bit. Though I embraced experimentation, I can't even remember being that dude.

Sex for me has never meant sticking my cock in some hole. It's always been her. From the time Fee and I were kids, she's been my person. Before I comprehended what that meant. Being with her was natural. Like breathing.

Being with anyone else ... isn't.

I'll never forget the time when we were fourteen. Making out by the campfire. My dick was so fucking hard, aching for her. Then her mom ripped us apart. Kept us apart. Stole our first time. The fallout from that night—from our parents— still reverberates to this day. I hate it. I hate what happened to us.

Hate that being married hasn't been a magic eraser.

"Zaney?" Fee's wiping tears from my face. I can't help it. I'm crying.

"Don't you get mad sometimes? About what was taken from us?" I cling to her like a lifeline. "I shouldn't be having a conversation with you about a goddamn bullshit sex club. I shouldn't have ever been there in Berlin. I shouldn't have ever put my dick into anyone but ..."

She presses her hand over my mouth. "Stop. I'm so sorry. I sometimes forget that you were heartbroken too. I keep seeking some sort of knowledge. Reassurance that I'm going to be enough ..." Fee removes her hand and kisses me. "God, let's just quash this. Tonight was incredible. We—I—just need to remember to stay in the present."

"If you ask, Fee, I'm going to be honest with you. I have no secrets. I never have." I lean my head against her chest.

Fiona strokes my hair for a while. It lulls me into a state of relaxation. My eyes are drifting shut when I hear her whisper, "I hate what they took from us too."

"We should tell them sometime. Maybe it would help our family heal." I'm half-asleep, but it's a thought that occurs to me often.

She kisses the side of my head. "You're probably right. For now, let's take the summer to just have fun. Think about it a bit."

"Sounds like a deal." I snuggle in closer.

Odds are, we'll never have a conversation with Carter. Lianne. Faye.

Still. Somehow, knowing it's even a possibility makes me feel just a tiny bit better.

Chapter Seven

A Couple of Weeks Later

I CANNOT BELIEVE I'M here.

Alinea. Recognized as one of The World's 50 Best Restaurants, but it's also Chicago's only location to have earned—and kept—three Michelin Stars.

My fucking dream.

Zane used his rockstar prowess to get us coveted seats at the chef's table. Deacon and Harper McCoy have joined us. He's the bass player in Oblivion. She's also a chef with a successful catering business. Juliet Reece, bass player of Warning Sign is also here with her partner, chef extraordinaire, Tristan Eves.

Over the years, LTZ has toured and played festivals with both Oblivion and Warning Sign, who are on the same record label. Of course I'm familiar with both bands, but I've never met any of the members until tonight.

Leave it to my husband to invite the perfect couples. The rockers talk shop. Us chefs lose our minds over the modernist cuisine. It's a perfect night out. With perfect food. Plus, Olga is watching all of our kids, so our minds are at ease.

The five-hour experience is unbelievable from start to finish. Chef Achatz creates a theatrical dining bonanza. All dishes are experimental and exciting, incorporating scented vapors. Molecular gastronomy. Whimsy. Beauty. Drama. Starting with Arctic char topped with crisped skin, glazed with maple syrup. Salmon roe suspended in smoke gel. Foie gras baguette. Wagyu beef with truffle and a crispy potato hash brown.

But it's the dessert that blows me away. The serving staff takes down a flat platter that we assumed was a light fixture and placed it in the middle of the round table we're seated at. The entire kitchen brigade enters our private room, one by one, creating a Jackson Pollock-esque food painting using sauces, blueberries, and a liquid nitrogen-frozen block of chocolate mousse that they smash to bits all over the surface.

Every single bite is divine. I'm so inspired. My mind whirls with possibilities. I scoff at my spreadsheets. I've worked at a three-Star Michelin restaurant—Le Bernardin—so I'm no slouch when it comes to fine dining. Even if it's been nearly a decade, I've got this.

Experiencing a Michelin Star restaurant as a diner is night and day different than cooking the food itself. Or reading about it. We're back in the Big Apple in next week. Zane booked us into Le Bernardin, my old place of employment. I can't believe I've come full circle.

"You look incredibly happy." Zane and I hold hands as we wait for our Uber to pick us up like normal people. Thankfully, despite the star power at our table, no fans bothered us tonight. The only rockstar moment was when the kitchen staff took some Polaroid pictures with our entire table.

I clutch a little bag of homemade candy presented to each couple at end of the meal. "Yeah, well, I guess you have your stage. I have mine."

"It was definitely your night." Zane twirls me around under his arm. "It was fun to see you chatting away with Harper and Tristan."

"God, I haven't talked shop in years. It was incredible. I've isolated myself a lot. I guess I didn't realize it." I snuggle against Zane's hard chest.

The Uber arrives. I lay wrapped in Zane's arms all the way back to The Four Seasons, where we're staying in a two-bedroom suite. Olga shuts off the reality TV show she was watching, says goodnight and heads to her own room. Zane and I check in on Mia, who should have been asleep for a couple hours, to find her wide awake.

I sit on the bed next to her. "Are you having trouble sleeping, Meems?"

"Where did you go?" She clutches a stuffed flea Zane gave her when she was a toddler. It never leaves her side.

"I took your mom on a grownup date." Zane leans back against the headboard and pulls her back against his chest. "Do you think we need to have a little daddy-daughter time tomorrow?"

Mia claps her hands and shrieks, "What will we do?"

"Well, I have reservations for tea at the American Girl store at eleven. Then, I thought you might want to get your ears pierced." Zane twirls a lock of her hair around his finger.

She squirms around and shoves Zane in the chest. "Don't tease me. Are you serious?"

"Dead serious." He boops her nose.

Mia whirls toward me. "I can get my ears pierced?"

"I guess so." I shake my head at Zane but can't help but laugh.

"Why isn't it morning yet?" Mia shoves her fists in the air and shakes them. "Why?"

Zane kisses the top of her head and gets up. Holds the blankets out. "In you go. The faster you get to sleep, the faster morning comes."

With Mia off to bed, we cross the suite to our room. I'm standing in a tank top and underwear at the bathroom mirror ready to wash my face when Zane moves behind me and wraps his arms around my belly. His palm spans my stomach. I've gained five more pounds with all of the huge meals we've been eating.

Funny, I don't feel self-conscious at all.

Huh.

"Hey." I catch his gaze in the mirror. "Whatcha doin?"

"Can we talk about making a baby?" Zane's long, curly hair melds with my magenta waves. His olive skin is in sharp contrast to my nearly translucent coloring. His sultry eyes bore into my blue ones. "Look at us. Can you imagine how good-looking our kid is going to be?"

I lean back against him. "That's going to have to wait until Gus opens, babe. Besides, when LTZ gets back together I wouldn't be super stoked about being on my own with an infant and a restaurant to run."

"We could travel as a family on the new bus." His hand works its way back to my belly. "I want a bunch of kids. We always talked about having kids."

He's so earnest. His voice nearly quivers. God, I love him. He's so fucking sexy. I tip my head up to kiss his scruffy chin. Run my nose along his jaw. His arms tighten. He cups my breast. Pinches my nipple. I gasp because it sends a zing straight to my clit.

"We're having so much fun practicing this summer, Fee." His mouth finds mine in a chaste, soft kiss. Then he gets naughty. He slips his tongue between my lips to dance with mine. Deepening. Building. Zane's thick cock nestles between my ass cheeks. "Maybe, if we're lucky, one of my swimmers will take."

Zane's fingers are now buried inside my soaked pussy. Tunneling. Scissoring. He yanks my panties to the side, bends me over the bathroom counter and buries himself inside me. "Holy shit," I cry out, spasming with gratification.

He ruts into me, balls slapping against my ass. Watches himself fuck me in the mirror. I didn't even notice he'd pulled my tank top up. My tits sway and bounce in time to his thrusts. "We're so fucking hot, Fee. Look at us."

We are fucking hot. I can't help but gaze at his beautiful face as he pounds into me. He's so into it. So into *me*. His face is in absolute rapture when he floods me with his come. He's magnificent. Eyes squinched shut. Lips pursed. Back arched. Taut arm muscles straining. When he's done, he holds me tightly, my back to his front. The smell of our sex is intoxicating. Our combined release runs down my inner thighs. Zane kisses my neck. Cups and squeezes my breasts. Worships me.

Loves me.

This is pure fucking bliss.

Minutes later, we fall into bed, wrapped together. I cradle his head against my chest. Stroke his soft hair with my nails. My words come out slurred. Happy. "I want us to have kids, Zaney. We will. A bunch of them. Give me a year or so. I'll still be young enough to bear an entire team of mini-Zanes."

"That's fair." He pulls me snug against him. "I'm so proud of you."

I rake my nails lightly against his pecs. "Why? I haven't done anything yet."

"Not true. You're a wonderful mom to Mia. You're a phenomenal chef. Sense of humor. Leader. Strength. Determination. Focus. But you're also soft. Sweet. Caring. Empathetic. Generous. You could have turned out a lot worse, considering." He peppers kisses on my temple.

I think about what he says. "Yeah..."

"No. Stop with the hamsters in your head." Zane tilts my chin up to look at him. "Tonight, for the first time in a long time, you were relaxed. Yet also fiery. Like your old self ... before. You were in your element. I hate that your confidence was damaged. It pisses me off. You didn't deserve for that to happen to you."

Tears unexpectedly fill my eyes. "I'm sorry ..."

"Oh, God, babe. No." He grips my jaw gently. "Don't ever be sorry for things that aren't your fault. Don't let me put my shit on you either. I guess with so much time on my hands I've been thinking. Reflecting. I've decided to schedule some sessions with Lisa Kincaid."

Lisa is Zane's therapist. She's helped members of LTZ over the years because her specialty is working with musicians and creatives. "Wow. I haven't heard you mention her in a long time."

"Well, you never made the appointment with the therapist your doctor referred. I'm not going to force you. You're not into it." His voice is a whisper.

"We've been a bit busy traveling around the country." I trace his nipple with my nail.

We lay quietly for a while. Finally Zane speaks. "Fee, it's okay if you aren't ready. As for me? I don't want to make mistakes with Mia. I'm going to talk to someone. I'm telling you this because know I can say anything to you and I'm safe. I trust you. Even if you get lost in your head sometimes, I hope you know I'm not going anywhere. Our bond is unbreakable."

Ohmygod. He knows.

Zane's fingers stroke my arm lightly. "Baby, here's the thing. You don't need to walk on pins and needles. You don't need to keep things from me. There is literally nothing you could do or say to ever make me leave you. Whatever obstacle we face, I know it'll be better if we tackle it together. Therapy saved my life as a kid. I have no shame in needing it as an adult."

"You want therapy for our relationship?" I'm stunned.

He props himself up on an elbow. Runs his knuckles along my cheek. "Mostly, I want it for me. I'm struggling with my own identity. I miss my band. I haven't talked to any of them in a month. Not even a text from any of them. It makes me sad. I feel displaced. I'm lonely without my band brothers. You're clearly struggling too. There's no judgement in that observation. I'd like us to be healthy. I'd like us to be there for each other like we always have been."

Holy shit, this man knows me so much better than I know myself. After Carter's overdose, Lianne put Zane into therapy to learn how to cope with an addictive father. I remember my mom scoffing at the idea. So many times she poked fun at "weak" little Zane. I think about all of the shitty little comments she'd make when we'd go on our summer vacations. It breaks my heart. Not just for him. For me.

Zane always took it like a champ. He knew that however many digs she made at him, she made ten times as many at me.

"Do you think I'm turning into Faye? Please tell me the truth. I'd die before I'd ever subject Mia to anything like ..." My eyes plead with Zane.

Since Zane and I got married, whenever I see my mother, it ends up in a fight. It's exhausting. Soul crushing.

He shakes his head vigorously. "No. The truth is you're nothing like her." He pauses, considering what else he's going to say. "In all fairness, I think you carry all of the lies she told you about yourself deep in your psyche though. I want to exorcise that shit out of you. Whenever I see doubt or fear or whatever in your face, it guts me."

"If you think I should go talk to someone—I'll do it. No excuses. Let's finish out our trip and we'll set it up for when we get back." I clutch his arms. "I love you so much, aside from my dad, you're the only one who's ever truly had my best interests at heart."

"I'll always have your back, babe. Always." Zane's entire body relaxes in relief.

"I've upped my dose rather than weaning off," I confess.

He nods. I knew it. He already knows.

"You weren't going to say anything?" I can't bear putting Zane through more addiction shit. He's had enough for two lifetimes.

Zane sucks in a breath. "Not yet. I know why you need them. I just wish you didn't. Or wouldn't."

Wow. Direct hit to the core.

I'll throw the goddamn pills out tomorrow and tough it out before I'll stress out my beautiful, sweet, sensitive, intuitive husband one minute longer.

He's got a point, though. There are alternatives staring me in the face.

The idea of dredging up old shit with my mom terrifies me.

But, he's worth it. So worth it.

And maybe—just maybe—I am too.

Chapter Eight

About a Month Later

WE'RE NEARLY OUT OF the woods.

Fee should have the fucking Xanax out of her system soon. Hopefully for the last time.

After Chicago, at her insistence, we postponed New York and flew back home so she could see her doctor and wean off again. I could tell she was shocked that I knew she'd upped her dose.

That's what scared me. It wasn't hard to figure out. Not at all. Fiona was noticeably loopy, almost like she was drunk. She was so tired. Sleepy. The biggest indication was when sarcastic, witty Fee was essentially replaced by her eerie twin, docile Stepford Fee.

I can't help but shudder.

Today marks her fourth week detoxing with four to six weeks to go—it's such a fucking long process. Fee's convinced she needs some sort of medicinal help so we researched alternative pharmaceutical long-term solutions. Zoloft. Lexapro. Klonopin. Midazolam. Holy hell. The meds are either highly addictive or come with brutal side effects..

Fee was distraught until my mom suggested we talk to a naturopath. Turns out there are great alternative medical options. We have an herbal remedy plan Fee is actually excited about.

I'll admit, I was a bit skeptical. Now, I'm convinced. Natural. Less negative side effects. In many instances, far better results in changing a brain's chemistry and how it responds to anxiety.

Fiona being fully invested is the key. She's taking Ashwagandha and Passionflower and will add in Valarian after the Xanax has worked its way out of her system. In the meantime, her naturopath prescribed herbal concoctions to take before bed if she needs help sleeping.

The extent and length of her anxiety continues to break my heart. The fact she's been living with it...

God.

In our first session, I learned Fee was prescribed a benzo years ago. To deal with our breakup. Then again after Gus died. To get through her grief.

It was surprising news. I thought we told each other everything.

I'm not mad. Or hurt. Mostly sad at the circumstances of why she didn't tell me.

The thing is, when I showed up for Fee at Gus's funeral, we hadn't spoken in over two years. I knew she needed me. I felt it in my bones. The energy between us was powerful. Charged. But our relationship was tenuous for a long, long time.

It took months for her to begin to trust me. We had to repair our fractured friendship. For Mia's sake. I certainly wasn't "Daddy" back then. She called me "Unka Zane" for fuck's sake. I wonder if she remembers that?

Anyway, it was well over a year before anything romantic happened between us. By the time we were fucking again, Fiona had long stopped taking Xanax.

So I thought.

When the custody situation took a turn, I knew she had a script for benzos to stay sane in the face of a terrible crisis. It made sense to me. She hadn't been sleeping. Her emotions were off the charts. The prospect of losing custody of Mia was...unfathomable.

Holy fucking shit, though. None of her doctors ever explained how addictive the stuff is. Or how dangerous it is to go off it cold turkey. Her magic solution for life's overwhelming moments has a steep, steep price.

It's been a stressful few weeks, but we're coping. Together.

As for now, I'm in my studio in our basement practicing. Tonight, Fractured is playing the Angel of the Winds Arena in Everett, which is an hour north of Seattle. They invited me to jam onstage. I love the band and I'm familiar with their music, but LTZ has never played a show with them so I haven't seen them live. I've been holed up for hours watching YouTube and learning their tunes.

"There you are." Carter raps on the door, strolls in and takes a seat across from me. "Fiona sent me down here to bring you up for dinner."

I grab my phone and see it's nearly five-thirty. "Shit. I got sucked in."

"Sounded great." He nods at me. His long, black hair flecked with gray looks tidier than normal. Trimmed. He's trying to impress someone.

Likely Lianne, my mom.

Ever since this past Christmas when she spent the holidays with us, I've felt a little weird around my dad. I'm burying my head in the sand a bit because it's clear there's something going on with my parents. Fiona thinks so and believes it's been going on for a while. I'm not so sure. When I brought it up to Carter, he brushed me off.

I don't dare ask my mom. I have no idea why she'd ever consider taking Carter back after all that went down. That being said, as far as I know, she's never had a long-term boyfriend. So ...

"Thanks. Are you coming with me tonight? Maybe you can play too?" I set my Gibson in its case. Throw in a pack of strings. All's that left to do is change and I'm ready.

Carter follows me up the stairs. "Nah. The TikTok generation doesn't want to see an old guy like me. Before you know it LTZ will be classic rock. What will that make Limelight?"

"Zaney!" My mom stands in the foyer. Smothers me as much as possible considering she's half my size. "I've missed you so much. You never text. You never call."

"I miss you too, Mom." I hug her back, looking over her head at Fiona, who rolls her eyes. Mia helps her set out the food on the island that tends to be our go-to surface for sexy times.

If my parents only knew.

Uh, *no*. Maybe not.

We take our plates of roast lamb, baby new potatoes, and green beans to the conservatory.

"Holy fuck, Fee," Carter says through a mouthful. "This is amazing."

Lianne touches his arm. "How are the renovations going? I heard there were some delays."

"We should be close to done with construction by October, November. We get back from New York at the end of the month and I'm going to hire a *chef du cuisine* and pastry chef to work up recipes here in this kitchen. As soon as we can, we'll move the test kitchen over to Gus." Fiona's smile is radiant. I know she's chomping at the bit to get moving.

Carter leans back and pats his belly. "I'll need to have a seat with my name engraved on it."

"The food's going to be much fancier than this, Carter." Fee slugs Carter in the arm.

"Ow. You're strong, Fee. Don't hurt an old man." Carter rubs his arm and then caresses Fiona's cheek. "Seriously, your dad would be so proud of you. I know it."

My dad and Fee's dad were best friends for their whole lives. As sweet as Carter's sentiment is, his comment hits me in a soft, tender place. After my mom and I moved to Denver, Fiona spent more time with my dad than I did. He'd miss my birthday yet be there for hers. I mean, he was a full-blown addict at the time, but still ...

"Babe, dinner's awesome but we've got to get to the venue." I stand and throw my napkin on my plate.

Fee nods. "Go change, I'll set the plates in the sink. Olga can load the dishwasher."

"Are you two coming with?" I glance between my mom and dad.

The look that passes between them makes my stomach hurt. It's how I look at Fee. No fucking question.

Shit.

"I'd like to see you play." Lianne rests her chin on her hand but doesn't pull her moony eyes from Carter.

I clap my hands to stop my eyes from bleeding. "Awesome. Okay, I'll text Tex."

"Text Tex?" Carter laughs.

"Yeah, Tex McLain. He's Fractured's me." I glance up from my phone as I send a message to the band's guitarist.

An hour later, we're pulling into the VIP parking at AWA. Zeke gets our passes sorted. We jump on a golf cart and are whisked to the backstage area. Seattle's new venue, Climate Pledge Arena, doesn't open until later this year, so most big shows have been diverted up here for the time being.

Fiona's hand is on my thigh. "Are you excited?"

"Yeah—but I'd rather jam with my guys. We've never gone this long without playing." My knees bounce. I fidget with my zipper. It's been a couple months since

I've received anything from my bandmates but a quick text. It bums me out to no end.

Carter cranes his neck from where he's sitting. "I forgot to tell you. Ty called. Says they're coming home in a month or so. Zoey's migraines are getting worse."

"He called you? Really?" Now I'm a little pissed. "Ever since he got back together with Zoey, it's like I don't exist."

Fee chortles. "Ah, Zaney. Is your boyfriend ignoring you?"

I stare at her, then burst into laughter too. Jesus. I'm acting like a jealous lover. He deserves to have some downtime with the woman he'd been unwillingly separated from for eight years. Thanks to my dad, which is *why* the call does niggle at me. Now's not the time. "I'm an asshole. Is Zoey feeling any better?" She had a scary fainting incident at an awards ceremony earlier this year.

"She made an appointment with a specialist to get to the bottom of things." Carter reaches down and takes Lianne's hand. Places it on his thigh.

My mom looks back nervously to see if I've noticed. I raise an eyebrow. "I know you guys are together, there's no need to hide it."

"We're not," Lianne says simultaneously as Carter gleefully proclaims, "We are."

"You two need help." Fee shakes her head. "Even if it's not official, you're fucking like rabbits. You're not hiding anything. Can you please put Zane out of his misery? Just admit you're in looooove."

"Fiona!" My mom's face reddens to a shade I've never seen. She's saved from further discussion when the golf cart pulls up to where a group of Fractured dudes are standing.

Tex approaches me. When I see him in person, I nearly fall over. He's the absolute double of Ty. His hair is a different color. Clothes are a different style. That's about it.

"Tex McClain." He holds out his hand.

"Zane Rocks. My wife, Fiona. My dad Carter Pope and mom Lianne Rocks." I gesture to my family.

Tex introduces us to his bandmates Connor Byrne, Noah Taylor, and Zac Ford, who lose their minds when they realize Carter fucking Pope is with me. "You've got to join us. We'd be so honored," Tex pleads.

Carter grumbles a bit but agrees. He may be a legendary guitar player in a band that doesn't tour much these days, but he gets his fuel from playing to a crowd just like me.

The four of us get settled into our own room before the Fractured dudes join us again. While the opening band plays, Tex, Connor, and I figure out when they want me to join their set.

"You're freaking me out, man," I say to Tex. "I swear to God, if you didn't have the southern accent I'd swear you were Ty."

"I get that a lot. Personally, I don't see it." He stretches his legs out. Shrugs.

I turn my attention to their singer, joking, "And you, why do you have to be named Connor? It's so confusing for me."

God it feels fantastic to shoot the shit before a show. Knowing there will be a show. And I'll be playing in the show. I need to hold on until I'm with my own band. I can get through it.

When it's time for Fractured to take the stage, Fee and I decide to watch from the sidelines. I hand Tex's guitar tech my Gibson, warning him that if anything happens to it I'll murder his entire family. Carter and Lianne sit on stools behind us. Mom's body language is cold. Dad looks miserable. I guess Fee's comment didn't go over well, but I don't blame her for making it. Whatever's going on between my parents is weird.

Ignoring their tension, I stand in between them and sling an arm around each of their shoulders. "Trouble in paradise?"

"Zane, stop it." My mom shoots me her most angry look, which isn't all that scary. "Don't be unkind. Your father and I are trying to figure things out. If you want to sit down and talk about it, let's do that. The passive-aggressive comments are not appreciated."

Carter blurts out, "I want your mom back. I've always wanted her back. It's no secret. It's never been a secret."

"Look, I'm married with a kid. If you're worried about permission from me, don't. I'm thirty fucking years old. I don't care what you guys do." I throw my hands in the air.

"Um, a little awareness of your surroundings? Maybe take this conversation somewhere else." Fee steps in the middle of us. "You're not being exceptionally stealth. Do you want this to end up on TikTok?"

I kiss my mom's cheek, I never want to make her feel bad. "I'm sorry. I'll back off."

Fee grabs my hand. We move closer to stage to watch the band. Well, I watch Fee. Her cleavage is out of control. I visualize cupping her big tits and sucking on those delicious nipples. My cock hardens. Shit, I'm going to embarrass myself and my wife if I don't refocus my energy on what I'm here to do.

Reluctantly, I turn my attention back to Fractured. Soon it's my cue and I join them. The crowd goes insane, which is a huge ego boost. But when Carter appears?

The roof nearly blows off the stadium. The old man still has it. We play with them for about twenty minutes, Tex, Carter, and I trade off in an epic three-way guitar showdown.

We don't hang around after the show, Fee wants to get home to Mia. When the car pulls up, we walk past a dozen fans or so who mill outside. I sign a couple autographs while Fee patiently waits beside me.

"Who's the fat chick, Zane?" A girl screams so loud it reverberates.

Fee stiffens. I grab her hand, squeeze and move us toward the car. No one gets to talk to my wife that way, but I know if I lose my cool our photos will end up all over social media making Fee a target. Unfortunately, me leaving doesn't go over well. A couple women join in the taunts at my wife. Ridicule Fee about her "fat ass." Call her chubby. Call me a "chubby-chaser."

I'm so furious. She's unbearably gorgeous in her green bustier and black jeans. I walk faster, dragging Fee with me. "Don't listen to them. Don't acknowledge them. They're just fucking idiots," I whisper to Fiona.

We make it to the car. Fee practically dives in. Lianne and Carter follow. Now that Fiona's safely inside, I flip the fans the bird before turning my attention back to my girl.

She's sobbing. Shit. Shit. Shit.

"Babe, don't let them get to you. They're jealous, mean, asshole people." I snuggle her to me. "You're so beautiful. Hotter than all of them combined."

She sniffles. "I've never felt so humiliated."

"Sweetheart, please don't take what they say to heart." Lianne's voice soothes. "Women will say anything to get under your skin when you're with a famous person. You've been with Zaney for a long time, you know better."

Tears stream down her face. I furiously dab them away with my thumb. Kiss her sweet face. I'm at a loss.

Carter, being Carter, somehow manages to bumble his way into the solution. "Fiona fucking Reynolds. You're a goddamn Michelin Star chef. Your job is to cook and eat food. My son has never had eyes for anyone but you. Be yourself. Live your life. Don't you ever let anyone bring you down. Don't you ever cry over a group of skanks who'd suck thirty dicks just to get backstage. Hold your head high, girl. You are stunning. Talented. Smarter than all of those hoe-bags combined. You are and always have been a fucking queen."

"Ohmygod, Carter." Fee's sobs turn into laughter. "Hoe-bags? Who are you?"

He shrugs. "Carter fucking Pope. I just call it like I see it."

My mom can't contain her smile. She reaches over and takes his hand, which makes Carter visibly happy. Maybe their reunion isn't such a bad idea.

I lean down and kiss Fee. She mutters, "Stupid fucking bitch. I'm the one sucking Zane's cock tonight. Or any night."

"I heard that, Fee." Lianne shakes her head.

Jesus. My family.

Unconventional. Complicated.

One thing's indisputable, we have each other's backs.

I'm one lucky sonofabitch.

Chapter Nine

One Month Later

To achieve my Michelin Star dream, the entire staff at Gus *must* be exceptional.

Front of the house is the wait staff, hosts, and sommelier. Back of the house is my entire team of chefs. The business manager will oversee the books, hiring and vendors. Finally, a public relations firm to get the word out about my restaurant. If I'm successful at bringing in top-notch candidates in all of these areas, Gus will have an excellent chance of making a mark straight out of the gate.

Once Zane, Mia, and I came home, my days were filled with endless amounts of paperwork. Zane got Mia settled into first grade while I was neck-deep in building the foundation of the business. It's intense. Employment agreements, training manuals and policy and procedure documents, liquor licenses, and LLC agreements.

My business manager, Emilie Fontaine, is an absolute rockstar. I met her when she was a bookkeeper at the restaurant I managed when I returned to Seattle. In the years since, she's leveled up considerably, earning a reputation for being a hard-ass, but fair, finance officer. I trust her implicitly, as does Zane.

Chef du Cuisine is a crucial role. It's important to hire someone as soon as possible. While I was away, Emilie prescreened to narrow down the field. We conducted Zoom interviews with the final candidates and have two contenders for the position. Petra Novak, who's held key roles at Atelier Crenn and Maude. Justice Abarca staged all over Paris, then Barcelona before spending the past couple years in New York at Per Se.

The Chef du Cuisine I hire will work with me to test and perfect recipes, recruit the rest of the team, train them, and get ready for service.

Gus doesn't have running water yet, so we're still weeks away from being able to use the kitchen. In the meantime, while Zane and Mia are in San Francisco for a show, I've flown Petra and Justice to Seattle to cook with me at the house for what is, essentially, a working interview. The fact that these two outstanding candidates are even considering coming on board blows my mind. I've been away from the restaurant scene for a while, but Seattle is a foodie town and the prospect of bringing a Michelin Star here is an exciting opportunity,

"Petra. Do you see value in the French system of hierarchy of the kitchen?" Emilie sits at the counter while the three of us tie on our aprons.

Petra is a slight, owlish woman with huge glasses who gives off a silent-but-deadly vibe. "Great kitchens are comprised of people who become like family. Dedicated chefs who work hard, play hard, and have a common goal of putting out perfect, delicious food. So, yes. Following the traditional hierarchy is important because it allows the team to focus on their role."

It's a great answer. She shares my philosophy, French food isn't synonymous with fine dining because there are better chefs in France. Or better ingredients, even. It's the rigorous, standardized training system that I experienced at Le Bernardin.

Emilie taps the tip of her pen to her lips. "Justice? Do you have any opinion on this?"

"Of course." Justice is extraordinarily handsome. Short, black hair. Huge blue eyes. Angular, chiseled face.

He exudes a calm confidence, almost like his superpower is to slow down time. His movements are elegant. Precise. As are his words. "The genius of the *brigade du cuisine* is how close it is to an assembly line. When the structure is fully embraced, the entire staff understand their role and are able to cook and serve perfect, delicious food."

Another great answer.

"I envision the brigade as follows. I am the Owner and Executive Chef. This is my concept. My vision. My recipes." I pace the kitchen. Back and forth. "Chef du Cuisine will oversee all daily kitchen operations including hiring, firing and scheduling, administrative operations, and ensuring my vision is executed day in and day out. I anticipate having several sous chef positions, line cooks. Dishwashers."

Justice glances around my ginormous kitchen. "What stations do you anticipate implementing?"

"Great question. We're in Seattle. Land of the most delicious seafood in the world. Probably the most important station will be the fish station. Sauces. Meat. Sides. Salad. Dessert ..." I trail off a bit. "I'd like to have innovation and cohesion."

Petra laughs. "Sometimes those are diametrically opposed, but when the team is able to embrace both concepts? Magic happens."

Oh, I like her. this decision is going to be tough.

"Emilie has explained how this weekend will go. Today will be a cooking skills day. Rather than reinvent the wheel, I have five one-hour tests. The most important is knife skills. I want you to prep ten vegetables in an hour." I hand each of them a printed list. "Next will be eggs. Please prepare a perfectly poached egg and a beautiful omelet. The third and fourth test will be combined. Roasted fish. Hollandaise sauce. We'll take a long break to hang out, eat, and visit. Later this afternoon, will be the consommé challenge."

Day to day, neither will be involved in prep or preparation of any of these things. However, if they have amazing skills they will insist on perfection of the staff. It will also give me a glimpse into how they work. Kitchen dynamics are nearly as important as skill.

To say I'm in my element is an understatement. I'm keeping a fairly decent poker face, but I haven't felt this excited about my career since before Mia was born.

Both Petra and Justice produce innovative, impeccable dishes. Thank God I have Emilie with me to evaluate because they are neck and neck. We send them upstairs to shower and change while we go out to my new greenhouse to chat.

"Justice's fish dish was so harmonious and balanced. The use of blood oranges heightened the dish. And his plating. Exquisite." Emilie sighs. "And wow, is he pretty to look at."

I purse my lips at her. "No fraternizing with the candidates, missy, but I agree with you." I stare out the glass for a second. "I agree with your assessment of Justice's food. As for Petra's dishes, every single one of the elements responded to each other. The sense of balance in each bite was extraordinary. She's so in tune with flavors, I get the feeling that if you blindfolded her and gave her little bites of food, she'd be able to identify anything. Her palate is incredible."

"Can we hire both?" Emilie stares at the two resumes. "It could solve the problem of staffing when you're on the road with Zane."

"It's unorthodox." I shake my head. "They're giving up current high-profile jobs to work with me, I don't want them to be competitive. It sets the wrong vibe for Gus."

"Yeah. I know. I just like them both a lot."

"I do too. Tonight let's show them the restaurant." We walk back to the house. "Then, let's just go about this weekend the way we planned and try not to become predisposed to either of them. Let things unfold the way they ..." I listen to myself speaking and realize I sound like the Zen version of Zane.

But hey! I'm not anxious. Or stressed. In fact, I haven't thought about anything but the task at hand for hours.

Holy shit. I feel normal and I haven't taken a benzo in nearly two months.

"Fee?" Emilie touches my elbow. "You stopped mid-sentence."

I shake the cobwebs away. "Oh, fuck. Sorry."

"Remind me of what the rest of the weekend looks like." She plucks a stalk of lavender from a bush we walk past.

"Tomorrow, they're doing the mystery baskets with a ninety-minute deadline." I've put together a bunch of weird ingredients like the show *Chopped*. "In the afternoon, we'll head to Pike Place Market to peruse the stalls for a bit of a break. This will give me the chance to see who I really vibe with, which is critical considering we'll be working so closely together."

She nods. "Or, people."

I laugh. "Or, people. Monday is the hardest day. I've given them each an envelope they're not supposed to peek at until that morning. The challenge is to provide a sample tasting menu for six they believe would be an excellent fit for Gus. I need them to cost it out. Shop. Cook. Prepare. It's an all-day thing. Zane and Mia will be back by dinnertime, so they'll help give feedback on the food."

Emilie scratches her cheek. "Who's joining us?"

"Ty and Zoey." I can't help but squeal a bit. "I texted Ty a couple weeks ago on the off-chance they'll be home. Turns out they're getting in tonight. We're all going to surprise Zane. He's going to be so excited."

"I'll get to meet Ty." Emilie bats her eyes. "He's so dreamy."

"And very, very taken. If you think Zane and me are bad, just wait. They never stop touching and making out and…it's quite something." I stifle a chortle.

She snaps her fingers like she's out of luck. "Damn. So he's truly into the girl he wrote the album about."

"You'll get to see for yourself."

We head back inside to find Justice and Petra deep in conversation at the kitchen island.

"Are you two ready for a real treat?" Emilie claps her hands excitedly. "Let's go tour the restaurant. Afterward, we're having a private dinner at Fee's other favorite Seattle restaurant, Altura."

As we climb into the car to begin our event activities, I realize I'm happy.

Opening a restaurant can be a huge stress.

For me, it's like a vacation after the shit I've been through for the past seven years.

I'm not even worried about what happens when LTZ reunites. I'm certain Zane and I will figure it out.

It feels phenomenal to be in charge. To be doing something I'm great at.

All of my dreams are coming true.

Chapter Ten

A Couple of Weeks Later

BOLD, BRAZEN FEE IS back with a vengeance.

I'm so goddamn happy. I knew she'd get back here if she believed in herself. Her passion for Gus is inspiring. The build-out is coming along. Her new staff members are fully committed. Her dreams are coming true. She deserves it. I fucking love her so goddamn much.

And today, my entire band is back in town. We'll be together for the first time in months. It's been hard to sleep, I'm so excited.

It's too early to call Ty, though. I check my phone. Seven. Yeah. Too early.

I can't begin to describe my elation at seeing Ty again a couple weeks ago when Fee surprised me. I love all of my bandmates, but Ty is like my real brother. It's been that way from the minute we met. We have this unspoken bond. We're on the same wavelength.

I know he's disappointed his travels with Zoey have been cut short. Her health issues were important to deal with though.

Knowing he's back at his Seattle house, which is blocks away from mine, tethers me. Even if we haven't seen much of each other since he's been back, him just being here has gone a long way to alleviate my own anxiety about LTZ's future.

Today, we'll devise a plan to get the band business rolling again and it comes at the perfect time. Fee's busy with Gus. Mia's back in school. I'm climbing the fucking walls. Time to channel my energy into our music again.

"Don't call him this early." Fee stretches and yawns. Shifts to her side so she can see me and lifts her eyebrow.

I trace my knuckles along her cheek. "Did I wake you?"

"Uh, fidgeting much?" She rolls her eyes. "Just wait an hour."

I reach down and fist my semi-stiff shaft. Pump it to a full erection. "I can do that."

"Whatcha doin?" She pulls the duvet back to reveal my activities. "Hmmm. What a mighty big cock you have there, sir. I could use a bit of that."

I lean back on the pillow and grab the headboard with both hands. "Well, then. Have your way with me, fair lady. It would be my honor for you to take what you need."

She kisses down my chest to where my dick is flush against my belly. Fee lifts my cock and licks her way up the underside. "I need this." She hums against my crown.

Holy Jesus. I can't help but fist a clump of her hair at her nape. Tug it a bit. Push and pull her up and down on my cock. Fee knows this game. She takes me deep. All the way down her throat. "Shit, Fee," I hiss and watch myself disappear between her lips. She gags a bit each time I hit the back of her throat, causing saliva to pool in her cheeks and drip down my shaft. Her mouth is pure, wet bliss.

Over the years, Fiona and I have shared thousands of euphoric sexual experiences. Our relationship's had tremendous ups. Downs. Even middles. None of it matters. I'll never, ever get tired of fucking my wife.

It makes me so hot when she's uninhibited and unashamed of her beautiful, lush body—like now. She's free to explore her sensuality with me, and she embraces that freedom. Fee slips her hand under my balls. Rolls them. Cups. Squeezes. She opens her throat. Braces her other hand on my stomach, swirling her nail around the fine hair. My cock slips all the way past her gag reflex into nirvana. My jaw clenches because I'm trying so hard not to ram myself all the way down her throat.

Eventually, she licks her way back up my shaft and suckles the crown, gripping the base with her fist. "God, I love blowing you, Zaney."

"Thank Jesus, because I will die if you ever stop giving me head," I moan. My hips rotate on the bed in tandem with her tongue drilling into the hole at the tip of my cock. So fucking intense.

Fee pumps me and takes me deep again. Bobs her head up and down for a bit before mumbling, "You have nothing to worry about."

"Climb on." My eyes are nearly rolled all the way back in my head. "Ride me. I want to fill your pussy full of my hot come."

It's been months since we've had sex in this position. It's my favorite. Her tits bouncing. Soft belly. Gah. My cock jumps at the thought of it. I hope she doesn't say she's too heavy...

Fee slings her leg over my hips to straddle me and impales herself. Splays her hands out on my ribcage and rolls her hips. "Like this?" she purrs.

My voice is guttural. "Yeah."

Ohmyfuckinggod.

She tortures me with slow, deliberate gyrations. She spends what seems like hours circling her pelvis. Finding the spot deep inside her and doubling down. Changing the angle. Repeat. I'm mesmerized watching my goddess wife take delight from my cock. Her eyes are locked with mine the entire time. We're in complete sync. When she comes, her head lolls back. Fee's nipples are hard peaks against her full mounds of deliciousness.

Now, it's my turn. I cup one breast in each hand and squeeze. Press them together and lean up on my elbows to tease them with my tongue. Fee winds her arms around my neck, fists my hair and brings her mouth to mine. We're grinding, kissing, biting, and sucking. She moans my name when she shatters for the second time, squeezing my cock with her inner muscles, giving me no choice but to let go. I shudder through my own release, spurting deep inside her. We're both panting. Tremoring. Spasming.

So. *Fucking*. Good.

Fee and I bask in our afterglow for a bit. She doesn't have much time to snuggle, though. This morning she's meeting with her new chefs, Justice and Petra, to go over the smallwares for the kitchen at Gus. They're also running into a couple of snags hiring a pastry chef and line cooks.

At least she has the two of them. "A dream team" as Fee calls them. They were both impressive during their interviews. The coursed dinner they prepared for us was simply stunning. Rather than decide, Fee hired them both.

While she showers, I make Mia breakfast so she'll be ready for school by the time Fiona needs to leave. The two of us have this parenting thing dialed in tight.

"Are you ready, Meems?" Fee whooshes into the room and begins gathering her things. Phone. Keys. "We need to get going."

Mia stuffs the rest of her peanut butter toast in her mouth. "Ready."

"You can call Ty now. It's officially not too early." Fee kisses me. I kiss Mia. Then, they're off.

Before I dial Ty, I see Connor's text requesting to move the meeting up an hour. I text Jace. He confirms. Next, I call Ty. It goes to voicemail. I dial again. Voicemail. Irritated, I hang up. What the hell is he doing?

Then I realize. He's probably still in bed with Zoey. I dial for the third time. "Yeah?" Ty's a bit out of breath, which means I was right. Exactly what I thought was happening is happening.

"We're all on the way, probably less than an hour. Connor's dad is having complications so we're moving things up so he can get back to his family. Jace is already on the ferry. I'm going to take a quick shower and pop over. Is that okay?" I word vomit all of the band business in about thirty seconds.

"Uh, yeah." He sounds groggy. "I'll need to have a shower too."

"I'm glad I called to give you the heads-up. We wouldn't have wanted to walk in on anything." I chuckle.

"Well, yeah. Zoey's boobs are off-limits from now on. Wait, what? Uh, give me one second." I can hear his muffled voice talking to Zoey before he returns to our conversation. "Zoey's going to meet her mom, so come over whenever."

Yes! I think but keep my voice somewhat tempered. "Cool. I'll be there soon."

After my shower, I walk the short distance to Ty's house just as Connor's pulling into the driveway. "Zane Rocks, how the feck' are ya." He slaps my back when he gets out of his Range Rover.

"Ready to meet the twins. When does Ronni get to town?" I lope toward the front entrance with Connor close behind.

He doesn't have the chance to answer because Ty appears at the door. Jace stands behind him. Holy hell, there are my dudes! My band brothers! I can't even speak.

Once inside, Ty leads us downstairs into his new home studio. He and I have jammed down here a couple times since he's been home. As of yet, Ty hasn't given any indication of where his head's at, claiming his focus is on Zoey. I can understand his position, but today's the day. It's time to be honest so we can figure our shit out.

God, I hope the guys are on the same page as me. I want to go back to work.

"My dudes, I hate to admit it but I feckin' missed you." Connor sinks into a chair by the mixing desk.

Just what I want to hear. I can't help it, I launch myself into his lap and kiss his scruffy, bearded cheek. "You're never allowed to fuck off to Ireland again. I don't care if you own ten homes there."

"You're a lunatic!" Connor shoves me off. We make a big show of him fending me off while I attempt to mount him. "For the record, it's just one house in Ireland. We're getting our new place ready in LA. Looks like it will be home base for a while, so it will. Ronni's pitching producing and potentially starring in a new series."

My heart sinks. I look over at Jace, who leans against the wall. He gives nothing away, the bastard. "The studio turned out awesome. Maybe we should just record the next stuff here. You have enough guest rooms, we could all just stay with you."

Ty's horrified look is priceless. I throw my arm around him. "You look like you're going to faint, Ty. Don't worry, he's just kidding."

"All of you are welcome to stay here any time. For however long you want." Ty pretend-chokes me. "Except you. I see you too much as it is."

Really? His words wound me. We've been at each other's houses once, maybe twice a week since he's been back.

"My dudes, please. Let's get down to business. Da's going in for his procedure tomorrow, so I gotta get back home." Connor motions for us all to sit.

Ty cuts to the chase. "My brothers, I'm just going to keep it simple. I need more time. I hope you understand."

"Thank God," I hear myself blurt out. "Fee is buried with everything that needs to get done for the restaurant opening. We need months to dial it all in."

WTF? What did I just do?

"I'm cool with that." Jace is so fucking nonchalant. He's living just across Puget Sound and he's been the most MIA out of all of us.

Connor breathes out a sigh of relief. "Aye. That's grand. The thought of going back out on the road right now? Feck no. But I do miss writing and recording. And playing if I'm honest. I want to come up with a plan so the kids can be with us. One that lets us take a lot of long breaks. I don't ever want to be gone for years at a time again."

Well, that's somewhat encouraging. I'm going to re-text him the buses I found tonight. "Ty, do you want to start writing? I have a few ideas." I'm suddenly nervous. Around a dude I founded the band with. A guy I lived with for a decade on a tour bus. "No pressure, just fun?"

"Yeah, I have a ton of stuff to demo." Ty smiles at me, making me feel slightly better. "Let's start in the new year, though. I want to finish our hiatus. To finish clearing my head."

"Is that what they're calling it now?" Jace snarks.

"He's clearing something." Connor's hearty laugh is contagious. We all join in.

When the laughter dies down, Ty takes a deep breath. "Well, it brings up something I need to tell you. Zoey and I are getting married sometime in the next couple of weeks. We just decided this morning, so I don't have the exact date. It won't be a big wedding. Just her family. Carter. All of us. The girls. The kids. I think that's it."

"Fucking awesome!" I can't help but jump up and hug Ty. If we have to take a few extra months off, at least we have a wedding to go to. That means we'll all be together.

Ty wrestles himself from my grasp. "Before we set the date, I wanted to check in with all of you to figure out what's most convenient for everyone."

"Dude, whatever day you pick, we'll be there. Text me when and where." Connor clearly has his family situation on his mind. "Seriously. Congratulations. I'm sorry but I gotta jet. Duty calls."

I'm bummed when he leaves. The entire meeting was a measly couple hours. Not how I pictured the day going. I'm dying to spend as much time as I can with my band, so I propose a surefire way to drag it out. "I'm hungry, feel like cooking, Ty?"

His eyes light up. "Sure. I think I have the fixings to make crab rolls. Homemade chips?"

Jace and I take seats to watch Ty cook. It's funny how alike he and Fiona are in the kitchen. It calms him. Soothes. He's always been an anxious person. Huh. I wonder why I never made that connection before. I can't wait to talk to Fee about it later.

"Sooooo..." I can't help but try to bring Jace back into the fold. "Double wedding? Alex and you. Ty and Zoey. Perfect, right?"

Jace looks around the room. "Uh...nah."

Ty has his ingredients organized and starts assembling. "I'm sure Zoey wouldn't care. I mean if we're all in town."

"See!" I make voodoo fingers at Jace. "Married life is awesome. Join us. Join us."

Jace is having none of it. "I don't think a double wedding's the way to go for us. Maybe we'll just elope."

"You'll be at our wedding though?" Ty glances at Jace.

He nods. "Of course, dude. I wouldn't miss it."

"Why would you elope? We hated missing Connor's wedding." I continue to interrogate him. He attempts to ignore me, which is a mistake. I wave my hand in front of his face. "Uh, Jace? You there?"

He bats my hand away. "It's just an idea. Let me work out the details with Poppy and you guys will be first to know. How's the restaurant coming? Is Fiona close to opening?"

"Fuck, no." I hate to share Fee's business woes, but I'm annoyed. "Between contractors bailing on us and failed inspections, it's been a nightmare. Neither of us has any experience with construction. Luckily, Connor's brother is on the job now. We should have brought McLoughlin Construction in from the beginning."

Ty sets down the crab. "Here you go."

"*Fuuuuck*. Ty. Be warned, Fiona's threatening to recruit you. She's having a hell of a time staffing up." I'm half-serious. "These are orgasmic."

Jace waggles his eyebrows. "You could just wear a wig. No one will recognize you. We all have some time on our hands now."

God, this feels so killer. Just shooting the shit with my band. I hope they have missed this as much as me. I decide not to worry. We're getting back together. Between babies and new restaurants and weddings, we do have so much shit going on.

Nothing's ever going to break up LTZ.

Why was I ever worried about something so stupid?

Chapter Eleven

A Couple of Weeks Later

CILLIAN MCGLOUGHLIN IS A feisty motherfucker.

Connor's brother pulls no punches with my former contractor who showed up to get paid this afternoon. I'm glad he stepped in to kick the bastard out. I'm crazy busy. Petra, Justice, and I are in the middle of preparing dinner for the entire band and their significant others. It's Ty and Zoey's joint bachelor/bachelorette party.

When Zane was stumped at what to do for his BFF, who decided to provide all of us with only three weeks' notice of the wedding, I volunteered. I love my husband, so...

I'll say it again. *I Vol. Un. Teered.*

Here. At Gus.

We are so far from being ready, it's laughable.

I'm such a fucking idiot.

Meanwhile, as Cillian rips the dude a new asshole, his crew is finishing the bathrooms, painting the office, installing the exit signs and ensuring all the final touches are complete. I mean, all of this needed to get done. I just didn't expect to feel so rushed.

I brought it on myself. Eleven courses.

Jesus.

"I've got most of the prep done, Fee." Justice is wiping down his station when I enter the kitchen. "Petra is butchering the lamb and deboning the fish."

"Great. I'll jump back in. I just want to write the menu down." I grab a Sharpie and a blank piece of paper. List each course. Each component. The accompanying wine. Shit. Wine. My heart stops. How could I have forgotten? My head snaps up to look around the kitchen frantically.

And there's Justice holding up a rare French burgundy. "I'm on top of it, chef."

There's no way I could have picked a better dream team. Justice, Petra, and I are in perfect sync. We work together so well it's scary. I'm so glad I didn't have to choose between them. Emilie helped me crunch some numbers. I discussed it with Zane. We had the answer.

Hiring both was the smart move. Together, we could get Gus on its feet faster. Selfishly? It frees me up. I want Mia and I to tour with Zane. He won't miss out on time with Mia and I won't be an absentee parent.

Eventually, I want to have Zane's babies.

Justice and Petra will give me the opportunity to have my cake and eat it too.

"We'll peace out so you can set up for dinner." Cillian joins me at the table where I'm finishing up my list. "You should be good to go for tonight. I'll stop in on Monday so we can put together the punch list. There's still quite a few things to do."

I follow him out into reception area. As he reaches for the door, I shock him by giving him a hug. "You've worked miracles. I appreciate all your help."

"It's my pleasure. We're all excited for you to get the restaurant and the club open. You're creating a true legacy here, Fee." Cillian's kind words are in stark contrast to his gruff treatment of my former contractor. He tips an invisible hat and is off.

My phone buzzes. I click on FaceTime. Zane's in our bathroom dripping wet from his shower. He sets the phone on the vanity so I have a great view of his naked chest. "Hey there, sexy man."

"Well, hello my sexy backdoor baby." Zane was so thrilled I let him fuck me in the ass last night, I probably won't hear the end of it.

Oh God. "Do NOT call me that tonight if you ever want in on that action ever again."

"You're no fun." He pouts.

I flip the camera around and pan the room. "Cillian and his crew just left, do you think this will be okay for tonight?"

"Yeah, babe. It looks phenom. I mean, there's still work to be done, but tonight will be a perfect testing point," he observes as he shaves his handsome face.

"How are you doing? Has Ty talked to you about his mom?" I'm not trying to interfere. Zane feels sad that Ty hasn't even mentioned his mother's shocking death.

His face falls a bit, but he recovers. "No. It's distressing. I don't want him to slip back into old patterns."

"Yeah ..." My Zane. Always worrying about the other people in his life and putting them first. I feel so protective of him and his generosity. He's been let down enough.

Don't ever forget, you're one of those people.

Zane finishes shaving and splashes aftershave on his cheeks. "It's going to be fine. He didn't have much of a relationship with her. I think I'll focus on being the *best* best man there ever was. He's going to be shocked when we surprise him with the dinner tonight."

"He will." I can't help but stare at my gorgeous husband. Zane's hair is still damp. He's clean-shaven. His brown eyes are like windows into the kindest heart that ever existed. "Plus, you're just doing what he asked. Trying not to worry about him so much."

He's in our big walk-in closet now pulling a T-shirt over his head. "I'm still thinking about what he said about being brothers at the wedding-suit fitting. We are brothers. I don't care if we're not blood related. It just ... meant a lot. I always wanted a sibling. Maybe he did too." Zane focuses on me.

"I totally understand." I smile at him through the screen.

"Yeah, I know you do. At least we had each other for most of our childhood." Zane puckers his lips and faux-kisses me. "By the way, if I haven't said it before, let me say it now. Thank you for getting yourself off that Xanax shit. Have you looked at yourself lately? You're so radiant and happy. Glowing, almost. You didn't need it. The light and fire is all inside of you, babe. You're my strong, feisty, gorgeous girl."

I can't help but blush. He's perceptive. I've lost the weight I gained when we were galivanting last summer.

I feel enthused. Clearheaded. Confident. Despite all of the stress and deadlines I'm under, it's a good kind of anxious. The motivating kind rather than a debilitating kind. "And you're my rock. Together we can do anything."

"We can. All because you hired both Petra and Justice." Zane rests his head on his hand and just looks at me. Like I'm the only person on the planet. "Fee, I'm psyched we're giving Mia a big family. Not just the babies you and I are going to make. Connor and Jace have kids. Ty's going to knock Zoey up any day now. I'd love for all of them to grow up together."

It's hard not to melt. "We will. We'll have all of that." We stare at each other for a bit. This year, we're killing it at life. A couple little bumps in the road, but manageable. Tonight's going to be awesome. The thought jolts me into reality. "Shit, babe. I've gotta jam. I have less than six hours."

"Thank you for doing all of this. You're the true rock-star between the two of us." Zane kisses the screen and we hang up.

Four and a half hours later, the place looks dreamy. I couldn't be prouder.

The plan is bulletproof. Ty and Zoey think she's having a bachelorette party with Ronni and Alex because I'm too busy with the restaurant. Which is true, obviously, but not for the reasons they think. Zane, Connor, and Jace are going to rouse Ty from whatever it is he does all day and take him for "dinner," since he doesn't drink. If all goes as planned, the boys will arrive , then the ladies. I'll join them for dinner and we'll celebrate the upcoming wedding.

"Go get ready." Petra waves a towel at me. "We're done with you."

"Fine." I take off my apron, satisfied that we're as ready as we will ever be. "You'll fill Daire and Jetta in on service?"

She winks. "If I must."

Jesus. I hope she doesn't have a crush on him. Daire was one of the best servers I worked with at the restaurant I ran for Tom Douglas. He offered to help out tonight. Secretly, I'm hoping to make him General Manager and to oversee all front-of-house operations. We're not quite ready yet, so it's awesome he's willing to be a server tonight and bring his sister Jetta along to help.

I can't focus on that now, it's showtime.

Minutes later, I'm in the walk-in cooler, thumbing the embroidered writing on my chef's coat. *Fiona Reynolds, Owner, Executive Chef,* when I hear commotion that can only be LTZ just outside the door.

"Want a tour?" I pop out to greet the guys. Zane takes his place by my side. He's so proud of me. It just shines in his eyes. Which makes me love him beyond measure.

Jace, who rarely shows any emotion at all, is stunned. "This is gorgeous, Fiona."

"When I was a line cook, I worked in some badass kitchens, but this is unbelievable, Fee." Ty, looking somewhat flustered, manages to hug me like he means it. "If you ever need a guest chef, I'm not worthy but I'd love to cook here."

I can't help but laugh. He could easily work the line for me. "Are you kidding, Ty? I might hold you to that. We've spent so much money on this place, I'll need to sell out two seatings for an entire year just to break even."

"Somehow, I don't think that's going to be a problem." He looks in wonder around the kitchen. Strokes the marble countertop where we'll eat dinner.

Out of the corner of my eye, I see Petra and Jetta gawking. Ty has that effect on people. He just radiates sex. Vulnerability. Over the years I've seen the lengths women will go to catch his attention. Unfortunately, for them, he only has eyes for one girl.

As if on cue, the telltale squeals and giggles emanating from the front door mean Ty's surprise is here. His entire body literally comes to life when Zoey enters the room with Alex and Ronni.

Zoey adorably flings herself at Ty, who holds her tightly against him. "Were you surprised? I've tried so hard to keep this a secret. Did you suspect something was up?"

As they kiss and snuggle like they haven't seen each other in decades, I greet Alex and Ronni. We had a blast helping Zoey pick out her wedding dress. I'm beginning to look forward to the times the four of us spend together. Such cool, accomplished, awesome women. When Gus opens, I'll finally be part of the club. "Welcome to Gus. I'm so glad we could make this happen."

"I'm so grateful for a night off. Connor's mom is watching the twins." Ronni, looks every inch the television star in a green sweater dress and knee-high Louboutin boots. She gives me a warm hug. "I was just telling Alex, we should get our kids together sometime before the holidays."

Alex, like Jace, is super laid back. "A couple of our horses are healthy enough for some human interaction. Maybe we could do a cute photo shoot at the ranch."

Huh. It actually sounds nice. Mia would love it.

After our band family is finished with the greetings, Ronni addresses the elephant in the room. She grips Ty's shoulder. "I'm so sorry about your mom."

Ty's face freezes. Then he puts on his rockstar persona to address us all. "Everyone, seriously. I'm fine. It was a long time coming. If you don't mind, I'd rather focus on the most important thing in my life. I'm finally marrying the most amazing woman in the world."

He bends down and kisses Zoey like no one else is in the room. It's so hot, I feel like a voyeur. Alex, Ronni, and I all mock-flutter our hands like fans. The guys make fun of them. My staff is stunned silent.

Zane whispers in my ear, "After that display, we might need a quickie over at the Mission before dinner."

"Not happening." I swat at him. "Okay, peeps. Please sit down and we'll get this party started."

When everyone is seated, my team goes into motion. In many ways, this is the inaugural soft opening to dial in the food and service. Petra and Justice are incredible, each detail is nailed. There are some tweaks I'm going to work on, but all in all I'm proud of the eleven-course feast.

Daire keeps the wine and mocktails flowing. Jetta is extremely competent and personable. It's just a seamless experience through and through. When we're finished, I move us into the lounge where we sit and visit in various groupings. Even after all of their hard work, my entire little staff volunteer to clean up and do the dishes, leaving me to relax with my friends.

Zane pulls me on his lap next to Connor and Ronni. I nestle into his strong arms, exhausted. Connor's half-asleep. Zoey and Alex, who have been best friends since they were little girls, are in their own little world. Jace and Ty are talking about some sort of certification thing.

"This is an incredible accomplishment, Fiona." Ronni takes my hand. "I was serious about getting together. I could really use some girl time."

"Really?" I look over at Zane to see if he's listening. Nope. He and Connor are talking about tour buses, so I focus back on Ronni.

"I'm trying to figure out this mom-work balance. You've been doing it for so long, I'd love to pick your brain." She seems so earnest, I get drawn in.

"Gosh, you just get through the day." I can't believe I've been a mom for nearly seven years. "Honestly? I have no idea. Help. Lots of help."

"I'm shooting a new series in Vancouver BC in the new year. I'll be in Ireland next summer for a movie. With the band situated here, I wonder if we should get a bigger place in Seattle. I'll keep my house in Malibu, of course, but we have a better infrastructure here." She pats Connor's knee. "It's a bit of an adjustment to go back to work when we had so much time off when the boys were born. I'm not sure how you do it."

I try not to scoff. She's one of the most famous television stars in the world. I'm, well, married to a famous rockstar. It's not like she and I are even close to equivalent. "How come you don't have help? You must have a fleet of nannies."

"Sadly, no. We're having a struggle finding someone in LA who isn't trying to fuck my husband or get his autograph." She shrugs.

I'm startled silent. Sweet, wholesome Ronni Miller just blew my mind. "Yeah, it's a real problem. I decided on an older, retired woman. I trust Zane, but I'm not taking any fucking chances. People will do or say anything."

"I didn't realize until recently you and Zane were childhood friends. It's so wonderful it blossomed into love."

"We've always loved each other. It sounds cheesy, but we were destined from the day he was born. He proposed the first time when I was six." I gaze up at my husband. It's hard to express how close Zane and I are. How intertwined our souls are. Few people understand.

So I explain. Ronni seems like someone I can trust. As I've learned more about her, I'm more and more impressed. It makes sense I'd like her. Just like I like Zoey and Alex.

The four men of LTZ are, essentially, brothers. All handsome, decent, loving, kind men with huge doses of integrity and talent. It stands to reason the women they've chosen for their committed, forever relationships share similar qualities.

As couples, we are family. Our kids will grow up together like cousins. We'll travel together. Experience life together. Celebrate our successes. Help each other through failures.

A lightbulb goes off. Our family isn't just biological. We have amazing people around us who truly have our best interests at heart. As we do theirs.

Zane and I are creating a life that is bigger, fuller and richer than anything I ever imagined.

What a difference a year makes.

Chapter Twelve

A Couple of Weeks Later

I'VE NEVER BEEN A best man before, my plan is to knock it out of the park. Ty's wedding is going to be epic, but tiny, so there's not much for me to do. I'm winging the speech, although I have a couple of bullet points written down.

Ty asked Carter to preside over their ceremonies. My dad's so fucking excited, it makes me a little ashamed I didn't think to ask him to marry me and Fee. He went online to get ordained by the Universal Life Church.

It's hard for me to say that without laughing. I mean, *c'mon*.

Anyway, I invited him to join Ty and me while we get ready. I thought he'd get a kick out of it. I didn't expect him to be emotional. I swear to God, he sounded like he was crying when I called.

Admittedly, this year hasn't been the best for us. Or for me and my mom. I'm feeling a certain kind of way about them being together. Oh, and they've been *together.* A lot. Now that Mom's taken a step back from her dance career, she hasn't been flitting all over the world doing ballet stuff quite as often.

Instead, she's been holed up at Carter's house. Flitting around with him when he plays Limelight shows. I half-expected them to elope in Vegas at some point. There must be trouble in paradise though. She won't be at the wedding. She won't be here for Christmas either.

Then again, maybe the opportunity to work with the London Ballet was too lucrative to pass up despite whatever their relationship status is.

Either way, it doesn't matter. I struggle with the idea of her taking Carter back permanently. I've come to terms with the fact they must have some sort of chemistry, though I don't see it. Not at all. It didn't occur to me they would keep in touch once I graduated high school, let alone become friendly again.

Romantic? *Gah.*

Kill me now.

Hell, if I hadn't been born they wouldn't have survived a year.

Then again if I hadn't been born Carter might also be dead.

He and I have been through our ups and downs over the years, there's no question. On the other hand, Mom and I have always been solid as a rock. When Mia came into my life, I realized why she left Seattle and Carter. To keep me safe. What a huge sacrifice she made. At twenty, she gave up her coveted position at the Pacific Northwest Ballet just to protect me.

Shit. I *totally* get it now. I would literally do anything for Mia. I love her so fucking much. She's in my bloodstream. Figuratively, I guess. I wish she were my biological daughter, but she's Fee's so it's as close as it gets. I couldn't love her more than I do. I know that for definite.

Admittedly, fatherhood has dredged up all sorts of confusing thoughts about how my dad treated me when I was little. I thought I was over it. Largely, I am. I've come to terms with the abandonment. The broken promises. The horror of him overdosing in the park when I was younger than Mia is now.

It's hard to believe we're approaching twenty years since he's been clean. Carter's mostly redeemed himself as a father. Some hiccups, of course, but he's a wonderful grandfather to Mia, and that's what's most important. I'm not worried about him relapsing. Not for years now.

It's no secret Fee's dependence on Xanax earlier this year was triggering. Even though we seem to be past it, I'm still in monthly sessions with Lisa Kincaid to keep my head straight. She validates my thoughts and feelings. Holds me to task when I veer off course.

Therapy's been such a positive part of my life from an early age.

I'd hoped Fiona would find it helpful.

She didn't though. One session and she was out. I can't—and won't—force her. Ultimately, keeping addiction out of our lives is what's most important. We've talked about it to death, though, and I *know* she feels the same way.

After all, she was with me in the park that day.

And, as a son of an addict knows, actions speak louder than words. So far, so good. She's back to herself. Confident. Sassy. Witty. God, she's so fucking sexy.

We're good. We are.

"When's your dad getting here?" Fee ties her bathrobe closed as she walks past me in our closet. "I want to be mostly ready. I'm mentally preparing to entertain the kids so the girls can get ready at Zoey's."

I spin her around as she passes. Lay a huge smooch on her lips. "Can you still taste yourself?"

"Can you?" Fee pulls away to sit at her vanity.

"Is it me or is our sex life the best it's ever been?" I walk behind her and rub her shoulders.

She looks at me through the mirror, lust in her eyes. "People say being married the first year is the hardest. In our case you're the hardest. All the time. God, my clit is still tingling."

"You can't say that to me and not let me fuck you again." I cup my cock, which is now, in fact, hard as steel.

She wags her finger at me. "Uh, I can and you won't. At least not now. Go think about some wrinkly grannies or something. There's too much going on. You're going to have to wait until we get back from the wedding."

"Fine." I cross my arms over my chest and pout.

Faintly, I can hear the doorbell. Olga or Zeke will let Ty in, but it's showtime so I sneak in another kiss with Fee and head downstairs.

When I'm halfway downstairs, I realize Ty and Carter are both standing in the foyer. It's funny, rock journalists always write about how much I resemble my dad but I swear I do a double-take. Ty and Carter look like actual twins. It's weird. I never noticed any similarities before. It must be the light.

I give them each a bro hug. "Are you hungry? Fee made Korean spiced chicken fingers, some sort of slaw situation and homemade rolls. I think Mia's having her lunch."

"Fuck, yeah. I was hoping she left something for us to eat." Carter bolts toward the kitchen. "Mia? Mia?"

Ty and I exchange looks and follow close behind.

"Grandpa, your beard is tickling me," Mia squeals when Carter picks her up and smothers her in kisses.

"Don't tell me you're too old for snuggles. You don't want to break an old man's heart." Carter boops her nose. "Or, maybe I smell bad. Do I stink? Tell me the truth."

Mia takes a deep, long sniff. "Nope. You're good."

Ty is still a bit awkward around my daughter, but he tries. "Are you excited to be a flower girl, miss Mia?"

"It should be fine." She rolls her eyes. "I've got to make certain Lena knows what to do. She's so little, it's a lot of responsibility."

God, I love, love, *love* her. "If you're finished, can you go upstairs and help your mom? We need to get your Uncle Ty ready to get married today. When Lena gets here, your mom will help you get ready in your room."

"Lena is here." Jace strolls through the door holding his sweet, blonde daughter in his arms.

Connor's behind him with Torin and Tristan, who are sound asleep in their car seats.

The afternoon is a whirlwind. Full of laughs. Mischief. Brotherhood. We manage to get dressed in our suits. Fee fixes all of our ties, leaving us four handsome mother-fuckers time to relax before walking the short distance to Ty's house.

"You nervous?" I nudge Ty.

He studies his phone. His face is serene. Calm. "Nah. I've been waiting for this day since I met her. She just read the note I left for her. I'm pretty sure this is gonna be the best day of my life."

"I'm so honored you asked me to be part of the cere-mony." Carter grabs Ty's hand in one of his. Takes mine in the other. "I will never forget this day. And what it means."

An unexpected wave of emotion whooshes through my body. I'm choked up looking into my dad's eyes. Glancing over at Ty, I can see he's emotional too. "We're family," I whisper.

Ty and Carter both nod. We all touch our foreheads together.

"So, uh...at risk of breaking up this special Hallmark moment, should we go and get you married, dude?" Jace claps me and Ty on the back and grins down at us. "I just got a text from Alex wondering where we are..."

Connor looms over us. "Of course, we can stay. Cuddle. You're bringing a tear to my eye, so you are."

"Fuck it. Let's get you married!" I throw my fist in the air and bellow, "Fee, we're ready to go."

Fee rolls her eyes. "You don't need to yell, I'm right here with the girls." She's stunning in a pinkish, flared dress.

Mia and Lena look adorable in fluffy dresses in the same pinkish color. I scoop up Mia. Jace carries Lena. We walk to Ty's house in giddy anticipation. Well, at least I do.

"You're adorable, babe." Fee kisses me when we arrive. "I love you."

I cock an eyebrow. "Oh yeah?"

"Yeah. You're in love with love. Take care of Ty. He seems calm, but this is a huge deal for him." Fee squeezes my hand and disappears upstairs with the girls.

I turn my attention to Zoey's dad, Mike Pearson, who embraces Ty and motions to the door. "Olivia just texted. We're ready. Carter, do you have what you need?"

"I do." Carter pats the pocket on his jacket. "I've got the vows ."

Mike shows me, Jace, and Connor where to stand. "Your wives will join you up here by the fireplace. Ty, you'll stand here, but before we begin could we have a minute?"

"Uh, yeah." Ty looks a little nervous.

Me, Jace, and Connor take our places and watch Mike speak to Ty. It appears to be a special and touching moment. It makes me so happy. For as much as Carter has served a role as stand-in dad, Ty's gaining a great father-in-law. Well, in-laws. Both Zoey's parents have fully embraced him, despite some of the bullshit he and Zoey have been through since they've been back together.

I know Ty appreciates it more than he'll ever be able to say. Despite the fact that he's arguably one of the most well-known people in the entire world, he's never felt like he belonged. Not really. Not until Zoey. And by extension, her family.

Fee returns with Ronni and Alex. All of our women are beautiful inside and out. But...Ronni's dress is something else. Her boobs are nearly bursting out of her top. I glance over at Connor, whose eyes are bugged out, he's so entranced by his wife's chest. He shuffles his feet a bit. Adjusts his tie. I nearly bust a gut when I notice him trying to discreetly cover the tent in his pants with his hands.

God, I should ignore it. Let Connor suffer in silence. But I can't. I just can't. I know I'm going to hell when I lean over and whisper Fee's advice from earlier today. "Just think about wrinkly grannies."

Connor's eyes widen. He's the sage old man of the group. The guy whose been in a monogamous relationship for most of the time I've known him. This turn of events is hysterical. I catch Fee's eye, flick my gaze over to Connor and back to her. Her eyes widen when she sees Connor's distress. I mouth, "Wrinkly grannies."

She chokes back a laugh just as Zoey appears in the doorway.

I'm going to hell. Yep. I've got a one-way elevator ticket down to burning hellfire.

Luckily, I get my shit together and focus on Ty, whose eyes shine with tears at the sight of his bride. I clap his shoulder and whisper, "She's yours forever. You're a lucky son of a bitch."

"I know," he whispers. "I hope I'll be worthy of her."

Ah, Ty. I won't ever let him feel less than. Not when we're all together. Not when we're on the brink of getting the band back together again. It's almost the new year. After the holidays, LTZ will go into the studio and tour. Life will get back to normal. Except, this time around, Ty will have Zoey by his side.

I can hardly wait.

Their ceremony is short and sweet. Heartfelt. Romantic. Carter is well-prepared and engaging. Ty's and

Zoey's adoration of each other is what novels are written about. Truth be told, the entire atmosphere is charged with positive energy. The rest of the night flies by. We eat an amazing catered dinner. The toasts and roasts go on for a while. I'm in my element. Laughter. Joy. Love.

I even manage to catch Connor and Ronni going at it in the spare bedroom.

A bit later, Jace, Connor, and Ronni are chatting at the fire when Fee and I join them. We chat about potential management, which makes me extremely optimistic that we're all on board to get back together.

Then I have to go and ruin it with my big fucking mouth.

At dinner, I learned news Jace hadn't shared so I decide to tease him a bit. I make a big show of being hurt. "What's this I hear about you being engaged?"

His reaction is unexpected. He's actually pissed at me for bringing it up. "Jesus. It's not like it's big news. I proposed weeks ago. We live together. We have a daughter. No big deal."

Ever my defender, Fee crosses her arms and levels her gaze at our drummer. "Stop it with the cool-guy stuff, Jace. At least you put a ring on it, we're all thrilled you got your shit together."

Fee's way off base. Jace has wanted to marry Alex forever. "Fee, we need to lay off. It's their business." I touch her elbow, hoping she'll take the hint.

But, nope. She goes full steam ahead. "Alex is the *best*, though." Fee's liquid-aqua eyes narrow at Jace like he's done something wrong. "I want her to be happy."

For fuck's sake. I do not want us to get in the middle of Jace and Alex's business. They are such private people. It's going to piss him off to think we're talking shit behind his back, which we are not.

"Did she say something to you? Because she's the one who won't set the date, not me." Jace crosses his arms over his chest, genuinely looking hurt.

"She's dealing with some health stuff, Fee." Ronni gently tugs on Fee's arm.

Wait, what?

Fiona's eyes widen with fear. "Oh, God."

Alex joins us. "What's going on?"

"I'm not sure." Jace looks distraught. Confused.

Fee rubs Alex's shoulder like she does for Mia when she's sick. "Are you okay, honey?"

Alex is caught off guard. She looks helplessly at Jace. "Um, yeah?"

"I think I said something I shouldn't have." Ronni looks truly bummed. "I didn't know you were keeping the situation private. I'm so sorry."

I have no fucking idea what is happening. My head is like a ping-pong ball. Fee is of no help, she looks like she just stepped onto a land mine too.

"What situation is that?" Jace grits.

She waves him off like it's no big deal, but I can tell that it is. "All of the girls were talking upstairs while we were getting ready. Fee, to catch you up, I'm having abnormal cramping and Jace and I are going to a specialist so I can hopefully get to the bottom of it this week. Basically, we're both tired of playing Internet doctor. It's scary out there."

"I didn't realize we were sharing yet, Poppy." The vein popping out on his forehead means Jace is now furious, but his voice is cool and calm.

Ronni's having none of it. "C'mon, Jace. Lighten up. Female-related health issues have been a taboo subject for too long. It's important we share these experiences. Keeping things like this secret is not okay. Did you know that the percentage of money spent on research into women's reproductive health is astonishingly low? You have a daughter. Think about it."

In my mind, the record scratches. I'm shocked. So is Connor. I get that Ronni has brought down one of the biggest assholes in Hollywood. She's a worldwide advocate for women. But, shit. She's gone overboard. My bandmates are not anything like Don Kircher, the misogynist pig who forced women to have sex with him for television and movie roles.

Holy baby Jesus. Fee high-fives Ronni in solidarity. I'm mortified. None of this is cool. This is *not* how our band works.

Alex rests her head on Jace's arm. "Jace isn't the bad guy here, Ronni. He's done more to help me than I've done to help myself. While I appreciate what you're saying, we'll make the best decision for ourselves. I'm happy to share what's going on, but our solution is not up for group discussion or debate."

I'm so fucking impressed. Alex diffuses the situation without shaming Ronni while also defending her man. Classy. All the fucking way.

Her comment also makes me realize something pertinent. It's not just the four of us in our band family. There are now twice, or three times, as many people. Wives. Children. Parents. All of whom will have a vested interest in LTZ's schedule.

Our lives have priorities outside the band. Which will continue as our families expand. Leading to more conflicts and resolutions.

I've wanted for the past year to pass as fast as possible. Mainly, so LTZ could be together again and we could go back to how things were. Recreate our magic and all that shit.

But things will not be the same. Never again.

Is that good or bad?

Neither, I decide. It just is what it is.

Desperate to find common ground at Ty's fucking wedding, I change the subject. "Maybe let's lighten the mood and play some music?"

Luckily, the rest of my friends agree.

And we do, play music that is.

Something's in the air though. As much as I want to bury my head in the sand, I can't deny it.

Doubt has creeped into my psyche.

I'm scared to fucking death.

What if this is the beginning of the end?

Chapter Thirteen

A Few Weeks Later

ZANE'S BEEN UNCHARACTERISTICALLY BUMMED for the past couple of weeks.

Apparently, his dad persuaded his mom to come back from London and spend the holidays with us, which includes my mom, Faye. There's always an element of tension when the three of them are together. Aside from that, I couldn't give a shit if Lianne's banging Carter. Zane's annoyed at the dynamic between his parents, so I'm just trying to be a sounding board as he works through it.

He's also been stressed about the way Ronni and I spoke to Jace at Ty and Zoey's wedding. I didn't think we said anything hurtful or invasive. Alex is the one who told us what was going on. Needless to say, he's been irrationally worried that Jace is going to quit the band.

It's part of the reason I arranged the horse photo shoot for the kids with Alex. I figure the four of us spending some time together will help alleviate his fears. It's my attempt to take care of him the way he likes to take care of me.

He's my other half, but we're also two sides of the coin in how we approach conflict. Zane tries to prevent bad things from happening. Smooths things over. Anticipates problems and predetermines his ideal solution.

I'm the opposite. I want conflict over and done with as fast as possible. I've always had the tendency to poke the bear, make decisions and let the chips fall where they may. His way is diplomatic.

I wish I could channel Zane's energy sometimes. It's just not in my nature. Take my relationship with my mom. I'm so tired of our conversations turning into a dissertation on what a shitty daughter I am. She hates not having control over me and I love not depending on her. Consequently, we rarely speak these days.

So fuck it. No matter what happens, I'm going to take care of my own family and spend the day at the ranch with Jace, Alex, and Lena. As a bonus, we'll all have extremely cute pictures of the girls dressed up for the holidays. It's going to be awesome.

"Can I ride horses, Mommy?" Mia asks from her booster seat in the back. We just drove off the ferry and are on our way to the ranch. She's adorable in snowflake leggings and a big red sweatshirt. I also brought a change of clothes so she and Lena can match in their pictures.

I turn to look at her. "Yes and brush them and make them pretty too."

"Wow." She shakes her head in wonder. "Best. Day. Ever."

Ten minutes later, we navigate the gravel driveway in Zane's ridiculous Aston Martin SUV. He's becoming so much like Carter. Collecting cars. Trading in one model for another. I can't keep up, but he's bored. I don't really care. He has the money, so who am I to nitpick?

Alex, Lena, and Mitch the dog greet us at the end of the lane. "Yay! I'm so glad you could come out. Jace is out running an errand but should be home any minute."

"I've not been around horses much, not since Zane and I went to a dude ranch when we were little, so this should either be terrifying or awesome." I glance back at her as I help Mia get out.

Mia leaps out and jumps up and down like a pogo stick. "Let's go! Let's go!"

"We will, miss Mia." Alex crouches to our daughter's level. "Before we go down to the barn, let's have some lunch and go over some very important safety information. Okay?"

Mia kicks the dirt. "Okay. That's fine."

Alex is an absolute natural at this horse stuff. You can tell she lives and breathes it. I'm so glad she took the time to teach us the basics. I would have never remembered to approach a horse from the side to avoid his blind spots. Or to speak to him so he knows you're there. We even practice how to touch a horse's neck and shoulder, using Alex as a model.

"I bet Jace would be pissed if he saw me petting you, Alex." Zane waggles his eyebrows as he strokes her shoulder.

She rolls her eyes. "He'd probably make you pet him."

"I'd love to see that." I chortle. *Oh*, how I would love that.

He's still not back forty-five minutes later when we finish lunch. I put away the food while Alex takes the girls to pee. I grab the cowboy hats I bought for the photos.

Alex looks at her watch. "I texted Jace, he's on his way. I think we should get started, it gets dark so early in December I want to make sure we have plenty of time for pictures.

Becca, Jace's sister's wife, who manages the ranch for Alex, waits with two beautiful horses. Samantha is light tan. Gloria is chocolate brown. While Becca shows Mia how to pet them for real, I decide to check in with Alex about the wedding night situation.

"Are we alright? Zane has been going out of his mind with worry that Ronni and I went too far the other night." I take her hand. "Mainly, I just want you to be okay."

She waves me off. "Yeah, I'm fine. Finding out you have health issues can be a bit of a shock. But, it's life. Jace is fine, he's just overprotective."

"I get it. Zane's the same. He's had a rough year without the structure of the band. I can't tell you how excited he is for LTZ to record again." I toss out a fishing line. Zane won't ask directly, so I might as well throw it out there.

She looks at me and sighs. "Jace misses the band a lot. I think the guys just need to get together again and talk, you know?"

"Yeah." I toe the ground. Think about what to say. I decide to keep to my own truth. "Zane and Connor have a crazy idea about getting custom buses so we can all tour with them. I'm trying to figure out how that's going to work with the restaurant. At least for the first year. I've got my core kitchen staff, but it's still going to be a ton of work."

Alex nods. "Zoey's bound to be pregnant any minute now if she's not already. Ronni has a bunch of TV and movie commitments next year. Jace and I are hoping—" Alex stops herself. "Well, my dream is to get this ranch certified for therapy."

"We all have a lot going on." I gaze out at Mia, who is enamored with Penelope the horse.

Alex starts toward the horses and gestures for me to follow. "We do. It doesn't mean LTZ is done. The guys have a bond that is special. Their music is special. A break is needed sometimes. It's never a bad thing to take a step back and reimagine, right?"

"Yeah. I feel the same way." I nod.

Alex leads Penelope into the small indoor arena adjacent to the barn. Becca boosts Lena and Mia up on the fence. I join them, glancing up at the house where Jace has just pulled into the driveway. Mitch takes off to greet him. I watch Zane and Jace embrace from afar. They disappear into the house so I return my attention to the girls and horses.

Alex is so incredibly beautiful in the ring. I'm not certain what voodoo magic she works on the horses, but upon her silent cues and hand gestures, they do tricks. They run around the arena. Bow. Stand still in a perfect line. Circle each other. All sorts of things.

It's so enthralling, I don't even notice Zane and Jace have joined us until Mia takes off running. "Daddy!" She giggles when he picks her up and kisses her cheek.

Jace waves at us and says to Alex, "Stuff's in the fridge."

"Took you long enough. It's time to dress up the horses for the pictures." Alex picks up Lena and walks over to the boys. Samantha follows and stands at her side.

She's such a rockstar. "I can't get over how cool you are, Alex. The Liberty horse stuff is fucking awesome."

"Well, I can't even boil an egg, so we're equally badass, just in different ways." Alex snuggles her daughter. "Right, Lena? Girls are badasses."

Jace laughs and takes her from Alex. "So, we're just embracing the curse words now?"

"I started swearing at a very young age, and I turned out pretty good." I wink at Jace and give Zane a huge kiss.

Zane yanks me to him by my beltloop. "One more of those, wife."

He's so fucking delicious. I can't help but kiss him again and again and again while we watch Alex teach the girls how to groom the horses. They braid red, green, and gold ribbon into the horses' manes and tails. Mia is mesmerized. So am I.

Alex is where she belongs.

Being here today gives me such a great perspective.

The men of LTZ deserve the awards, accolades, and wealth they've achieved with their band. But, so do all of us. Zoey and the foundation. Alex and her horses. Ronni and her television and movie projects. Me and the restaurant.

We're all badasses in our own way.

We matter. What we do matters.

All of us, together, matter.

Feeling on top of the world, I follow Alex and the girls inside the house to change. We wear matching velvet T-shirts, and I don't even care that she wears size XS and I now wear 1X. We're both beautiful. Our girls are beautiful. The pictures turn out beautiful. Spending the afternoon here on the ranch was the perfect medicine for Zane. And for me too if I'm honest.

It's amazing what following your dream can do for a woman. It's as important as unconditional love. This past year has been rocky, but it feels like the cloud of doom that's followed me for so many years has given way to bright-blue skies.

"Whatcha thinking?" Zane takes my hand on the ferry ride back to Seattle. Mia's zonked out in the back, so we just stay in the car for the half-hour trip.

I lean my head on his shoulder. "How happy I am." I angle my neck to look up at him. "Really and truly happy."

"I love you, Fee." He presses his lips to mine.

"You love me so well, Zaney. You always have. You give me everything. Always. I hope I do for you." I stroke his long hair. We press our foreheads together in a head snuggle.

He nuzzles my ear. "You don't need to give me any-thing. You're already inside me. Coursing through my veins. Your love is in my bloodstream. In my cells. In every organ of my body."

Wow. Just. Wow.

And he thinks Ty is the lyricist of the band.

"So you do feel me inside you." I wind my fingers around his curls. "I'm Fiona Reynolds Rocks, the in-vasive love virus."

He snorts. "Yes, that's it. I've got a case of ILV."

"Just to make sure, maybe I should guarantee the virus takes." I trail my fingers down his chest to his cock. Squeeze. Run my thumb along his crown through the denim.

He flicks his eyes to the backseat. I do too. Mia's still sound asleep. She snores softly. We have easily fifteen minutes before the ferry docks. He leans down and whispers as I stroke him. "We better stop."

"Yeah, I know." I remove my hand. We'll need to pick this up later when Mia isn't in such close proximity.

Zane takes my chin with his thumb and forefinger. "We have eternity, Fee."

I can't help but beam at him.

It's true.

And, I intend to enjoy every single second.

Chapter Fourteen

A Couple of Weeks Later. New Year. New Attitude

WOEBEGONE ZANE *BE GONE*!

There's too much to do. I've come to terms with the fact LTZ will be on hiatus longer. The holidays gave me perspective. And faith. We all want to reunite and make music. But, we have families now. New priorities. Spending time with them made me realize we can accommodate all our shit if we work together.

We're brothers after all. So, we'll focus on the things we need to focus on and reconvene when we're done.

I'll admit, my peace of mind is largely because we've decided LTZ will play on opening night of Gus.

Shortly after the Fourth of July.

It's going to be epic.

In the meantime, Ty and Connor are producing Connor's brothers' band, Fireball, next month. I may even head to LA to help for a couple of days. After the album is done, Connor's temporarily moving to Vancouver with Ronni so she can focus on the television series she's producing for Netflix. Alex's health issues seem to be a bit more serious than originally thought, so Jace is needed on the ranch.

This frees me up to help Fee. She has a calendar chock full of things to do between now and when Gus opens in six months. I'll take over The Mission business until then. Hire a booking agent and fill up the calendar. Interview a general manager. If I take that off her plate, she'll have time to spend on the restaurant. And time to spend with Mia and me.

It's also time to find new management for LTZ. We've been talking about leaving Katherine forever and haven't quite pulled the trigger because of our indecisiveness. I'll do my research on alternatives.

My favorite part of the day, other than making love to my wife, of course, is taking Mia to school. And picking her up. Just like my mom used to do for me.

She must have ESP because my phone buzzes. "Hey, Lianne. What's shakin?"

"Zane, you know I hate it when you call me by my first name." Her soft voice seems unusually vulnerable. "I'd like to see my son, are you home?"

Shit. Time to dial my snark back. "Yeah, I'm finalizing the design on my tour bus. Come over. Fee's going to be at Gus until late."

"Great, thank you, baby. I'll be there in a half hour."

I change out of my stay-at-home-dad track suit, which is fucking badass because it has skulls all over. Throw on jeans and a slim-fitting black sweater. Maybe it would be fun to take Mom out to lunch. Might as well be ready. I've resumed picking out my bus amenities when the doorbell rings.

Lianne Rocks is stunning. She always has been. Her strawberry-blonde hair is pulled back in a low ponytail. She wears a shocking-blue cloud-like coat cinched in at the waist. Slim black pants tucked into knee-high black riding boots. I squeeze her to me. "Hi, Mom."

"Zaney." She clutches my cheeks and kisses both of them.

"I made coffee." I pull away and gesture to the kitchen. She takes off her coat, revealing a long tunic sweater in the same blue hue. I hook it on the coat rack in the foyer.

We settle in the conservatory and she pulls no punches. "I want to know why you're so angry with me."

"Uh..." I'm a little taken aback.

"What did I do so I can fix it? I miss you." Her eyes well up. "Ever since your wedding, I've seen so little of you. And when we do, you're so distant."

Ohmygod. I can't take making my mom sad. I jump up and sit next to her. "No. Mom. No." I pull her to me. "You haven't done anything. I'm just dealing with some things ..."

"Fee?" She sniffs. "Is she still upset about what happened all those years ago? I wish I could have fought harder. Made Faye see ..."

Fuck. Fuck Fuck. Fuck. Fuuuuuuuck. I slump back in the couch. Bring my fists up to my eyes. Shit. Are we *really* going into all of this? I focus on my breathing. Get my heart rate under control. When I feel calmer I place my hands in my lap and look at her. Tears stream down her face.

I make a decision. If we're going there, it might as well be now. Get it out of my system. Maybe put it to bed. "The custody shit took a huge toll on us. Mostly Fiona, obviously. But me too."

"Of course. I totally understand." Mom settles back against the couch. We both turn to face each other. "Tell me what you feel safe revealing. I'd never ask you to betray her trust."

I take another moment to think about what to say. Because it's not all about Fee. "She went on anti-anxiety meds, and it messed her up. It scared the shit out of me. It took months to deal with, but that's behind us. You've seen her, she's better than ever. Having Gus be a real living, breathing thing to focus on has been miraculous."

"Oh God, Zaney. That breaks my heart. Does Faye know?" Mom has always considered Fiona her daughter. I'm positive this worries her as much as it did me.

I fiddle with the bracelets on my wrist. "We're not seeing much of Faye. It's triggering for Fee. She's always berating her for her weight. Her lack of ambition. Her poor mothering skills. *Me*. Fuck, it's exhausting. We hired Olga to help us out when we moved in here. It's been life changing not having Faye's nasty energy around us and Mia."

"I'll never understand what happened to her. She used to be eccentric, but in a fun way. When you were little, she helped me so much. It's like she changed overnight into a person I didn't recognize." She rubs her temples, shaking her head.

I bite my lip. As an adult, I realize Faye showed my mom the sane side and nothing else. "She didn't change. She was always an asshole." I close my eyes, remembering all the little shitty comments she'd make to me when I was little. "Did you not hear the things she used to say to me?"

"Like what?" My mom's eyes widen. She didn't know.

"It's not important. Just know that she fucking hated me. Always insinuated I'd grow up to be just like Carter. That I was a loser. Shit like that." I shrug. "It was basically just comments under her breath, but I heard them. Fee did too."

"That fucking bitch." Mom stands and goes to the window. Mutters. Paces. Shakes her head. Then buries her face in her hands and cries.

I jump up and join her. Hug her. "It's okay, Mom. It is. I didn't think you knew, and I was too young to fully understand it. I think now that I'm officially Mia's dad, many things I was salty about make sense to me. I'm working with Lisa Kincaid, the band's therapist occasionally when I want to talk things through. Fee knows."

"I'm so sorry, baby. I just can't believe poor Fiona was stuck with her up in Bellingham. That bitch kept her from Gus. Kept her from you. I should have fought harder." She looks crestfallen.

I move back to the couch and pat the seat beside me. "Well, there's something I've been feeling. I don't want to hurt you, but I might as well be honest."

"*God.*" She sits. Rests her head on her elbow. "Spill."

"I fucking hate that you're back with Carter. Don't ask me why. I just do. It's why I don't have you guys over. I'm working through this too, but I don't have any answers yet." It actually feels freeing to just tell my mom what I've been feeling for over a year.

Her entire face reddens. "I. Uh ..."

"You're sleeping with him, yeah? Since last Christmas?" I tilt my head. "But you're you, so you want a commitment. Amiright?"

"I'm *me?*" She's confused, annoyed.

"Yeah." I actually don't know what I mean. I hope my mom will fill in the blanks.

"Oh, jeez." She lies back against the cushion. She flings her arm across her eyes. "Sometimes I wonder why I was so fucking transparent with you about sex. I blame it on the fact that I was just a baby when I had you. I grew up when you did."

I don't say a word. I just look at her until she moves her arm and sees me staring.

"Fine. You want to know? I'll tell you." My mom doesn't stop her stream of consciousness for a long time. She tells many stories I hadn't heard before. Her move to Seattle. Life at the ballet company. How free she felt living on her own. All about Carter. How they met. How their relationship evolved. Answers my questions.

It's a lot of information.

I'm overwhelmed.

"It's always been Carter for me. Me for Carter. Just like it's always been Fiona for you and you for her." Her voice is soft and loving. Just like I remember when she explained how Carter was a drug addict and what that meant.

"It's not the same ..." I protest.

She grips my wrist. "No, it's not for one very important reason. Carter made choices that were not safe for me or for you, and I had to sever ties. Not completely, because he's your dad. It took eons for us to be friends again. Remember how surprised you were that he and I spoke at night when you lived with him?"

"Yeah. You told me when I visited you in New York after that summer. Remember? I asked if I could live with him."

"Yes." She brushes a hair from my face. "And we *still* kept in touch from that point forward. Throughout high school, of course. And after. Mainly, for me, it was to talk about you. How amazing you were. LTZ. The tour. All of it."

I squint at her, confused. "You and I talk all the time, I told you all that stuff."

"You did."

"And you're telling me you talked to Carter too?"

"I did."

"So, are you sleeping with him? You're implying its none of my business, I know. But, maybe it kinda is." I wince. No one should ever ask their mom about her sex life. Then again, not many people are as close with their mom as I am.

"Yes. On and off for years." She looks at me somewhat furtively.

It's like a bullet to my heart. "Wait. What? What the fuck?" I sit straight up. I feel like I'm going to hyperventilate.

"We slept together after your high school graduation. As I said, on and off ever since." She manages to keep eye contact with me, though I can tell this conversation is painful. Maybe embarrassing. Well, for both of us.

"So, you're telling me you've been together for years? Didn't you think I might need to know this information? I hate lies." I shout so loud our neighbors could hear through the walls.

Her entire face reddens. "Uh, no. I didn't. Because we weren't together. We're not together now."

"Oh God. My mom and dad are *FWB*. Why the fuck did I even ask?" I squeeze my eyes shut and put my hands on my ears. "That's even *worse*. I cannot believe my mother has been hooking up with my dad for years and I had no fucking clue. I'm such a fucking *idiot*."

When I open my eyes again, she's regarding me thoughtfully. "Zane, you have been an adult making your own decisions for over a decade. Immersed in your own triumphs. Heartbreaks. Successes. Problems. Do you think I'd ever dump my own shit on you? Burden you with it? Of course I wouldn't. My job is to be your mother. To be *your* support system, no matter what." She takes my cheeks in her hand and looks me dead in the eye. *"I take care of you.* Just like my own mom takes care of me. Just like you'll take care of Mia. And any other children you and Fiona have. Do you get it?"

I just look at her. Absorbing.

She releases me. "Let me be clear. You do not need to worry about me. Whatever is going on with your dad and I is our business. I know it affects you, but I can assure you we are not a couple. You'll be the first to know if and when that happens."

"It's tough to comprehend. I'm just being honest." I feel strangely emotional. I want my mom to be happy, but it seems to me that she and Carter are in a constant state of flux. "Carter hasn't been with anyone that I know of since I moved in with him. I'm sad he's alone. He shouldn't be. Neither should you."

She nods. The tears well up again. "You're right."

"Look, I'll try to stay out of it. This is a lot to take in. We've been talking for hours, do you want to come with me to pick up Mia? Maybe we can pop in on Fee and you can see how Gus is coming along. It's been a long time." I stand and hold my hand out to her.

She allows me to pull her up. We hug for a long, long time. I love my mom so much. Adulting is hard. Sometimes I forget that she's just doing the best she can. It's time to take her off the pedestal I've put her on and have a real relationship with her. Like I do with my dad. Or, at least like I thought I had with my dad.

It occurs to me that Carter has protected my mom's honor for years.

Holy shit.

My mom has a point. They are like me and Fiona. I'm going to have to unpack this insanity with Fee later.

"I'd like that. I miss Fiona and Mia so much and I don't want us to ever have this separation again, Zane. You're my son. You're my sweet Zaney." She wipes the tears I didn't know were falling from my eyes.

And I get it. If Mia avoided me when she was my age, I'd be devastated.

Looks like my new attitude is going to include resetting my relationship with my parents.

It's probably time.

Chapter Fifteen

A Month or So Later

NUMBERS AREN'T MY THING.

I've got to make them my bitch though. It's an expensive proposition opening a fine dining restaurant featuring seasonal, high-end regional food. The investment to take things to the coveted Michelin level is astronomical. From the decor to the food to the staff to the marketing. Zane and I are spending a fortune, and there's no guarantee we'll ever make it back.

Emilie's working hard to keep us on track, but self-doubt is a bitch. I worry that this is a vanity project. I wonder ... Gah. I can't say it out loud.

Is all of this worth it?

God, it is though. Gus could put this region on the map. Seattle has delectable cuisine. World-class restaurants. Celebrity chefs. Hell, I worked for one of the best. Currently, we have no Michelin-Starred restaurants. The Guide doesn't even *cover* the Pacific Northwest.

This whole endeavor feels like an insurmountable uphill battle.

The Michelin Star situation is so weird, it's almost hard to believe the story. The Guide originated in France over a hundred years ago. It was a free publication put out by the Michelin tire company for car travelers and featured lists of restaurants, hotels, gas stations, and instructions on how to repair and change tires. Kind of like an old-fashioned paper GPS.

The star rating system for restaurants was implemented when the Guide used a single star to denote restaurants they deemed "fine dining establishments." A few years later, they expanded the ratings to three stars, which is the best you can get.

Receiving a Michelin Star is a great honor. The rarest of accomplishments in the restaurant world. Le Bernardin, where I worked for many years while in culinary school, has three stars. I truly believe my experience there is the reason I have a chance at accomplishing my dream here in Seattle.

I'm confident I'll have the service, staff, and food dialed in but it's crucial to get sufficient publicity to gain the attention of the Michelin Guide team. I suck at marketing and public relations. I need help.

Big help.

Enter my own personal knight in shining armor. Through his rockstar connections, Zane helped me identify the four top hospitality PR firms in the country, arranged for them to pitch me and convinced Jace to sit in on the meetings.

He might be the drummer for LTZ, but his background in marketing helped catapult the band to the top when they were just starting out. He singlehandedly managed all their social media, press, and positioning until the band became too famous for him to keep up.

"So, I'm not up to speed on the Michelin stuff, can you fill me in on the top-level shit before the interviews begin?" Jace reclines in my office chair. His hair is tied back in a low ponytail. He's wearing gray jeans and a black sweater. Thick black reading glasses. He looks a little like a hipster ad executive, which is perfect.

I hand him four folders containing the presentations of each firm. "Michelin has a secretive process. They select just a few restaurants to be inspected. If Gus makes the cut, multiple reviewers will make reservations and eat here just like any other guests. All reviewers are religious about maintaining anonymity. They go to great lengths to come across like any person eating at the restaurant."

"Tell me the process." Jace chews on a pen while perusing a folder.

Using my fingers I count out the criteria inspectors use to determine who receives a star. "There's five elements they grade on. First, quality of products. Second, mastery of flavor and cooking techniques. Fourth, value for money. Fifth, consistency between the inspectors' visits."

He scrunches his nose. "Uh, what's the third?

"This is the one that's going to be the death of me." I suck in a breath. "The *personality* of the chef representing the dining experience."

"Seriously?" Jace cocks a brow. "That's a criteria?"

"All *five* are. And I get why you're skeptical about my personality. I'm a lot. I need the most help with that one." Fear gnaws at my belly.

Am I enough?

I must look a little freaked out because he suddenly leans forward. "Oh, Fee. That came out wrong. You're awesome, but so many chefs are a little...eh."

"Hotheaded? Prone to drama? Arrogant?" I purse my lips.

He laughs. "Uh, yeah."

"This shit is hard mental work. We earn the right to be all those things." I stab my pen at him faux-threateningly. "In all seriousness, it's expensive and grueling to keep consistent enough to meet all of the criteria every single day. But, if you're able to get a star, revenue goes up. If we're able to get two or three, it skyrockets. Michelin Stars mean diners travel here just to go to Gus. If we're the first restaurant in Seattle—well, the entire region—to earn the stars? We'll be booked out solid for years." I lean forward and speak quietly in case any of the staff are listening. "We've spent so much money on this place, I just want to get to break even. This is not a rockstar wife's cute little hobby. It's my dream. My passion. Ever since I was a teenager. I want to make Zane proud."

I want to make myself proud.

He nods as he scribbles down notes. "Got it. I imagine you want to have it dialed in from the get-go so if these anonymous inspectors come in Friday at eight or Tuesday at five-thirty, they expect the same experience."

"Yes, exactly."

"What skill set are we looking for in these PR folks?" Jace flips through another folder. "They all represent Michelin Star restaurants."

This is the point of the conversation that makes me cringe. I wish Zane were here with me, but he's in LA for the day to help Ty and Connor record one of the songs on Connor's brothers' album. "I feel like I can get the service, food, and experience where they need to be, but I have no clue about promotion. How to drum up interest. Get the word out. All the things that will make Michelin want to include this region in their Guide."

"Okay. Is that all?" Jace glances up at me.

"I need help ..." I gulp. God this is so stupid. "... making me into a personality." I bury my face in my hands. I'm so fucking embarrassed. Zane is the public figure in our family.

"Uh, you're already a personality. Piece of cake." He laughs.

I'm stunned silent. My mouth lolls open.

Jace stops laughing and tosses his head. "You don't think so? I don't think I've ever been in your presence without you saying something insanely snarky and hilarious. Your observations about all these things are legendary. Mia is just like you. It's eerie."

"Wow." I seriously have never seen myself this way. In my mind, I'm a somewhat chubby introverted nerd with pink hair who speaks without thinking and lucked into being loved by the most handsome man alive who probably wouldn't give me a second look if we hadn't been BFFs from birth.

He throws the folders on the desk. "You just need some media training. All of us had to go through it when we started selling records. It's not hard. The PR team can find someone to work with you. Train you. Better yet, you should have your top employees go through the training with you. Alex told me you're nearly staffed up."

"Yeah, you met some of them at Ty and Zoey's dinner thing. I'm still hiring a pastry chef, but my management team is dialed." I glance down at my phone. "Shit. The first candidate will be here any minute, do you want to take a break? I better check on Cillian and call Olga."

Jace gets up and rummages through his backpack to find his own phone. "Good idea, I'll see how Alex is feeling. My sister's with her, but she's still recovering, which she hates. The woman cannot sit still."

"Is she okay though?" I know Alex had a procedure, not much else.

"Yeah. She's fine." He nods, giving nothing away.

I'm not overly close with Jace and don't want a repeat of how I reacted at Ty and Zoey's wedding, so I touch his shoulder to show support rather than hug him. "I'll call her. Please tell her I'm thinking about her and hope she's feeling better soon."

"Sure will. Catchya in a bit." He ducks out.

Six hours later, we're exhausted but the decision is clear.

I'm in awe. Jace is seriously the most silent but deadly dude I've ever met. He has a way of asking insightful questions without seeming like a creeper. He knows when to speak and when to shut up and listen. It's fascinating how he—deliberately—either puts a person at ease or intimidates them, depending on their level of genuineness or schmooze.

Clearly, I've never given him enough credit. He and Alex make a lot of sense now that I've spent an entire day with him. I'm a thousand percent certain the reason we're getting the best PR team with the most perfect scope of services is due to Jace.

"So, Calibrate PR?" Jace flings his backpack over his shoulder.

I can't help but beam. "Yeah, they're perfect. Thank you so much. You have no idea how much I appreciate your help."

"Not a problem." He shoots me his sly grin. "Hopefully, Alex and I can be guests on opening night."

I almost fall into his trap and correct him when I realize he's teasing me. The entire band will be my guest of honor on opening night, all of the band members and their wives. Three additional spots hopefully occupied by the most coveted food critics in the United States who will lose their minds at eating with the most famous rockers in the world.

Jace and I walk through the kitchen. The smells are scrumptious. I realize I never ate today and it's almost seven. "We always have a ton of leftover food. We donate most of it to shelters, but I'm going to pack some to go for our dinner. Can I pack some up for you, Alex, and Lena?"

"Hell yeah." He nods. "That would be awesome. Poppy and I are terrible cooks."

Justice has already gone home, so I introduce Jace to Petra. She's fan-girling so hard but tries not to show it. I find it so funny. I've known the LTZ guys way before they were famous. It's always amusing to me when someone I know loses their shit over one of them. Jace is gracious, though. Of course he is.

When he leaves, loaded down with containers of food, I text Olga and pack up my paperwork for the night. Whenever Zane is away, I like to eat dinner with Mia, help her with some homework and finish up my work once she's asleep. He'll call me after ten, we'll have phone sex and then talk until we fall asleep. I'm on my way out the door when Petra stops me.

"Do you think we'll have a shot?" She's putting away pots and pans.

"There's a method to my madness." I set my stuff down to chat with her. "It's a long shot. But, I want us to operate Gus the way we intend to run it forever. Consistency is the key. That's why we prepare recipes over and over and over again. It's why I'm working with Daire and Jetta on service. Putting every detail in a manual so we can train. Seattle will have never seen anything like this."

Petra grabs her coat and purse from her locker. "You can tell me to fuck off, but you and Zane must be spending an absolute fortune. Between this and The Mission."

"Most restaurants have financiers. He and I have been fortunate in our lives." And not so fortunate, though I don't say so out loud. I think of how I received the money to fix this place up and the blood, sweat, and utter torture I went through to gain custody of Mia. "This is my dream. It's my one shot to do it right. So, I'm assembling a team of badasses to make it all happen."

"I just want to thank you for giving me this opportunity." She's bashful. But sincere.

"Don't thank me yet, we're coasting. The real work begins next month." I pick my stuff back up again. We walk to the back exit.

She holds the door for me. "I'm all in on this. I couldn't think of a better mentor. I feel like the most fortunate woman in the world."

"Petra, you're more than proving yourself. I am so grateful you said yes to working with Justice." I lock the restaurant up and we walk to our cars.

"He's so great." She smiles.

"The team is top-notch." I get in the car. "Four and a half months. Are you ready to put Gus on the map?"

"Fuck yeah." She fist pumps me. We say our goodbyes and I'm finally on my way home.

I fight giving in to fear. Every. Single. Day.

For so long, it felt like nothing was ever going my way. Almost like I was swimming in mud. My fears were actually justified.

Now finally. *Finally.* The stars are aligning.

I won't allow self-doubt to rule my world.

Never fucking again.

Chapter Sixteen

A Few Weeks Later

I'M CONVINCED ZOEY IS pregnant.

Fiona, Mia, and I are at Ty and Zoey's for Sunday brunch. Since they returned from LA, we're hanging out quite a bit. At least once a week or so. Usually on Sundays. Ty cooks, which Fee appreciates. It's often the one day Fiona has downtime, and not always for the full day. She has so much shit to do before Gus opens this summer.

I had my suspicions about Zoey for a week or so, and today I'm certain. For one, she and Ty keep shooting each other smoldering looks. Well, more smoldery than normal. For another, he's over the top checking on her comfort. Bringing her herbal tea. Covering her with a blanket. Stuff like that. Finally, Fee brought over some bourbon chocolates she wanted her to try. Zoey made up some excuse and declined.

I have never, ever, ever seen Zoey turn down any form of chocolate. *So*. I'm a genius sleuth. She's definitely pregnant.

While I keep Ty company in the kitchen, Fee and Zoey watch some Bravo housewives show with Mia. They FaceTimed Alex earlier. Then Ronni. It's fucking cool that all of our women are friends now. It will make touring together so much fun.

"My brother, if you want to hear the final mixes of Fireball, the files are on my phone." Ty looks up from the vegetables he's chopping.

I grab his phone and punch in the code—he and I have no secrets—and scroll through his music files and press play. I close my eyes and let the music wash over me. Four songs in and I'm blown away. Ty's talent as a producer is fucking masterful. I stop the music for a second. "Dude, this is incredible."

"Yeah? I'm happy with it. I know Zoey's happy I'm done with it." He smiles then resumes bustling around the kitchen.

I go to press play to listen to the rest of the album and happen to see a text pop up.

Zoey:

I want to tell Fee.

"Aha!" I jump up and fling myself at Ty. "I knew it."

Ty drops the chunk of cheese he's holding on the floor when I crash into him. "Jesus, Zane. What the fuck?"

"Zoey is preggo. I'm so happy for you guys." I grip his face and kiss him full on the mouth.

He twists away from me and wipes his mouth. Not mad, flustered. "Um ... what?"

"Zoey just texted you." I hold up the phone. "What would she want to tell Fee?"

Ty hasn't moved. He swallows. Looks around. "I ... um."

"Dude, it's so cool. You've wanted to be a dad for so long. You're making your dreams come true." I resist hugging Ty again, clearly he's discombobulated. "Look, I won't say anything."

"What won't you say, babe?" Fee wraps her arms around my middle. Zoey and Mia stand next to her.

Shit. I didn't see them come in.

Zoey rushes over to Ty. "What's wrong?" A look passes between them. I can't quite put my finger on it, but there's a vibe.

"Nothing. I was listening to music on Ty's phone and saw a text come through." I shrug. "No big deal."

Ty looks down at Zoey and nods. She sighs and looks over at us. "We were going to say something when we were eating. I'm pregnant. Due late fall."

"Did you hear that, Meems? You're going to have another cousin." Fiona's pink hair is long and flowy today. She's like a gothic fairy princess in her oversized black shirt and leggings.

Ty picks up the cheese. Doesn't visibly react to their big news. "Food should be ready soon." He tosses it in the trash and grabs a bag of shredded cheese from the fridge. Cracks a load of eggs. Buries himself in food prep while the four of us stand around the kitchen.

"Should we finish the show? The commercial is probably over." Zoey tugs on Mia's pigtail.

Fee shoots me a look when she follows Zoey and Mia out to the living room. When I see they're settled back down watching their show, I move over to where Ty is slow-scrambling some eggs. It's like he's in a trance.

"Are you okay?" I pat his back. "I'm sorry if I said something that made you upset."

He sighs. "I'm so fucking scared."

"About being a dad? You'll be ah-maz-ing." I hope my voice is super encouraging.

Ty sets the pan of eggs aside. Takes out bacon and sausage, which are cooking on a sheet pan, from the oven. "Yeah, I want to believe that. Don't get me wrong, I'm fucking psyched. You know how much I love that woman." He points to Zoey. "I'm going to do right by her for the rest of my life, I just have all of these thoughts lately. Memories. It's fucking with me. I've been talking to Lisa again. Zoey doesn't know."

"Why not?" I grab a piece of bacon and shove it in my mouth. I'm glad he's talking to Lisa. *So* glad.

He tilts his head and just looks at me. "I can't stress her out. She's pregnant. God, we've been through too much with the accident and my part in it. I just don't—"

"It doesn't work that way," I interrupt, frustrated with his constant need to bury shit and not deal with it. "She's gonna *know* something's fucked up. Look, Fee was struggling last year and tried to play it down. She seriously thought I wouldn't notice. If you love someone hard—and you guys fall into that category just like we do—you're connected in a seriously intuitive way." I tap my head. "Ty, trust me. Honor her. Tell her what's on your mind, even if it's painful."

Ty scoops the eggs out on the platter. Arranges the sausages and bacon on another. Shoves them in the warmer and stirs the pancakes. We stand in silence while he ladles eight dollops of batter on the flat grill. Flips

them. Puts them on a new platter. Repeats. He's process-
ing, it's his way. It's against my nature, but I know when
to stay silent.

Finally, he looks up. "I'll try to talk to her. I just don't
want to screw anything up."

I listen to him ramble a bit and debate giving him sage
words of wisdom. Something along the lines of: Zoey
worships the ground he walks on. She loves Ty for the
man he is, not the heartthrob rockstar fans think he is.
She's not going anywhere. Ever.

I'm about to tell him to take his head out of his ass
when Mia runs up and stands before us. She's not happy.
"Uncle Ty, I'm *hunnnnngry*. Breakfast is taking so *looon-
nnng*."

Ty crouches down and hands her a tiny pancake.
"You're such a patient girl. This will tide you over. Can
you go tell your mom and Aunt Zoey breakfast is ready."

"Thank *Goooood*. Thank you, Uncle Ty." Mia kisses
him on the cheek and runs back to where Fee and Zoey
are watching TV.

Ty touches the spot where she kissed him. "I can't wait
to have this baby."

"Mia is pure magic," I agree. "When your kid is born,
you'll never be the same. In an amazing way."

"Fuck it. Help me set this food on the table. I'm so
sick of myself. This is supposed to be a happy time and

I'm going to enjoy this experience with my wife and my family. And that includes you, asshole." He shakes his head, clearly annoyed with himself.

At least he recognizes it when his mind spins these days. When LTZ was on the road, sometimes there'd be long stretches when he'd be so inside his head, we'd worry he wouldn't make it to a gig. Or worse, that he'd quit. Or hurt himself. It was a constant stress, at least for me.

He always came through, but some days it took every single ounce of his professionalism to walk up the steps to the stage. And shit, he'd *slay* the show. I mean, Ty's front-man status is legendary. Afterward, whoosh. He'd be gone. Back to the bus. Or his hotel room. I guess it's no wonder he turned to substances to quiet his mind. That led to its own set of problems.

He's been clean for so long. It occurs to me that emotions—fears—I have about Fee's Xanax use are tied into Ty's addiction issues just like they are Carter's.

It's exhausting worrying all the time about three of the closest people in my life.

Come to think of it, is there a time in my life when I haven't worried? Huh. I can't think of one. Shit. Something else to talk to Lisa about.

Luckily, the rest of the morning and early afternoon are calm and peaceful. Mia and I clean the kitchen. Fee watches a show with Ty and Zoey. I find a way to slip in my ideas about the new custom buses. We even look through the prototype designs I've been working on. By the time the three of us head out, I'm convinced Ty and Zoey are on board.

When we get home, I go to the studio to jam for a bit while Fee and Mia hang out and watch a movie. The day I spent helping Ty and Connor produce Fireball in LA was inspiring. My creative juices are flowing. I make demo tapes of riffs, progressions, and solos. Don't put any sort of restrictions on myself. Let the music flow, so to speak.

"That sounds haunting." Fee stands in the doorway. I was so immersed, I didn't even see her.

I switch off the amp and set down my guitar. "Yeah, I like it though. I'm just messing around with it."

"I love you." She smiles. A genuine, brilliant, loving smile. My favorite kind.

I motion for her to come close. She crosses the room and stands before me. I take her hands in mine. "I *love you.*"

"Mia's asleep." She brings our hands to her lips and kisses my ring-covered knuckles. "It's nearly eleven. I have a big day tomorrow, I just wanted to say good-night if you're going to be down here for a while."

"Shit, is it seriously that late?" I cup her cheeks with our hands still entwined. Pull her lips to mine. Little nibbles. Then our tongues touch. Tentatively. Teasing. Just the tips. We play for a bit until we can't resist. Our kisses become super intense. I suck on her lower lip. Then, we devour each other.

Fiona pulls away and straightens up. "I have to get some sleep."

"Let's sleep then." I stand and hold my hand out to her.

We climb the two flights of stairs to our master bedroom, which we've decorated in plush, soft shades of purple and gray. Each of us go through our bedtime routine. Fee climbs into bed. I decide it's time to unveil a little surprise for my wife. In my walk-in closet, I strip naked and come out with my toys.

She's under the covers reading something on her iPad when I return. Without saying a word, I take it from her and set it down on her nightstand. "Time to play."

"Oh, Zaney, it's late ..." she says, but her eyes spark.

I pull back the covers. Fee wears a long T-shirt. I toss my surprises on the bed next to her, grab the hem with both hands and pull it up over her tits. "Take this shit off."

"Bossy," she grumbles but holds her arms up so I can tug it over her head and throw it on the ground.

I shrug. "I'm about to give you half a dozen orgasms. In this case, bossy is going to work in your favor." I hook my fingers on her underwear and slide them down her legs. Kiss her toes when I lift her legs up one by one to divest her of the panties.

"Zane ..." She looks down at herself and then at me. "Ugh. I've put some weight back on ..."

I run my palms up along her delectable, creamy thighs and I push them apart. Bend down and inhale her arousal while my hands continue their journey over the swell of her belly. Up her rib cage to her breasts which, I knead with both hands. Pinch her nipples into hard beads. Look into her bright-blue eyes and plead, "Please believe you're the sexiest woman in the universe. Do not go back to a place where you forget this is me and you are you. I dream about your beautiful body. I am not complete unless I'm balls deep inside you. Do not forget that. *Ever.*"

"But ..." She tries to sit up, but I press her back against mattress.

"You want it up your butt?" I reach for the little tube of lube and the rose-shaped clit teaser I bought online. "Nah, tonight it's all about your sweet pussy."

Fee's eyes widen when I squeeze a generous dollop of the liquid and spread it around the device. Turn it on. You can barely hear the slight buzz when I place the opening to her clit. The airlike suction simulates intense oral sex. I cycle rapidly up through the levels until Fee can't help but squirm and thrust, trying to make contact. I hover it just above her little nub until she's so turned on her focus is in how she feels, not how she looks.

Her body reacts, unencumbered. She writhes. Mewls. Grips the sheets in her fists. Digs her heels into the mattress. I plunge two fingers inside her. Hook my fingers against her G-spot, then, using my thumb, I turn up the stimulation mode to the next level. Hover. Press. Thrust. Hover. Press. Thrust.

She's stunning. Sexual. Womanhood personified.

Mine. Mine. Mine.

Her entire body twists. Her hips sway and circle. "Oh shit. Oh, holy shit." Fee's forgotten all about her insecurities. Her arms are thrown over her head in abandon. She squeezes my fingers in her channel. "Oh, holy motherfucking shit ..."

I turn it up to the final setting. "You're stunning, baby. You should see yourself. You have no idea how fucking hard I am. Let it go." She bites her plump lower lip. Her hips cant. "Yeahhhh. Just like that ..."

"Zane. What are you doing to me?" Her hand clamps over my wrist to keep the suction in place. Seconds later, Fee's entire face squinches. She literally jackknifes and thrusts against my hand when she comes, drenching me.

I shut off the rose and gather as much of her cream as I can and suck her deliciousness from my fingers. Lean over and give Fee a taste. Run my hands all over her body while we make out.

"We're not done yet." I reach for my other toy. I lube up the vibrating clit-flicker cock ring and roll it over my erection. "Thought it was about time to try this."

We love to play with toys, but we've never done this before. "God, it makes your dick look massive." She licks her lips when I kneel in between her spread legs.

Fiona's so aroused, her wetness glistens. "If it takes me fifty years, I'm going to fuck your bullshit body image issues into oblivion," I say when I bury myself in her heat with one thrust, making sure the little prongs hit her at just the right angle.

"Oh holy ... Ahhhhhhhhhhhhhhh ...." Fee screams. I'm so glad we soundproofed the hell out of this room. There's nothing hotter than when Fiona is uninhibited and loud during sex.

I press her knees high against her tits. Ram into her. The cock ring is incredible. It's vibrations stimulate my entire shaft and actually collect blood at the base, which makes me ginormous and I'm no slouch to begin with. My dick is darker. Thicker. Longer, if that's even possible. It intensifies how *in-fucking-credible* Fee's velvet pussy feels so much, my eyes nearly pop out of my head.

When I drive into her, the little pulses from the silicone prong press firmly against Fee's clit. I can feel it all the way to my balls.

A couple of pumps and I'm a wild animal. She's there with me. The sounds we're making are feral. Clawing. Grinding. Biting. Scratching. Fee shrieks when she comes again. And because I cannot stop pounding into her, she cannot stop coming. And coming. And coming. Her pussy is so fucking tight around me, I'm afraid my dick's going to explode.

I'm out of my head. Operating on pure instinct. Superhuman. I grip her ankles. My hips slap against her. I yank her ass up against my thighs and gyrate like a hula dancer on speed. Fast. Hard. Harder. Faster.

And she's *still* coming, Her head thrashes from side to side. Her tits shake. Her stomach contracts with each orgasm. Her words come out like babbling. I'm chasing. Chasing. *Chasing*. It's nearly there and I know it's going to ruin me.

A white-hot, icy jolting sensation takes root at the base of my spine and simultaneously races through my balls down my taint to my asshole and up the length of my shaft. I erupt like a volcano, a literal volcano. My hot lava fills Fiona and overflows. I've never splooged so much in my life.

Our combined release runs down her thighs and pools on our sheets, still damp from the last go-round.

And ... apparently, I'm not done. Christ. I simply can't stop coming. It's so—gah. Too much. Unreal.

"*Feeeeeeeeee*," I moan. And cry. Tears run down my face. "I'm having an out of body experience ..." I almost wince when my dick spasms and spurts again.

Even after the second orgasm, I'm still rock hard and feel a third coming on. I can't take another one, it will kill me. I manage to pull out and roll the cock ring off my shaft. I flop over on my back, exhausted. My chest heaves. My cock twitches. My hair's wet from exertion.

Best. Sex. Ever.

I have no idea how much time goes by before I'm able to glance at Fiona, who's in the same babbling state as me. Her eyes are closed. She rubs her clit in slow circles, not to get off but to come down. Her lips move in some sort of silent chant. Little aftershocks occasionally zing through her body.

Neither of us are in a position to change our ruined sheets.

I don't think either of us cares.

I'm not certain when we manage to fall asleep.

All I know is that there's no one but Fee.

My Fee. My Fee ...

Chapter Seventeen

The Next Month

I FEEL LIKE CRYING from joy.

The buildout is complete. It's spectacular. Each detail is exactly how I pictured.

I'll be fully staffed up next month. Followed by two months of training.

Training. Training. Training.

I *cannot* believe I'm less than 90 days away from opening my own restaurant. And the new Mission.

God, my dad would be so proud.

My mom? I haven't heard from her in months. Not a fucking peep. The correlation between my mental well-being and not having her toxicity in my life isn't hard to see. I'm confident. In control. I don't second-guess myself quite as much.

Like letting my executive team do screening interviews with staff from around the country for the non-leadership positions. The positions are highly competitive, so to ensure Gus attracts the best candidates, I'm offering nearly fifty percent above market rate for all wages with health care, generous PTO, 401K benefits, and performance bonuses to sweeten the deal.

I'll fly those that make the cut to Seattle in a couple weeks so I can make the final decision. Then it's *go* time.

My goal is to create a workplace where a core staff stay for at least three years, if not longer. Consistency of food quality and service is crucial to attract and earn a Michelin Star. If I pay top dollar to retain the best team in the world, it will streamline my timeline significantly.

This approach is most definitely *not* something I learned in my business classes at culinary school. Quite the opposite.

I'm not stupid. I'm sure some critics will assume Zane's backing the restaurant even though I'm investing every penny of my settlement money from Corey into this venture.

Social media is up and running. We have a great initial following, so there's a buzz. The PR push hasn't even begun yet, though interviews and articles are scheduled.

We're moving in the right direction.

Far more exciting is my new hire—a remarkable pastry chef.

Wolf Woodrow, whose tasting menu is—was—the most coveted seat in the world, is joining me at Gus. A month ago, Zane and I took Carter's jet to Berlin to meet with him. Luckily, his sister is a huge fan of LTZ, so he made room for us that night last minute, even if he was only peripherally aware of the band.

Wolf's dessert philosophy is revolutionary—in his mind, it's more than just a final course. In fact, many of his dishes are not even all that sweet. Using simple techniques, he prepares fresh chocolate by hand every day incorporating natural ingredients. Same with jellies. Pastries. Pies. He eschews refined sugar. Scoffs at artificial flavor.

Every single element is executed with flawless technical skill.

By the *grumpiest* man I've ever met.

After the meal, I knew I had to have him, though. No question. When I proposed a partnership, Wolf laughed at me. Actually laughed. He was so rude, I thought my nonviolent husband would beat the shit out of him.

But, no. Zane stayed out of it. He has so much faith in me, he let me handle my own business and went back to the hotel while I pitched Wolf. He and I sat at his tiny four-seat bar and drank artisan whisky. Talked food philosophy for hours. Shared stories of our respective culinary journeys.

It was nice. We opened up to each other in a way you can do when you're strangers and have nothing to lose. As it turned out, Wolf endured his own special brand of hellish heartbreak. He also confessed that the stress of keeping his unique conceptual dessert-themed restaurant staffed was slowly crushing his soul.

That night, we realized we were kindred gastronomic spirits. Wolf's entire gruff demeanor softened. He was interested in joining forces, becoming an investor and partner in Gus. We finalized our partnership agreement and are in the process of fast-tracking his E2 Investor visa. We'll be cutting it close with respect to Gus's opening, but it will be worth it.

By the time I get home, I've had a twelve-hour workday, factoring in a two-hour visit from Alex and Zoey sandwiched in between. I'm fried. No sooner than I walk through the door, Mia rushes down the stairs and says in hushed voice," Mommy. Mommy. Grandma's here."

"Oh yeah? Is LeeLee with your dad?" My brain cells are not firing on all cylinders. I can't even think. I drop my tote bag and kick off my shoes. All I want to do is hang out with Mia and Zane for an hour or so, then go to bed.

Mia shakes her head. "No, *your* mom."

Instant. Tension.

"Oh, how nice. Where is she?" I try to keep my annoyance out of my tone. Why is she *here*? She didn't even call. Or text. A drop in? Kinda rude, in my opinion. I hear voices coming from the conservatory. Gah. The tone of my mother's voice. I pinch my nose with my thumb and forefinger. "Mia ..."

My daughter is so fucking intuitive it scares me and breaks my heart. "I *know*. Adult stuff. I'll be in my room. Daddy told me to stay there, but I was listening for you."

"Oh, Meems." My heart hurts. I never want my daughter to be wise to the drama between me and my mom. I've got to do better. When I was her age, I knew way too much about fighting and family tension. So did Zane. We've vowed not to let Mia experience any of that shit, and yet ...

She dashes up the stairs and looks back at me. "Don't worry, Mommy. My work here is done. Peace out."

I can't help but gawk after her. My child. You'd think she was a teenager and she's barely seven. Nevertheless, I'm going to handle this tomorrow. It would kill me if Mia felt about me the way I feel about my own mother most of the time.

Speaking of which. Just when my life is going well, *she* shows up. I can't afford to let her derail me. Not again. I also can't let her take out her shit on Zane.

Fuck.

I scurry to where the voices are coming from.

"You're a liar. You got what you wanted, my daughter doesn't even speak to me," Mom hisses at Zane, who stands across from her with his palms pressed to his thighs. "There's no coincidence when that all started. Your *wedding.*"

To his credit, Zane keeps calm. "Faye, I don't interfere in your relationship with Fiona. That's all on you."

"How dare you." She lunges toward him.

He retreats. "Don't. Not in my home. With my daughter here."

"She's not your fucking daughter. It's a goddamn blessing she's not yours. It's a goddamn *blessing* my daughter is on birth control. God forbid you get her *pregnant.*" My mom's so worked up spittle flies from her mouth.

"Stop." I hold my hand out like a shield. "Enough."

My mom and Zane spin around, stunned to see me.

"Fiona. Baby." Mom's crocodile tears appear. "I've missed you so badly, why haven't you called? Or texted? I had to come check to see if you're okay."

"No. I'm not fucking okay."

Mom whirls around to Zane. "I *knew* it."

"Can we please sit down?" I gesture to the sofas. "Mia is awake, and I would like to have a civilized conversation using indoor voices to stop this madness once and for all."

Zane plops down. Leans back. Spreads his arms along the back of the couch, unbothered. "Yeah. I think it's time to just get things on the table. Once and for all."

Faye looks back and forth between us and sits, reluctantly, on the edge of a chair.

"I have tried to have this conversation with you so many times, Mom. I'd appreciate if you'd let me say my piece." I take the seat next to Zane but lean forward and clasp my hands.

My mom points at me. "I will not be made out as the bad mom in this..."

"You *are* a bad mom," I state simply. "You have some motherly instincts, but mostly you are abusive, shaming, judgmental, and unkind."

Her face reddens, her voice raises an octave. "How *dare* you. After all I sacrificed for you."

"No. That does *not* fly with me. I'd sacrifice anything to protect my daughter. *Anything.* And I wouldn't *dream* of making her feel like shit about herself. You don't get to talk to me about sacrifice." I shake my head, careful to keep my voice calm.

"Without me, you'd be on the street." Faye clenches her teeth. "You'd have seven kids out of wedlock. You'd be nothing."

Zane can't help himself. "Oh, hell no ..."

"Babe, I've got this." I grip his hand on the back of the sofa. He sighs, but nods.

Faye stands. Nearly bares her teeth. "I'm not going to listen to anything you have to say. Clearly, I'm not welcome. I should have taken the money Corey offered, at least then I could see Mia when I want to. Hell, I'd probably have *custody* of my grandchild. A mansion to raise her in. But no good deed goes unpunished."

"Holy shit. Do you actually hear what you're saying?" I'm stunned. Utterly stunned.. I had no idea Corey tried to buy her off. It's hard to know if she's lying. When she's in a mood, my mom says horrible, shitty, untrue stuff. It's been this way my entire life. Then she'll be nice, helpful, agreeable, and pleasant for a while like she's changed. Eventually the hurtful, abusive word vomit explodes again.

It fucks with you. It really does.

Mom sneers. "Don't be such a fucking baby, Fiona. I'm venting. I have every right ..."

"No, you don't. Not in my house." I'm so done with her.

"It's not your house, it's Zane's house." She laughs. "When he fucks around on you—he did it before so he'll do it again—you'll be shit outta luck. Where you gonna live? At your fancy new restaurant he paid for? Talk about self-indulgent and entitled. Who the fuck do you think you are?"

"It's time for you to leave." I stand and gesture to the stairs leading to the kitchen, where it's a short walk to the front door. Ruing the day I ever told her about why Zane and I broke up. I *knew* it would bite me in the ass.

She doesn't move. "You're not going to kick your own mother out. Even you wouldn't stoop that low."

Zane gets up and puts his arm around me. "Faye, you always take it too far. And you're never self-aware enough to see the path of destruction you carve."

"Shut the fuck up, you red-blooded bastard." She lunges toward us.

Zane steps in between us, spitting mad. "Wow. Fucking wow. Racist much? Tell me how you really feel, *Faye.*"

I'm horrified, but not surprised at my mother's hatred directed at Zane's indigenous heritage. But it's also horrific because it's partially mine too on my dad's side. I push Zane aside. "Mom, I'm dead serious. You just can't stop yourself. And now I'm D.O.N.E *done.* That's it. The end of our relationship. You will not speak to me or my husband that way in *our* house. Your racist, cunty ways are no longer welcome in my life. I can't risk you being around Mia. Or any of our future babies unless you make some serious changes. I mean it."

"I'm not leaving until I see my granddaughter. If you won't let me, I'll sue," she screams. "I'll fucking *sue*."

I'm all tapped out. "Do your worst. I've been through it all. Your threats mean nothing. Please leave, or I will call the police."

"You'd do that?" She finally stands and her entire demeanor shifts again. "To your own *mother?*"

"You're not my mother unless you make changes." I shrug. "Until that time, yes. I would. Gladly."

She gasps. Starts to cry. No, she sobs. "I'm sorry, Fiona. Please ..."

Zane senses I'm on a razor's edge at this point, and I am. But I also know my mother. I can't allow her manipulative ways to put him in harm's way. "Babe, please call Zeke."

'Oh, right. Yeah." Understanding washes over him. He punches in a text.

Two minutes later, Zeke appears. Assesses. Sends his own texts, then addresses Faye. "Ma'am. I've called backup."

"You, *what?*" She's shaken, that much is clear.

"I'm not safe with you, neither is my family. It's clear you do not have our best interests at heart, so it is what it is. Please get help." My head is absolutely pounding. I just want her gone.

Zane bands his arm around my waist. I sink back into him. He kisses my temple. Whispers, "I love you, I know this is excruciating."

"Yeah." I stave off tears, which will come later. For sure. I focus back on my mother. "Mom, you need to leave. Now."

She shuffles away with Zeke following several paces behind. Zane and I trail after them. At the front door, Zeke holds it ajar. Just when I think she's going to finally get the fuck out, she turns. "You'll regret this, Fiona. I'm your only family. The one who *truly* loves you. Don't you get fooled into thinking all of this is your real life. You've never done anything in your life to deserve being this rich. It's obscene. *You're* obscene. A fat, lazy, insecure little bitch who couldn't accomplish a fucking thing on her own. You'll never get a Michelin Star. You should never have been born, you utter waste of human space."

I gasp. She's stabbed me a million times in the past and again tonight with her words. It feels like the final blow. I literally crumple to the ground. She flashes me a triumphant sneer on her way out.

If that weren't the worst thing that could happen, I see movement on the staircase. Mia. She heard everything.

Zane sees it too, he frantically looks at me and then up at where Mia was. Back again. He's conflicted, but I'm not. "Go to her, please. I need a minute."

"Fee, you *know* what she said isn't true." He crouches down and takes my face in his hands. "She's lost control of you, she'd say any fucking thing to get it back."

My head knows this, but my heart hasn't caught up. Doesn't matter, Mia's who is most important. "Please, babe. Can you check on her? Give me a chance to shake this off and I'll be right up."

"But ..." He's so incredibly pure and sweet.

I must release him from worrying about me. For both our sakes. "Zane, Alex had a miscarriage. Zoey and Ty are dealing with his past issues with a mother who actually physically abused him. Ronni has a nanny who's obsessed with her husband. I'm fine. We'll talk later. Please make sure our daughter is okay. I'm holding it together for her. Believe me, I just need to have a cry and I'll be better. I don't want to do it in front of her."

"Okay, babe. Okay." He kisses me deeply. "She's horrible." Kisses. "I love you." More kisses. You didn't deserve *any* of that."

I nod, unable to say anything.

He runs upstairs, which gives me a great sense of relief.

At least for my daughter.

Zane is the best father she'd ever hope to have.

Her mother, on the other hand, is a fucking mess.

Chapter Eighteen

A Couple of Weeks Later

Two months.

The day I've been obsessing about is two months away. So much crazy shit has happened to all of us this past year or so. It's a miracle we're still on track.

My band's agreed to a schedule. After The Mission show, we're going to write. Play a couple of unannounced festival shows. Then record. Hopefully release something before Christmas.

Now it's me who's freaking out a little bit. I haven't said anything to anyone, but ...

I'm really worried about Fee.

"Meems, are you ready?" I tap on her door. "We need to leave a little early, your mom left her tote bag and she needs it."

Mia emerges from her room. Black-and-white knee-high socks. Pink tutu. Purple sweater. My darling rock goddess. "Can you put my hair in space buns?" She holds out two pink elastic bands.

"Of course." I move behind her, tie her black hair back into two ponytails then wind her hair around itself and secure it. Floof out the ends for a bit of flair.

She dashes back into her room to inspect the style from all angles, declaring, "Oh, it's *good*!"

"I'm the official space bun guy then?" I call after her as she flies past me and slides down the stair rail. "Hey, your mom doesn't like it when you do that."

"*You* don't care." She shrugs and puts on her backpack.

Oh boy. I made the classic rookie parenting deflection boo-boo. Now, I've got to adult. "Uh, yeah. I *do* care. For one, whatever your mom and I decide goes. For two, it's dangerous. You could get hurt if you fell off, and I would cry if you got hurt. So would you."

"Okay. I'm sorry." Mia watches me intently as I descend the stairs. Our daughter hasn't seemed to have internalized anything after Faye's visit. Her behavior most stems from missing Fee, who's essentially living at Gus.

I grab my keys, wallet, and luckily remember Fee leaves Mia's meals in the fridge so I whoosh into the kitchen and grab her lunch. "Ready?" I say as I open the front door.

"Uh, Mommy's tote bag?" She holds it up to me.

Jesus, Fee's lost without it. "How are you so fucking smart?" I kiss her forehead.

"Inherited." She flounces to the car.

Have I mentioned how fucking much I love my daughter?

I consider bringing Mia with me to give Fee an extra moment with our daughter. *No*. Today, I need that second for myself. I decide to take Mia to school before I drop the tote off.

There's no way after what happened with Faye that Fee's okay. She's been doubly—no triply—driven ever since the incident. We barely have sex, and we're back to doing it in the middle of the night with all the lights off when we do.

I've asked her how she feels about what happened. She blows it off. Not in a mean way. More indifferent. Or, "I'm too busy to worry about it."

"Same old. Same old," is her direct quote.

I want to believe her. She's so relaxed. Controlled. Focused. *Excited*. Yet, something doesn't make sense.

How can she be so calm about Faye's special brand of assholery? She said some pretty unforgivable things ...

Unless ...

Fuck. I'm super conflicted. There's no denying it's crunch time for the restaurant. Her whole team is working as hard as she is. I'm trying to support whatever she needs to get Gus open on time. For now, that means taking care of Mia, which is a joy and pleasure.

I'm definitely the one winning in this situation.

I pull into the back lot and park my Aston Martin next to Fee's Toyota Highlander. Glance over at her tote bag. Hate myself for what I'm about to do and yet, I do it anyway.

Because I've got to know.

I look inside. Poke around. It's mostly filled with brochures. Business cards. A couple of notebooks. Bottle of 222s, over-the-counter painkillers from Canada. Pens. Thermometers. Hair ties. Sample menus. A fancy chocolate bar. Aw, a little daffodil keychain I gave her for her twenty-eighth birthday.

Thank God.

I fucking hate myself for snooping in Fee's things. It's just ... She's so composed. Should she be? Am I being an asshole?

God, I don't know.

"Zane?" Justice knocks on my window. "Are you okay?"

Shit. I motion for him to move so I can get out. "Yo, Justice. Uh, yeah. I just have to drop Fee's bag off, she left it at home."

"Oh, that's awesome. She said she left a couple of recipes we worked on yesterday at home. I think they're going to make it on the menu, we need some more practice to be sure." He holds out his fist.

I make a fist and knock mine to his. "Cool. Glad to help. Plus, it gives me a chance to give my wife a kiss, so I'm all for her leaving something behind."

"Man, I don't know how you guys do it." Justice shakes his head as we walk into the back entrance. "Relationships are tough for full-time chefs."

I'm not about to discuss my relationship with one of Fee's employees, but I'm happy to let him ramble on about his own experiences. "Yeah? Have you lost a significant other because of your job?"

"Nah, I don't do relationships." He takes off his jacket and puts it in his locker.

I crane my head to look for Fee. "You're missing out, man."

"Someone's going to grab your heart one day, Justice." Wolf appears in the doorway to the office. "Trust me when I say, you'll be powerless."

Justice waggles his eyebrows. "Not a chance, I like power too much. If you know what I mean."

I can't help but laugh.

Fee must hear the commotion. She pokes her head out of the office. God, she's pretty. Her pink hair is tied into two braids. Pouty lips. Chef coat with "Fiona" emblazed about her left boob. I'm a little moony, it's been a couple of weeks since I've seen her in the daylight. She's long gone by the time Mia and I wake up.

"Oh, thank you, Zaney." She reaches out and takes her tote. "Wanna try something? In my office?"

Holy crap, she walked us into that one.

Of course, her entire brigade makes "woo-ing" noises and slapping sounds, to her great embarrassment.

Not mine, though. "Children, children. If you aren't trying something in the office, you're not living." I clap my hands together three times. "Back to business. While I try whatever Fiona has in store for me."

"Jesus." Fee can't help but laugh along. "They already worship the ground you walk on, do you always have to be so fucking cool?"

I hook my arm around her neck. "I was born cool."

"Now, I know you're full of it." She elbows me in the side. "I was the one born cool, I had to give you cool-guy lessons."

"Ah. I remember that now." I hold my finger up into the air.

She sits at her desk. "Did Mia get off to school okay?"

"She slid down the fucking banister again. I scolded her. Hopefully she won't do it again." I sink down on the couch adjacent to the three desks. "Other than that, yeah. It's all pretty chill."

"We're setting up the dining area today. Most of the serving plates and dishes have arrived. They're stunning." Her grin is from ear to ear. She doesn't look stressed at all.

"I'm glad she worked out." Fee hired an elder from the Puyallup Indian tribe to create all of the pieces she'll serve her courses on. A friend of Carter's aunt.

She touches her dad's photo, which is framed on her desk next to a picture of the three of us. "It seemed like it was meant to be."

I glance around the office, which is now set up not just for Fee, but also Justice, Petra, Daire, and Wolf. "I haven't been back here in a couple weeks. It's a perfect setup."

"Right?" Fee stands and locks the door. "I figure if we can go at this pace through summer and into fall, we'll get service dialed in. Then we can switch the main schedule and settle in."

I must zone out or something because she stops talking and looks at me. "Zane?"

"Yeah?" My elbows rest on my thighs, my hands clasped. "Sorry."

"Are you okay?" She sits next to me on the couch.

I can't figure out how to describe what I'm feeling. I'm always the positive guy. I work hard at it. It just feels like my entire world is a little off-kilter. It occurs to me I might be projecting my own shit onto Fee. Reading into things that aren't there because her career is all in front of her.

Fuck. Am I envious?

Not exactly. No. I'm the one who's struggling to adapt to the changes in our lives.

"Zane?" Fee puts her hand on my thigh. "Talk to me."

"I don't know, babe. I think maybe it's the band. Something's off on the timing for the band. Jace all but said Alex isn't on board with touring., so he won't want to go You know what's happening to Ronni. She's dealing with so much legal shit. Which means Connor won't want to be away from her."

"Yeah, but Ty is on board, isn't he? They'll need a little downtime after Zoey gives birth, but she'll be excited to go on the road." Fee turns sideways. Rubs my thigh to comfort me. "And Mia and I will be with you as much as possible."

I lean in and kiss her. She's trying so hard, but I'm just blue today. "I know. I guess after what you just said, I'm settling into the reality you won't exactly be available at will. If I'm honest, after an entire year hanging out with Mia every day, I can't imagine being away from her. Maybe this is the end."

"*Zane...*" Fiona's eyebrows crease.

I take her hand and bring it to my lips. "I want you to have Gus. You've worked so hard. It's time. I've lived my dream, Fee. You deserve yours too."

"God, remember how much we wanted to grow up so we could be together when we were kids?" She leans her head on my shoulder. "I can't believe we're older than our parents were when you moved to Denver. How did we get to be grownups? It's not as easy as we thought it would be."

I press my forehead down toward hers for a head snuggle. "Time keeps on going by, but I never love you any less. In fact, it feels like each day we're together my love for you multiplies, if that's possible. I want you to know that if something happens with LTZ, or any of the guys decide to peace out, I'll be okay with it."

"Zane..." Fee tilts her head up. I peer into her blue eyes, which are flecked with so many hues it's breathtaking.

"I mean it." I snake my arms around her so her entire upper body is pressed against mine. I whisper in her ear, "I mean it."

She hooks her arms around me and buries her face in my neck. Looks up. "My love for you is so ... so ... all-consuming. Knowing you're always with me, even if we're not in the same room, city, country. Feeling that you're part of me. You know that, right?"

"I do, Fee." I trace her cheekbone with my thumb. "I feel you too. That's the best part about being your other half."

She nods. "We're so fucking sappy."

"Yeah, we might be." I kiss her, savoring her lips. "What we have is worth billions. I sometimes have to pinch myself that we're fucking married. Really married. We have Mia. We have businesses. Homes. God, we are living the dream."

Her smile is brilliant. Unencumbered. Free. "We do. So let's maybe try not to control all the things. We don't know what's going on with any of the guys or their part-ners. Not really. I have faith that things will happen the way they are supposed to."

"Well, if you're supposed to get this fucking Michelin Star, I guess I should let you get back to work." I lay another smack on her lips and stand.

"I'm okay, you know. I get that you're worried." She holds her hands out to me and I pull her up.

I wince. "I looked through your tote."

"Why?" She's confused.

"I thought maybe ..." I bring a fist up to my eyes.

A flash of hurt then understanding washes over her face. "Zane, you can look through anything I have. My phone. My underwear drawer. My tote. Whatever." She grips my wrist. "Hiding things from each other isn't an option. You never need to do that. Just ask."

I can't help it when a wave of shame floods my body. Tears threaten to spill. "I'm sorry, baby. I ..."

"I get it." Her grip on my wrist loosens. She skims her fingers up my palm and threads them with mine. "We both have so much shit in our past that makes us question things sometimes. I'm not mad. I never want you to feel worried about me. I'm your rock too, you know. I'm not some fragile butterfly."

God. My Fee. She's the one who kept me going when we were kids and no one liked me. I'd almost forgotten that kid ever existed. We *are* each other's rocks. Knowing this, deep inside, comforts me. "I'm scared about my band, baby. I've been scared all year. My connection to the guys is slipping. We're all drifting away from each other, and I can't stop it."

"My sweet Zaney." She pulls me to her. "I love you. I'm here for you. Lean on me."

And I do. I fucking do.

It's such a relief knowing that she's got me.

She always has and she always will.

Chapter Nineteen

The Next Month

WHY DO I DO it to myself?

I'm less than a month from opening Gus and I offer to host a fucking baby shower? And do all the cooking? When I haven't finished training the staff yet?

I'm such a fucking idiot.

Oh, I'll make this fucking shower my bitch. No one will see me sweat. As far as the ladies will know, it's effortless. Easy.

Then, and only then, will I have a nervous breakdown. The heaviness I feel now is...gah.

At least Zane is with me and we have world-class help.

Wolf made a five-tiered topsy-turvy red velvet cake covered in light-blue-and-green argyle fondant. He also baked mini-cupcakes topped with extraordinarily cute zoo animals. As avant-guard as his desserts usually are, his cute decorating skills are on point..

Justice and Petra helped me prepare the food. An organic chicken roasted in locally sourced Ship-wreck Honey, salt and cayenne chopped into a sal-ad of cucumbers, local greens, and rainier cherries. Fresh-baked cheese biscuits. Three tartlets out of homemade puff pastry filled with goat cheese and fig. Spiced lamb and chutney. Roasted eggplant and feta. Petra curated the most incredible charcuterie tray filled with meats, cheeses, nuts, and spreads sourced from local farmers. She arranged them as a giant baby buggy.

It's seriously next level.

Zane and Mia made a huge banner in blue let-ters spelling out "Baby Rainier." Mia, who's beginning to show an aptitude for art, drew in little Ty, Zoey, and baby characters. This morning Ronni and Connor stopped by early to help set up. The men are outside putting up giant balloon displays.

If only their fans could see the heartthrob rockstars now.

"Can I help? I can't promise anything, my kitchen skills are nonexistent," Ronni offers.

She's dressed in a beautiful, white designer suit. I'm not letting Ronni near the food. "Are you any good at table design? Maybe set the table for ten?"

"You got it." She seems happy to be able to contribute.

I give her twenty minutes before bringing her a glass of wine. "Well, there's a talent I think you've got down pat." The table is impeccable, sophisticated and inviting. "Alex just texted, she's on the ferry. We have about an hour or so before they arrive."

"I'm so in awe of you, Fee. You're so incredibly talented." Ronni clinks her glass to mine.

God, coming from an actress with a million Emmys—high praise. I know my face is red. "Smoke and mirrors. I feel like I'm always on the brink of disaster."

We end up having a deep conversation about motherhood and trying to balance our shit. We're so much alike in many ways. Ronni trusts me enough to confide some shit, which opens my own floodgates. I didn't realize how awesome it was to have a close girlfriend to talk with. Especially one who understands balancing life as a rockstar spouse with your own hopes and dreams.

I love Zoey and Alex, but they've been BFFs since birth. Maybe Ronni and I could be BFFs too.

No time to contemplate, though. I leave her to check on the guys while I change my clothes. I no sooner come downstairs and Lianne arrives. Then Zoey's mom. Then Alex's. The women are milling about the kitchen as if we have all the time in the world.

I waggle my finger at Zane, who rushes to my side. "You and Connor should get moving."

"Oh, shit." Zane bellows, "Connor? Let's roll."

With the guys gone, we're finally in full baby shower mode. "Sparkling rosé anyone? Miraval? A little nod to Brad Pitt. He may be old, but he's hot and makes a fine wine."

After a toast, I take a bite of hand-crafted raw milk cheese from Chimacum Valley Dairy. The ladies are still just standing around so I decide to break the ice. "Ronni. Tell me the truth. How tough is it having twins? Zane is so jealous, he can't stand it. I'm stressing about having one baby, but two would put me over the edge."

It does the trick. Each woman shares her own stories about motherhood, getting us in the mood to welcome Zoey into the fold.

That is, until Lianne pipes up. "It's not easy being on your own with a baby. Carter was so involved when Zaney was an infant. By the time he turned two, Limelight was on the road, leaving me to fend for the both of us. I was just lucky Fiona's mom, Faye, helped out so I could still dance. Otherwise, my career would have been shot."

I munch down another square of cheese. No one but Zane knows what's gone on between me and my mom. I thought he told Lianne about the incident we had a couple months ago. Maybe not. In either case, Zoey's shower is not the time to bring everyone down with my family drama. So, I speak the truth. "Yeah. I couldn't have made it through Mia's first years without my mom."

"Wait, is Faye your mom, Fiona?" Alex's mom, Andrea asks.

"Sometimes. Depends on the day," I can't help but snark just as the door sounds. "Ooh. Saved by the buzz."

"Oh my God, you guys." Zoey's eyes are huge when Alex brings her in. She scans the room, wiping tears as they fall down her cheeks. "This is amazing."

I can tell she's truly touched—and maybe surprised—at the effort her girlfriends have made for her. I want this to be a special afternoon welcoming her into the motherhood fold. One of the reasons I volunteered is both Zane and I have noticed Ty's past issues bubbling up in unexpected ways during our weekly brunches. His moods are a bit, uh, unpredictable.

Zoey never, ever complains. Or makes him feel less-than. She just loves him as he is, as Zane puts it. He's her biggest fan for that reason. And so while we don't have the type of friendship where she'd necessarily confide in me, I knew she probably needed a day of sisterhood and celebration.

Nevertheless, this shower is eating into my strict schedule. I have a shit-ton of work to do later this afternoon and they're easily twenty minutes late. It's time to gracefully move the day along. "Okay, ladies. Now that you're here, lunch is served."

Ronni stands and taps on her glass with a spoon. "Zoey, on behalf of all of us here, we welcome you to the mother club. It's an experience like no other."

"Absolutely. And to your third trimester. Heartburn, constipation, giant tits, and the inability to ever get comfortable," I add, hoping to keep things lighthearted and sarcastic. I'm not in the mood for sappiness.

To my delight, it works. Zoey cups her ample boobs. "I'm up two bra sizes."

"I'm sure Ty's not complaining." Alex, who isn't quite as blessed in that department, casts her eyes to the ceiling.

"He's not." Zoey grins cheekily.

Olivia is mortified. "TMI. The last thing you want to hear about is your child's sex life."

"Mom, I'm pregnant. How did you think it happened?" Zoey laughs.

Her mom fixes her with a scolding glare. "Divine intervention."

Lianne, who's trying to keep herself from laughing, shakes her head. "Zane has always been TMI with me."

"Ah, well that's Zaney." There are days when I can't help but admire my mother-in-law. At a really young age, she kept her shit together during some trying times. Unlike my mom, she always put Zane first. "You did a good job with my guy, Lianne."

To my surprise, she embraces me. "He's *always* been your guy."

Her words strike a chord.

I think back to when Zane and I were little. He and I always used to sleep in the same bed, which continued even when we'd go on summer vacation with our moms. One summer we were, God, twelve? Thirteen? My mom was adamant we were too old and she wouldn't allow it. Neither of us understood why, so when they went to sleep we crawled into bed together anyway. It was all so innocent.

Thank God it was Lianne who caught us and not my mom. She wasn't mad, she was...touched? I remember the look in her eyes. It's the same as it is now.

She always knew we were meant to be.

I'm snapped back into reality by Alex, who's been unusually quiet and contemplative. "Enough of the sappy shit. Presents. Now."

It gives me an opening. "We're set up in the other room. Head in there, I'll bring some drinks in a minute."

Most of the ladies make the short trek from the conservatory to the living room. Zoey, on the other hand, plops back down. She's out of breath.

"Are you okay, honey?" Her mom rushes over to her.

"I'm fine. That was just *weird*, I felt like I was going to faint." Zoey shakes it .

Olivia helps Zoey to her feet. "Let's get you into the living room. Once that belly pops, the discomfort starts. Get used to it."

"I'm getting so fat. Ty doesn't seem to mind, though." Zoey looks down at her bump. Pats it lovingly.

Ronni rolls her eyes dramatically and pinches some nonexistent fat. "You should have seen my belly when I hit five months. I never thought I'd look like myself again. Well, I don't, but man, I was twice your size. The twins, God love them, have fucked up my body big time."

"Go on ahead. I'll be right there." I shoo them away so I can mix up a batch of orange and passionfruit juices and seltzer "faux-mosas". As I stir, it's hard not to let negative self-talk creep into my mind. Ronni and Zoey's weight comments stun me. Do these ladies truthfully see themselves as overweight?

I run my hand along my soft torso. Though I'm doing my best to hide it, my body image is back to shit. I feel self-conscious. Compared to those two, I'm huge. Both women are—at the most—a size four, maybe six. When I tried on clothes for this shindig, I discovered my 1X dresses are all snug. If they truly believe they're heavy, I can't imagine what they think about me...

No, stop thinking that way.

I take cleansing breaths. I just need to get through another hour. I finish the drinks and bring them into the living room with a smile. "With those stupid migraines, I'm so glad you're taking such good care of yourself, Zoey. When I was pregnant with Mia, I developed preeclampsia. I don't want that for you. Not with all of the complications that go with it. It fucking sucks."

"Yeah. Well, Ty's taking good care of me." She smiles at all of us. "He cooks for me every night. Massages. Foot rubs ..."

"Sex." Alex and the rest of us—except Zoey's mom, who hides her eyes—laugh.

God, we're terrible. As is typical with our group, the stories get a little raunchy. A bit squealy. The moms wisely keep their lips zipped because—*ew.*

When the topic turns to pregnancy woes, Lianne, Andrea, and Olivia join in. We're graphic. Disgusting. Hilarious. Because, face it, it's a rite of passage at a baby shower. One I never had, considering my own particular circumstances, so I get a little bit of a macabre thrill participating now.

Zoey is clearly horrified but has no power to stop the share-a-thon.

Thankfully, the rest of the afternoon passes quickly. Ty and Zoey have a ton of stuff for the baby, who she calls "Rufus." All the women leave on time except Ronni, because Torin and Tristan are upstairs with Mia and Olga. Connor is on his way to pick them up.

"You doing okay?" Ronni picks up a couple of trays and takes them to the sink.

"Thanks." I put the trays in the dishwasher. "Yeah, I'm totally fine. It's crunch time. The kitchen staff is plating the menu tonight. They're going to serve me, Zane, Carter, and Lianne as test diners. That way I can tweak whatever needs tweaking."

"Oh, so you have things to do tonight. Where's our invite?" She winks.

I snap a towel at her. "You and Connor will be in next round. I promise."

Connor and Zane burst through the doorway.

"Zoey's on the way to the hospital." Zane grabs a tartlet and stuffs it in his mouth. "I don't think we need to worry. It's just precautionary."

Connor wraps Ronni from behind. She grips his forearms and looks up at him. "Good, so they're okay?"

"Aye." He takes a slice of salami.

"Ty's in excellent spirits," Zane confirms.

Ronni disentangles herself from Connor and gestures to the stairs. "Fee and Zane still have restaurant stuff tonight. Let's get out of their hair so they can hopefully have time to relax."

"Oh, aye." Connor nods at me. "I'll go get the boys."

Zane winds a lock of my hair around his finger. "Thank you for doing this, Fee. It meant a lot to them. To me. Leave the rest for Olga."

I nod. The best thing I could do is put my feet up for a while. Hang out with Mia before I go back to the restaurant.

As successful as today has been, Gus is going to take most of my time for the foreseeable future. Family time will be essentially nonexistent.

It just makes me determined to have it all. Soon.

The faster I get my Michelin Star, the faster Mia and I can travel with Zane and the faster we can expand our family.

Seems like the best motivation around.

Chapter Twenty

One Month Later

HIATUS IS OFFICIALLY FUCKING over.

Hallelujah.

God, I'm so psyched. I'm not certain why I was ever worried. Me, Ty, Jace, and Connor are fucking magic. I'm as pumped today as I was all those years ago when LTZ first played together. No other band has our vibe. Our energy ...

LTZ is *special.* We always have been. We always will be.

Standing here onstage at the new Mission, I survey the showroom floor. Shit, I feel like bawling. *This* is what I was missing. My band. The adrenaline before a show. The anticipation of being on stage.

Two shows a year? Five? Fifty? Doesn't matter. As long as we're together and making music regularly, my life is complete.

As happy as I am to have such a huge part of my life back, being there for Fee over the past year has been totally worth it. Her soft openings have gone perfect. The press adores her. Her staff is impeccable. They'd follow her anywhere. They trust her. Not many chefs have the luxury of eighteen months to focus on one restaurant concept and execute it. Fiona has made use of every single minute.

It's a monumental night for my family.

"Nice article in *People*, asshole." Jace flings a copy of the magazine at Connor. "Way to steal Fiona's thunder."

Connor catches it easily in midair. "Not my idea. Ronni had to do damage control for being forced out of her *own* feckin' movie."

No. No. No. Today is not the day for any outside drama.

"Uh, guys? Look around us." I gesture to our crew. The bar staff. The kids from Ty's foundation who are going to kick off the show. "I know you all have shit going on, but please. Can we leave it behind for a day?"

We're sitting on the edge of the stage waiting for Ty. To their credit, Jace and Connor take my comments to heart. As they should. I don't ask for a lot, but today is all about LTZ. Gus. Fee. The Mission. What we've accomplished is ... unbelievable. Gus is a legacy and homage to Fee's dad. The Mission is a huge part of my dad's band's legacy. LTZ's legacy too.

It's all about the fucking *legacy* tonight. Nothing else.

The nightclub has the look and feel of the old Mission but modernized. I point out the mural comprised of posters from the most important Mission shows. Including several Limelight shows from the 90s, and of course the LTZ show that set our career in motion. I'm so fucking proud.

"This is fantastic, Zane, so it is. But where the fuck is Ty?" Connor glances toward the load-in dock.

"He's still in the car talking to Zoey. She's not been feeling well again. As soon as he makes sure she's okay he'll be here." I strum a chord on my precious Gibson, excited to plug in and run through some songs. Just then, I get a text from Ty. Of course he's not at the loading dock, he's at the entrance. "Ty's out front, I'll go get him."

Predictably, he's still in the car with his security guard, Sergey. I jump in the back seat and hold out my fist. "Hey, my brother."

"Ready, my brother?" Ty is so genuinely excited, it infuses me with energy. He's dressed in his trademark ripped blue jeans. White tee. Black leather jacket.

Taped-up green Doc Martens. "My dude!" I point to his boots. "Are those…"

Ty just smiles. God, I love this man. He doesn't need to say a word. Wearing the boots that made him a star tell me all I need to know. He's all in. The final piece of the puzzle fits. LTZ is *back.*

Jace is up onstage setting up his drums when we go back inside. He's between drum techs and very specific about his setup. Ty shouts up to him, "Well, humping our own gear feels like déjà vu. Other than that, this Mission is a hell of a lot nicer."

Jace flips him off. Unbothered, Ty stops to chat with his foundation students. I met them earlier. Lake Lyon is a twenty-year-old guitar whiz. I'm excited to hear Candy Crushed, an all-girl glam-metal band. Rounding things out is Velocity 7, two sisters and two brothers who, apparently, harmonize like nobody's business. Who knows, maybe one of them will be the next LTZ?

My guitar tech, Pokey, motions for me to come over to my stacks, so I jog ahead to approve his setup. Just like old times.

Connor steps out from the wings. "Hey, my brothers. Feels feckin' good to be back up on stage, not gonna lie."

"My brothers. I'm so fucking excited. I'm ready to go." Ty finally strolls toward us. Pumps his fist in the air. He's in front-man mode and I'm all for it.

Tingles run up and down my spine. This is it. We're doing this. My leg bounces. I'm so keyed up, I might explode.

Ever the task master, Jace keeps us in line. "While the gear's getting set up, let's have a quick meeting. We're all together, and it's time we finalize some stuff with the band."

I lead the band and crew to the green room where we've set up some hospitality. I'm fucking proud of the space. It's high tech. Clean. Hospitality area. Shower. Plenty of space to spread out. Amenities touring bands need.

We pull our chairs into a circle. Jace continues his organizational ways. "Isis Management. Discuss."

This. *This*. We've danced around it for weeks, and now we're making *plans*. I didn't even have to initiate the conversation. It's all I can do not to kiss my band mates on the lips. I'm going full blown moony, and I don't give a shit. I deserve to be this happy.

"I'm on board, they've been feckin' great for my wee brothers' band." Connor clasps his hands together.

I look at each of the guys in succession. Try to hide my enthusiasm with business talk. "So, finally Katherine is out?"

"She's pressuring us to do all the things that burned us out over the years. We're not kids starting out anymore. It feels like the time to make a change." Ty bops his head up and down like he's thinking on the spot. Stops. Sets his jaw the way he does when he makes a final decision for himself. "After all, we're all family men, or soon-to-be family men now."

Jace jumps in. "Yeah, but I still want to play. And tour. Are we all up for that?"

Yes. Yes. Yes.

Connor cocks his head. Crosses his arms over his chest. "Aye. I'm on board on *one* condition." He looks at me, specifically. "We each need our own bus. If we can agree on that, I'm cool because I plan on having my family with me if we're gone for longer than a couple of days. That's my non-negotiable. You don't want to be woken up by my evil twins. Trust me."

Ty's face lights up. "Yeah, and we'll have our tiny little guy."

"Ty and I have written some songs. I know we've all been working in smaller groups, but it's time to get into the studio and work it all out." I gesture to Ty. "Last fall at your house, when you showed us the new gear, Jace joked that we should record at your house. Honestly, I think it's a cool idea. It would be the least disruptive to our families in the short term."

We chat about logistics and make plans to take a trip to LA next week on dates that coincide with a festival at the Hollywood Bowl. Some artists we've toured with over the years are playing, which makes it likely we'll be able to jump on stage and perform a couple of songs. While we're down there, the four of us will meet with Isis Management to finalize our decision.

I wave to Carter, who wandered in while we were in the middle of band business. He leans against the back wall while we get ready to run through the set list. Ty sits cross-legged, writing out said set list, looking like his heart is about to burst from joy. He pulls out an envelope. Looks at it. Puts it back in his jacket.

Jace kneels down next to him. Nudges his shoulder. "What's got you so happy?"

"Life, man," I overhear Ty say. "It's fucking awesome."

"Yeah, sure is. Hey, you forgot to include *Butterfly*, we should play that tonight." Jace points to the playlist.

Ty scribbles it down on the pad. "Yeah. We should. Good?"

"Yep." Jace returns to his kit.

These little exchanges warm my heart. We all know one other so well. Each of us has our own special friendship with the other. Our common bond is so present. Why did I spend the entire year scared that LTZ might never get back together?

I decide to go check on Fee. Maybe give her a kiss. My hand is even on the door handle when I decide not to interrupt her. My job tonight is to play the show on time and get the guys over to the restaurant. I've tried to take care of her all day. Tonight's her night.

I text her instead and wait for her reply.

By the time I get back, we're all set up. Jace clacks his drum sticks together. Connor plays the opening to *Down.* I jump onstage just in time to plug in my Gibson and play my part. Minutes of chaos give way to that magic moment the music clicks.

Ty watches all of us lock into the pocket then grabs his mic. "We're fucking back, my brothers."

"Feckin right we are," Connor's low voice resonates throughout the club.

Before I know it, we've gone through our entire set without stopping. I'm flying. I gesture for the guys to bow at the front of the stage just for grins. The foundation kids stare at us slack-jawed, they came here for sound-check and just had a full-length private LTZ show. My dad beams. I'm psyched we haven't lost a beat over the past year and a half.

I've never felt so exhilarated, I swear.

Well, no. The definition of feeling exhilarated is this morning when I was balls deep inside Fee. Then again, it's not fair to compare.

Carter approaches the stage where Ty's texting some-one. Probably Zoey. I decide to join them. "We sounded dope, man."

"You did. How does it feel to be back on stage?" My dad pats me on my back.

I cannot contain myself. "Amazing. The show's going to be perfect. As excited as I am to play, I'm so proud of Fee. She's worked so hard for tonight to go smoothly."

Carter and Ty both look at me, amused.

"Can I talk to the two of you about something?" Ty seems a little nervous.

Carter seems surprised. "Anytime. What's up?"

"It's kind of private, but I'd love to get your advice." Ty points to the green room. I'm intrigued. The three of us head back to where we had the band meeting. Once inside, Carter and I take seats. Ty locks the door and sits across from me. He fidgets. Glances around the room. Seems nervous.

Carter's oblivious. He scans the entire room. "I can't get over how high-tech this is. It's nothing like the old Mission, that's for damn sure."

"Well, it's thirty years later, Carter." Even though I always seek his approval musically, I'm still slightly annoyed with my dad about my mom. It's probably time for he and I to hash things out months after mom and I had the talk. "Okay, Ty. What the hell is up?"

Ty tells us an unbelievably insane story about a meeting he had with an estate attorney. Carter and I sit in utter shock when we learn about his mother's family, apparently one of the wealthiest in all of Seattle. "I've inherited some money. Apparently, my grandparents left it in trust for Jada if she ever got clean. Obviously, she didn't. Now it's mine."

"Holy shit, Ty. That's fucking nuts. All that time you struggled, and your grandparents were rich?" I slug him in the arm. While I'm confused why he's picked now to tell us, it does explain his great mood. Not that he's hurting for cash.

Ty nods. Punches his palm with his fist. "Yep. And I'm going to do great things with their stupid money."

"Is that what you wanted to talk to us about?" Carter asks the exact question I had swirling around in my head.

Ty swallows. His entire demeanor changes. It's hard to pinpoint. Detachment? No. Embarrassment. "Uh, no." He reaches in his pocket and pulls out the envelope I saw him looking at earlier. "Apparently, the grandparents also had my mother followed by a PI for most of her life. I learned she ran away from home when she was fifteen.

Hung out on The Ave. Slept with all of Seattle and got pregnant with me. She never knew who my father was, but my grandparents did. They kept it secret from her. But, these are the paternity results."

"*Whoa.*" Every single hair on my body stands on end. My stomach fills with acid.

Ty casts his eyes to the ground. Looks up at the two of us. "Yeah. Whoa."

"Did you open it?" Carter leans forward to get a better look at the plain envelope.

He shakes his head. "Nah. But I've seen some pictures of her when I was a baby." Hands a photo to Carter. "I got a package of her stuff over Christmas from her sister. Fucked me up for a while. Brought back shitty memories. The estate woman's card was with her shit. So was a Limelight flyer for one of your shows at The Mission. Zoey convinced me to meet with her so we could try and put my past behind us. "

A light flashes behind my eyes. Nothing good is going to come of this, somehow I just know. I don't want to be here.

"Holy shit." Carter scans the photo. Squints. Holds it closer to his face. "She looks really familiar. Maybe she hung out at The Junkyard back in the day. Shit, Ty. When I went to see Jada when you started hanging around, I never put two and two together. They don't even look like the same person."

Wait, what? Carter saw Ty's mom? Why didn't I know this? I'm trying to stay cool but I'm ready to explode.

I'm not cool. Not at all.

"Well, that makes sense. She was a junkie. Only sixteen when she had me and a little worse for wear by the time I was in high school." Ty shrugs like this information is NBD.

Carter keeps staring the picture. "When I went to see her at the bar, she looked—and acted—rough, but I remember thinking at the time I might have known her at one point. Huh." He bores a hole in the photo with his laser-beam eyes. "You have the paternity info? I wonder if maybe I'll know the dude. You're, what? Three months older than Zane? Limelight was still playing the clubs around then. It's certainly possible."

No. No. No.

Ty fidgets a bit. "The main reason I wanted to talk is to confess something else that happened when I started spending time with you both and Jada realized who you were, Carter. She demanded that I steal Limelight stuff from your house. She said the band 'owed' her.' I promise, I never took anything. I would never ..."

Carter scoffs, "Of course, you didn't."

"I'd never think that." I'm now on complete autopilot. All of this is...a lot. It's not the time for this conversation.

Today is my day. *Fee's day.* I'm bordering on pissed.

Ty shifts in his seat. Pauses. Shakes his head and looks at Carter with slight trepidation. "Is there any reason she'd say that? Before I open this, I thought I'd better ask if she knew the other guys in the band? I mean, you were with Lianne? ..."

"Fuck. Those days are a blur. But, yeah. It seems about the time when Lianne and I were together." He scrubs his chin with his hand thoughtfully. "Man, she played hard to get, I was so fuckin' smitten. We were together for only a minute before she got pregnant with Zane."

Ty and I exchange glances, both of us suspecting the old "wear a condom" lecture is coming on. A lecture I feel a certain kind of way about.

Carter's gravelly voice warbles on. "I cleaned up for her. She was worth it. Before that? I was no angel. None of us in the band were. There's a reason I lectured all you guys about wearing condoms. We all fucked all the women. We snorted all the coke. Smoked all the weed. Drank copious amounts of alcohol. I remember so little of it. Fuck, man. I'm surprised we were productive at all."

Jesus God. I can't take this much longer.

Ty waves his hands at my dad to stop the madness. "I didn't mean anything by it, Carter. I just don't want to ruin some guy's life. Especially if it was someone in your band."

"It's fine, Ty." Carter's voice is calm. soothing. "You can't change the past, you have to own up to it. I fucked up a lot of relationships. With Lianne. Zane. My band. Doesn't change the fact that back then it was nonstop partying and fucking. None of us cared about consequences. We didn't even think about them."

Kill me now. I'm a fucking consequence, doesn't he see how hurtful these comments are?

Ty flaps the envelope around. "Well, anyway, these are my paternity results. As I said, I'm afraid of fucking up some guy's life who has no idea he has a kid. Or another kid, as the case might be. I thought, since you are both dads, and you're basically my dad, Carter, I'd ask for your advice. What do you think?"

"*You're* gonna be a dad. What do *you* think?" I half-heartedly knock his shoulder with my fist.

"I'd wanna know." He nods. Then owns it and says definitively, "I'd wanna *know*."

Ah, fuck it. Now I wanna find out which of Carter's bandmates is Ty's dad. "Me too."

"I'd want to know." Carter stands. "But, yeah. Once you find out, you'll have to decide how to approach it."

Ty waves the envelope. "Should I open it? Now? Rip the bandage off?"

I change my mind again. This is a terrible idea. "Uh, maybe you should do this with Zoey."

"Zoey and I discussed talking it over with her first, but I think she'd be okay with me doing this with you guys. In fact, I think she'll be proud of me." Ty grabs a plastic knife from the hospitality table. Slices open the envelope. He faces me and Carter, pulls out the paper. Shakes it.

Stares at the paper.

I stare at Ty.

Watch his face morph from curiosity into utter devastation.

Then white-hot rage.

The next three seconds are a little like this: You're driving a hundred miles an hour. Racing down the freeway. You press on the gas. Accelerate. And then, all of a sudden, you see it. The brick wall that's a hundred yards away. In front of your windshield. It gets closer and closer. The car's going so fast, you aren't going to be able to stop. Your body knows this. Your mind knows this.

Somehow, you don't even want to.

Stop.

And then ...

You smash into it.

That's your last memory.

Before your entire life falls apart.

Chapter Twenty-One

The Same Nght

I FEEL THE BEST I've ever felt in my life.

This morning, I woke up early with Zane's head in between my legs. He treated me to thirty minutes of his special brand of pussy worship. Rolled on the cock ring and fucked me for an hour. Made me come half a dozen times. He called it his "opening day" special.

I'll say.

God, I needed it. Our sex life has suffered for a while now. Spending fourteen-hour days prepping a fine-dining restaurant and rock club to open on the same night will do that to you.

After our morning sex marathon, Zane helped Mia get ready and arranged for breakfast to be brought in for the three of us. My daughter presented me with a beautiful painting. An abstract watercolor of various herbs in my greenhouse. I plan on hanging it above the door at the restaurant for good luck. In our scurry to get over here, I forgot it at home. I'll bring it tomorrow.

Not that we need it. I'm ready. My staff is ready. Gus is booked up for the next two months. Both seatings. It's crazy.

My PR team did their job. Ronni arranged for her people to make me over. Other than when I splurge and get my nails done, I've always been a staunch DIY girl, to Zane's horror. He's thrilled I've gone to the dark side and bought a few designer pieces for interviews.

Add in professional hair color. Media training. My profile is definitely on the rise.

Suddenly, I'm being compared to some of the most famous chefs in the world. Netflix wants me for an episode of *Chef's Table* and the new *Iron Chef* series. The Food Network contacted me to create a new show. My face is on the cover of *Food & Wine*. Next month, *Bon Appetit*. All of the food blogs have added Gus to their "must" lists. James Beard reached out.

It's a good way to get on Michelin's radar.

I'm mortified to admit that my self-esteem about my appearance is at an all-time high. It's the press coverage. I've been called beautiful. Sexy. Sultry. One article stated that Zane was lucky to be with *me*. I'm trending as #hotfee on socials.

Gah! I should want the focus to always be on the food, and I do. Publicly, that's what I tell everyone, including Zane. Oh, I know it's all fleeting and fickle, but damn. It sure feels good. There's plenty of substantive coverage of the restaurant, a girl can secretly feel hot because strangers are telling her so, can't she?

None of that matters in this moment. I still have a couple hours before service. Alex and Ronni are in front waiting for Zoey. Zane and the rest of LTZ are next door at sound check. I'm bummed I won't be able to see their show, but I'm needed here.

Their show begins early and should end around nine. Half hour later, Gus will open its doors. Tonight's service is just the eight of us. Plus three prominent Seattle food writers. Tomorrow, the national food critics will arrive. By the end of summer, the reviews will come in.

Then, I cross my fingers. And toes. Hopefully, Michelin will reach out.

As owner and head chef, my role is like the ringleader of a circus. I'll jump in and demonstrate cool techniques, but Justice and Petra will oversee all of the stations and the staff. Daire and Jetta will handle the entire customer experience. Wolf will present his mini three-course dessert tasting with our new sous chef, hired just to execute his vision.

I've pulled together the greatest culinary team I could ever have dreamed of.

I grab a bottle of 1980 Vintage Dom Perignon from the wine cooler and eyeball the dining area before I join the ladies. "I thought we deserved to have a little toast with the expensive stuff. Zoey can't drink anyway, so we won't feel bad she's not here yet."

Alex and Ronni hold out their glasses. I pour. We clink.

"Holy shit. I haven't tasted this stuff in years." Ronni shuts her eyes in bliss.

Her reaction is why I love fine dining. That level of utter indulgence is *everything*. "Well, this is it. I can't believe tonight's the night. The social posts about LTZ go live in an hour and then all the chaos begins. I've put my heart and soul into this opening. I hope everyone loves what we've prepared."

"O.M.G." Ronni scans my menu and looks at me in awe. "Crab with avocado, ginger lime, and cucumber? No, wait. Foie gras seared with sunchoke, dates, and water chestnut? I'm going off my diet to eat this, Fee. It's going to be sooooo worth it!"

I can't help but preen a bit. "I'm most proud of the duck dish. I've roasted it with endive, which is like radicchio and Marcona almonds. I've braised it with foie gras and potato. I think the desserts are incredibly special too. Obviously, we have Wolf. We managed to poach the sous pastry chef from Alinea. She's created this amazing fondant of maple she's braised in a bourbon barrel with milk for the past week. We're serving it with shaved ice."

"A lot of this is over my head, considering my skills are limited to heating up soup. I'm looking forward to such a well-thought-out feast, Fee. Bravo." Alex raises her glass but doesn't drink it. Hmm.

"Are you nervous?" Ronni swirls her champagne. Sips.

I don't get a chance to answer. The entire restaurant reverberates with what sounds like a catastrophic crash next door. My entire body goes into fix-it mode. I run to the secret room located at the back of the dish pit. I press my ear to the wall. Look back at Alex and Ronni, who've followed me back here. "This is a hidden door to the green room. We're planning on using it for catering big shows."

For the most part, the main showroom of The Mission is soundproofed. The green room on the other side of this door is where LTZ is set up tonight. My assumption is the guys are messing around and knocked something over. The noise is somewhat of a design flaw, though.

Gus won't get a Michelin Star if sounds from that room can be heard in the dining area.

I mean, fights and band shenanigans aside, I've fucked Zane in the dressing room a time or two. I guess my staff might have heard something they shouldn't.

But, no one wants to hear that when they're enjoying a three-hundred-dollar tasting menu.

I press on the button above the keyhole. Nothing. Goddamn it. It occurs to me I did forget something tonight.

"Fuck." I bang my fist on the door, hoping someone on the other side will hear me. "Zane has the master key. We haven't gotten copies made yet."

Ronni and Alex watch as I call Zane. No answer. I shove my phone back into my pocket. "Can either one of you ladies call your man? I don't want to make a big scene by going through the side door, but it's kinda crucial for me to know what's going on."

Both of the ladies pull out their phones and make calls. No answer.

Now fear prickles my neck. This isn't good. What the fuck happened over there? My entire Gus staff is gathered around just standing there. Waiting.

"Fuck." I shake my head. Nothing is going to derail tonight. I've got to take control. I'm about to call out an action play when the sounds of Ty screaming obscenities at the top of his lungs are followed by the distinct sounds of fighting. I hear Zane yelling. It's absolute mayhem on the other side of this wall.

For a moment, I feel paralyzed in fear. Crime in Seattle is at an all-time high. What if someone is holding them at gunpoint? What if Zane's in danger?

Ohmygod. Nothing, and I mean nothing is more important than my husband. I'm a fucking leader. I've got to lead.

Now.

"Justice. Petra. Daire. Gather the brigade into the staff lounge. Stay there until I say otherwise." I deliberately keep my voice calm. Like I'm calling out orders during service. Everyone immediately snaps into action.

Slowly and methodically, I walk back to the door where Alex and Ronni stand with their ears pressed against the panel. I'm so fucking pissed I can't get in that way. I'm not sure if it's dangerous to go out the front. Or the back, for that matter.

Connor's low voice booms through the wall. He's shouting at the top of his lungs, but we can't make out what he's saying.

"What the fuck is happening?" Ronni loses her shit at the sound of her husband's voice.

Before I can stop them, Alex and Ronni take off running though the restaurant and out the front door. Shit. I've got to go with them. I'll suss what's happening. Sort shit out. Get back on track. My team is safe in the staff room. Until I know what's what, I refuse to allow any more negative thoughts into my head. Time is of the fucking essence.

The second we're out the door, I hear sirens in the distance. Lots of them.

Oh, God. This is bad.

I join the ladies at the front door of The Mission. Thank God the social post isn't live, or this place would be a madhouse. We all pound on it in between frantically texting and calling the guys. No one is answering.

Ironically, Zoey's texting Alex. She's almost here and has no clue what she's coming into.

"Let's just go around to the loading dock." I motion to Alex and Ronni. We jog around the building to a sight no business owner should ever see.

Five police cars scream into the back parking lot, followed by two ambulances. They burst into the building through the roll-up door. I catch a glimpse of a bunch of people standing around like zombies. I catalog whether they belong. Crew. Staff. Opening bands.

No one stands out. My mind spins into a little bit of a vortex as I take it all in. Not understanding what's happening. Not quite sure I want to.

All of the weight of the past year and a half catches up to me when I realize there will be no opening night tonight. Everything I've worked so hard for has gone up in flames. I can't help but sob at the fear and the anger.

I call Zane. Then Carter. Zane. Then Carter. No one is picking up. I'm out of my mind with worry about my husband. My father-in-law.

Also, self-pity. In this moment, it feels like no one gives a *shit* about me.

Your mom was right, you fucking idiot.

Just when I think I've never felt lower, I see the EMTs carrying Carter out the back on a stretcher. Zane's running behind them, wailing the identical cry as he did at six when his dad overdosed at the park. It feels like all the air is sucked out of my body and I'm floating above this entire scene, watching this melee from the sky.

It's hard to comprehend how much time passes. I feel like a ghost. I watch Carter get loaded into the ambulance. Zane jumps in the back with him, not even a glance around to look for me. A couple of officers shove Ty, who is handcuffed, into. a police car. Jace and Connor stand on the loading dock looking shell-shocked, with Ronni and Alex at their sides.

Ah. LTZ drama. On Gus's opening night. Fan-fucking-tastic timing.

Funny, suddenly I don't feel a thing. I'm numb. "I'm going back to the restaurant," I say to no one in particular and walk around the building and back to Gus. On the way, I call my PR team and tell them to cancel the critics.

It's peaceful inside my beautiful business. I look around. Dinner service is ready to go. We were planning to serve our summer tasting menu tonight, of course, but we also prepared a beautiful meal for the entire staff, crew, and the bands.

A wasted effort.

I sink into one of the plush couches. Look around at this opulent place. Jesus. Who the hell do I think I am? I laugh maniacally. Then, I can't stop. I'm laughing so hard, I'm shaking. I nearly lose control of my limbs. My stomach muscles ache. I can hardly breathe. Doesn't matter. There's nothing I can do.

Emilie tentatively approaches me. Daire is behind her, followed by Justice, Petra, and Wolf. They all look so concerned. So worried. So ...

Jesus, I burst into another uncontrollable fit of giggles. My entire staff stares at me while I lose my mind. None of them know what's going on and why I'm behaving this way until I explain what's happening in between bouts of laughter.

Finally, Wolf boldly makes a move to sit next to me. He wraps his arms around my shoulders.

His simple gesture unleashes my anger. Rage. Sorrow. Agony. Fear. My laughter turns into horrible, wracking cries of agony. I'm having a mental breakdown in front of my employees. If I didn't think Gus was ruined before, I sure as hell know my professional dreams are dead now.

And Zane. Oh God, Zane. Tears stream down my face. How did I let Zane just go like that? I'm a horrible, horrible, undeserving asshole. My entire body shakes uncontrollably.

I've got to get to him.

"Hey." Wolf holds me tightly against him. "We're all here, Fee. It will all be okay."

I shake my head. "I'm so sorry, everyone. I don't even know what to say. I...I've...I've let you down." I can barely form a sentence.

"This was out of your control, Fiona." Daire crouches down next to me. "Don't stress, we can figure all of this out."

I take a deep breath. Regain an ounce of composure. Wipe my tears. "We need to clean up. Pack up. All the things. If I could just get a few minutes..."

"We're on it." Justice waves the staff back to the kitchen. "We'll be in the back if you need anything. What should we do with the food?"

"Plate it up. You guys can eat it. We can feed the crew next door. I'll figure it out in a bit." I wave him off and pull out my phone to call Zane.

I plunk down on the couch in the foyer and see my Zaney's already texted me.

Zane:

> Fee, I'm at the hospital. Carter had a heart attack.

Zane:

> Baby, i need you call me.

I dial Zane's number. No answer. I try a couple of times before he answers.

"Fee." Zane is clearly in tatters. His voice is ragged. Hoarse. "It's a disaster. Carter's in ICU. He'll make it, but he's *so* messed up."

Holy shit. "What?" It's all I can muster.

"Ty found out he inherited a bunch of money from his mother's family. The executor had his paternity test. Ty asked to talk to me and Carter after sound check, he opened the results..." Zane chokes back a sob. "Fee, Carter is Ty's biological dad. He fucked a teenager when he was dating my mom. Ty's my...*brother*."

I just can't. It's too much. What the actual fuck. "Okay..."

"It was such a perfect night. Why? Why did this happen?" Zane's voice is so tiny. I want to be there for him. I do. All my reserves are used up, though.

I take a deep breath. "I'm closing Gus, Zane. The night is ruined. I can't do this again."

"No, Fee." His voice is strong. "We'll be okay."

"Just finish the story, Zaney." I don't want to argue the point, I just want to get all of the shit on the table.

"Ty lost his mind. He attacked Carter like a wild animal. I had to fight him. I hurt him bad. He quit the band. Said horrible things to the guys. He's in jail." Zane sounds so lost. "God, he's my brother, Fee."

"Unbelievable. Let me close up, babe. I'll meet you at the hospital. Where did they take him?" I pinch my nose between my finger and thumb.

An unmistakable hospital beeping sound is in the background. "You can't. Lianne's here. Only two of us are allowed in. I'm sorry, Fee ..."

Thank God.

"Zane, I love you, babe. If you've got your mom there, I feel better. My entire staff is here. The band is probably next door. Don't worry, I'll deal with all of this. Focus on your family." The weight of the evening is beginning to press down on me in a way that is suffocating. I just want to climb into bed. Pull up the covers. Sleep for a year.

The best I can do is curl up on this couch. Shut my eyes.

I feel someone sit next to me. Gentle hands slip off my hat, which I didn't realize I was still wearing. Soft fingers brush stray hairs from my face. Ronni's soft, soothing voice is like a balm to my soul. "I know you're not okay."

"I'm trying not to make this whole thing about me, but fuck, Ronni. Whenever I think my life's finally on track, the rug's pulled out from under me. It's hard to keep fighting." I sit and collapse against the cushion. "I'm trying not to feel sorry for myself, but there's a nugget of rage bubbling inside me. Why tonight? Why? I called the food critics to tell them we weren't opening. Based on the reaction I got, it's unlikely they'll give me another chance."

Ronni shifts so she's sitting across from me sideways. "This is just as much your loss as Zane's, babe."

"I know, it's not that. It's everything. Zane texted me from the hospital. I'm sure Connor told you, but Carter had a heart attack." A fresh wave of grief washes over me. I can't help it, I start crying again. Ronni holds me against her. My God, I've never lost it so completely the way I have tonight.

Ronni's voice is strong. "Carter will be fine. You'll re-open. The band will work it out."

God. She has no idea. "Zane needs me, but they won't let anyone else in Carter's room. He's just wrecked. It's like déjà vu." I find myself telling Ronni all about the day Zane and I found Carter in the park. As if that has some sort of relevance to what is happening. Or does it? All

I know is my world is in upheaval. "I just don't know if I have the stamina to do this again from scratch. I put every ounce of myself into tonight."

"Just take some time." Ronni's compassion triggers something in me. She's in the middle of a terrible lawsuit. Fielding horrible international press. Yet, here she sits with me. Comforting me.

I grab her hand. "Shit. Ronni. I'm a bad friend. I haven't even asked you about all of what you're going through."

"Oh, it's all legal bullshit." She waves me off.

I can't let her do that. As women, we always stuff our own feelings down. "Uh. No. Try again."

"I've been asked to step down from the movie I was producing for Finnegan O'Rourke." Ronni's voice falters. "I'm beginning to wonder if all the work I did to bring these bastards down was worth it."

Shit. We're in the same goddamn boat.

"I never thought about how the allegations would affect your work." It makes me feel somewhat normal knowing that I'm not the only one going through a huge pile of shit. Maybe we can help each other get through it. "Are people truly believing it?"

Ronni laughs. "You *have* been in the dark. Yeah. The tide of public opinion is most definitely moving against me. Kircher has social media bots trolling me. Spewing out trending hashtags. It's a lot."

"You seem so poised. How are you getting through this?" I'm in awe of her, she's so—Fonzie.

Ronni's face lights up. "Connor."

Holy shit. Yes. I have to call Zane back. I hate how I left things. "Zane's always been my person, you know? Do you mind if I go call him? I should check how Carter's doing."

"Don't ask a second time. Go." She shoos me away.

I turn back. "Go get everyone, we have a shit-ton of food here. I don't want it to go to waste."

What a total fucking whirlwind.

I've experienced *all* the emotions today.

It's not over yet.

I might as well feed people while I wait for the other shoe to drop.

Chapter Twenty-Two

The Next Morning

GOD. WHY AM I sitting here in ICU with my dad? I don't care that he almost died. I'm trying to find compassion, empathy ... anything.

Nope.

All I feel is fury. This man, who I share DNA with, always finds a way to fuck up my life. He doesn't even have to try. It just happens.

Literally, anything that's ever gone wrong for me can be traced back to Carter. Come to think of it, Ty and I have that in common.

What if ... he hadn't cheated on my mom when I was a baby.

What if ... he hadn't overdosed in the park that day.

What if ... he showed up for me when I was a kid.

What if ... he hadn't deliberately broken up Ty and Zoey.

What if ... he hadn't fucked a teenage runaway and gotten her pregnant.

My mind is spinning. I haven't slept. I just want to get out of here. I need Fee. So badly. She's the one who'll make sense of all this. She's been there from the beginning. God, I need help to get me through. This mess is so hard to process. I can't begin to comprehend the past twelve hours.

In one rip of an envelope, all of my dreams have been destroyed. Fee's hard work rendered useless. Gus is forever tainted. LTZ is broken up.

All because of Carter.

No wonder Ty went ballistic. His reaction last night was completely understandable. Thirty years of trauma all came to a head. If I feel this angry, it's not hard to imagine why he beat the shit out of my—our—dad. Carter fucking deserved it.

My reaction, on the other hand, was abhorrent. I'm ashamed. It was like an out-of-body experience. I don't remember much. I know I was pummeling him. Screaming. Hurting him. Physically. Mentally. With intention. The man's been through enough. Now he's in jail. I'm devastated to know I'm capable of such destructive behavior.

Just *devastated.*

But, not surprised.

Impulsiveness has always been something I've struggled with. I get it from Carter. It's the trait that makes him do terrible, selfish things without regard for consequences.

"She seemed vaguely familiar ...."

God, he makes me sick. I'm a fucking mess.

My phone pings.

Fee:

Connor and Ronni are still here. They don't want to leave me alone, when can you pick me up?

Me:

I'm leaving in a few. Waiting on some test results.

Fee:

Okay, I'll just call Zeke.

Me:

No. Wait. Please.

Fee:

I'm exhausted, babe. Do what you need to do, if I can't be there with you I want to be with Mia.

Me:

> I'll leave now. Mom's here, she can just text me.

Fee:

> Are you sure?

Me:

> Yeah. Be there soon.

I've got to pull my shit together. It's my job to be there for Fiona. She's who matters, not Carter. I should not have left her to deal with the aftermath of our businesses on her own.

Fuck this. I'm leaving. I push through the ICU door. God dammit. Zoey sits with my mom just outside. I wonder why she's here and not with Ty, but I don't think I can face her to ask. Their backs are turned so I skulk back behind the door. It's not my proudest moment, but I listen to their conversation like a fucking creeper.

Mom cries over Carter *again.* "Just when I think he can't hurt me any worse..."

"It did happen before you were with him, right?" Zoey's surprisingly kind. She shouldn't be after what I did to her husband. "Ty was born before Zane."

"I know." My mom shrugs.

Zoey takes a deep breath. "It still hurts?"

"So much." Tears stream down my mom's beautiful face. It breaks my goddamn heart. "We were in such a new relationship when I got pregnant with Zane. But he was the hottest guy in town. I thought I was the shit. God, I had this idea we'd be Seattle's 'it' couple. I guess I should have expected he was fucking different women. But getting some underage street girl pregnant? I just can't fathom."

Yeah. Me either. It's a knife to my heart.

Zoey takes her hand. "I think you and I are a lot alike, Lianne. *And,* I think Carter and Ty are a lot alike."

Jesus. I can't take any of this. She's fucking comparing them? Like this is normal? I want to punch something. I'm getting the hell out of here and let the chips fall where they may. I push through the door, my mom and Zoey look around. Startled to see me.

It takes all I can muster to acknowledge them, though I don't look either of them in the eye. "Hey, Mom. Zoey."

"Zane. I'm sorry about Carter. How is he?" She's literally the nicest person alive. How can she be this sweet in the face of such madness?

I stand there like a fool. Then plop down next to my mom. I still can't look at Zoey, so I cover my eyes with my hands. "Sore. Sad. Shell-shocked." I should shut up, but no. I word vomit. "What the fuck is happening? I can't comprehend that Carter is Ty's father. That Ty is my *brother.*"

Mom draws me to her and kisses my head. Like I'm five. But, I need it so I lean in. Close my eyes. She speaks so softly. "Were you able to talk to him about it?"

"No." I don't want to admit that most of the night I sat with him in hatred, not love. "It's not the right time. He needs to get his strength back."

I make the mistake of looking at Zoey, who's watching me. Her hazel eyes are so sad. She rubs her bump. God. I put a pregnant woman's husband in jail. I put my brother in jail. I'm so upset, I almost don't hear her when she asks, "Zane, do you mind telling me what happened?"

Shit. It takes me a minute to gather my courage. "Well, it happened so fast. Ty was just telling us about the meeting you had with the estate lawyer. He showed us a picture of Jada with Ty as a baby. Carter recognized her as a girl who came around The Junkyard." I stroke my stubble as I recount the story, ending with the DNA results.

When I'm done she looks devastated. "I had no idea Ty brought that envelope with him. I thought we'd open it together."

"Zoey, in all honesty, I don't think I can take much more today. I want to be with Fee. And Mia. I think all of this is going to take a little time." I stand and pinch the bridge of my nose. "Carter needs to heal. Physically. Mentally. He loves Ty, he'll want him in his life. I do too, it's just? A lot. Can we take a rest until we know where Ty's head is at? Is that okay?"

Zoey nods. "Of course. I have to get home too, my dad's bringing Ty home from ...*jail.*"

"I'll keep you up to date on Carter." My mom hands Zoey her phone. "Program your number in here."

While they're exchanging numbers, I slip out. I'm on the way to the parking lot when I realize I came here in the ambulance. My head is such a mess. I call Zeke. Sure enough, he's already in the parking lot and arrives in under a minute, thank God. Fifteen minutes later, I let myself in the back entrance at Gus.

The place is spotless. Like opening night never happened.

I guess it didn't.

I push open the door to the office. Fee's at her desk. I see the back of her head, which rests on her forearms on top of the desk. Maybe she's sleeping.

"Fee?" I whisper.

She rolls her head around to look at me through half-mast eyes. "I'm kind of awake."

"Babe." I rush over to her side. Pull her against me.

She buries her face in my neck. "How's Carter?"

Always about fucking Carter. "Two stents. He's in ICU. Ty's in jail."

"Yeah. I know. Connor told me he got arrested." Her eyes flick to the door. "Speak of the devil."

Our big bass player stands there, his hand in a fist poised to knock. "Just wanted to tell you we thought we should head out now that you're here."

"Thanks for staying, man." I don't know what else to say.

He cocks his head. "I overheard about Carter. He's okay?"

"He'll be in the hospital for days." I sigh deeply. I'm exhausted.

Connor looks like he's about to speak then thinks better of it. "I'll call you tomorrow. You, me and Jace should check on Ty."

"Zoey's dad is bringing him home." I rub my temple.

Fee nods. "Zoey just sent a text asking if you got here okay. I'm not going to answer. I can't get sucked into a big text string. I'm too fried."

Connor takes a step back. "Yeah, I get it." There's an awkward pause. "I'll just ... go." He leaves with a wave.

Fee gets up. Stretches her back. Starts gathering her stuff.

"So ..." I scratch my head. "Zeke was waiting for me. I rode in the ambulance."

She glances up. Starts to laugh. "Of course. Fuck. Of course."

"Where are the keys to the car?" I wince. I literally have no idea.

Fee throws her hands up in the air. "I have no clue. None." She plops back down at her desk. Buries her face in her forearms again, this time laughing ruefully. "Figures. It fucking figures," she mumbles.

I don't find humor in any of this.

"Let's go to Hawaii. Or something." She pounds her fist on the table. "I put the staff on paid leave. We can deal with all of this shit in a few weeks. Okay?" Fee's blue eyes search mine.

I've got nothing. How she's even thinking about traveling, I do not know.

"Oh fuck." Something catches her eye. Fee reaches down and holds up a Valentino purse. "This is Ronni's. I better get this to her before they leave."

She jumps up and darts out the door toward the dining area. I trail behind her in clothes I've worn for nearly twenty-four hours. I'm so fucking over all of this. I'm done peopling for the day.

Connor stands behind Ronni, massaging her neck. She winces. "This wasn't the best place to sleep. My purse is back in the office, though."

"I've got it." Fiona holds out the purse to her as she approaches them.

Rather than take it, Ronni throws her arms around my wife's neck. "Babe, are you okay?"

"Honestly? No." Fiona steps away. Crosses her arms around her middle. "We're going to close the venue and postpone opening the restaurant until later this year. I want to get out of here for a while. Maybe Hawaii. I think the three of us need to get away and do nothing. Recalibrate."

I feel like I'm living in the twilight zone. We haven't talked about this. Hawaii? When my life's fallen apart? Goddammit. I just want to go home.

Luckily, Connor takes his cue. "We're off to retrieve our wee boys. My ma wanted me to invite yous over for some Irish stew tonight. Just us, my folks. I think Cillian and Seamus might join. Might be an opportunity for us to have a peaceful night."

Sounds. Fucking. Awful.

I'll say anything just to get this conversation over and them gone. "Can I call you later? We need to go back to the hospital for a while. My mom won't leave Carter's side. I don't get it. She just found out he fucked an underage homeless girl and fathered a child a couple of months before she was pregnant with me. Why she didn't fly back to Denver, I don't know."

Unfortunately, my shock-them-the-fuck-away approach backfires. It has the opposite effect.

Fee caresses my cheek. "She loves him, Zaney. He's her person. It's not all that different than our story."

WTF? Has she talked to my mom about this? Their sentiment is nearly identical.

"It's not the same," I protest. "It's not the same."

She pulls me against her tits and I melt into her against my will. I'm so fucking tired. "It's going to take a bit for this to all sink in. Our family has so much healing to do. It's hard to fathom that Ty…"

No. Just fucking no. I do not want to be soothed by family healing. Not on your life. Just the thought makes me want to beat the shit out of …

"Fucking Carter." I pull away and smash my fist against the table. I can't let her say another fucking word.

Connor, Ronni, and Fee all visibly jump. Eyes wide. *Fuck.*

I bow my head. I'm a monster. A horrible fucking monster.

I feel a big hand on my back. "Aye. Feckin' Carter."

When I look up, Connor's toothy smile surprises me. My band brother. He knows me. He gets me. I stand up and shake out my arms. Hook my arm around Connor's neck and raise my fist in the air and scream, *"Fucking Carter!"*

When I look over at Fee, she just gives me a sad smile. "We should let them get their kids, Zane. I'd like to pick Mia up from my mom."

God, the two of us. We're a regressive mess. Mia's at home with Olga, not with Faye. She's running on fumes, it's the only explanation why she'd forget that her mom's not in the picture. Oh well, we're finally going home, no need for me to make a big deal.

The four of us shuffle out. I lock the door behind us. Fee looks around the parking lot, which is empty except for Connor and Ronni's Mercedes, my Aston Martin, and Carter's Audi. "Thank God the press is gone."

"They were here?" I hadn't even thought about it. I haven't been online since the incident at The Mission.

Ronni rests her head on Connor's shoulder. "It was nuts out here. All of this is worldwide news."

Great.

Connor and Ronni get into their car. I shove my free hand in my pocket to grab my phone so I can call Zeke and discover a set of keys. They're not mine, but I recognize them. I hold them up and jingle. "I've got Carter's keys. Might as well take his car until we find ours."

So that's what we do.

All the way home, I pray we don't hit another brick wall.

Our family won't survive it.

Chapter Twenty-Three

Latert the Same Day

TALK ABOUT A COLOSSAL meltdown. My staff and friends must be so proud.

Way to hold it together, Fee.

Well, I was scared. No, terrified.

God, there is no excuse. It shouldn't have happened. I'm mortified.

It had been a monumental grind for months to get Gus ready. Not just for me, for my entire team. The reward was supposed to be a successful opening. Great reviews.

Happy diners. All of these things motivated my staff to work hard for so long.

My entire team upped its game. Topped ourselves on a daily basis. It was awesome. We were so fucking ready.

Only to watch it all fall apart in an instant.

No doubt they rue the day they decided to leave their prestigious culinary jobs all over the world to work for me. I'm such a joke.

Fuck. When I looked around at my dream-team—the executives, Justice, Petra, Emilie, Wolf, Daire, and Jetta. The all-star staff, sous chefs, dishwashers, servers. All I could think about was the time and effort I put into recruiting each person. How awful it would be to lose any one of them. Especially after they rallied around me despite my despair and their own personal disappointment.

I made a snap decision, I offered each staff member six months paid vacation complete with benefits if they'd come back to help me reopen next year. They all agreed. They believe in Gus. Somehow, they believe in me. In fact, they encouraged me to take a break. And they meant it.

So, that's what I'm going to do. Our family is in shambles after what happened. I don't want to give up my dream, but it's time to focus on getting healthy. Mentally and physically. I'm the heaviest I've ever been—two months of eating without any exercise will do that to you—all the glowy "she's hot" press aside, last night put me right back into a shitty headspace.

Somehow, I need to find strength to take care of my family. Get healthy. Most importantly, show Mia how to face disappointment with grace. Teach her what it means to pick yourself up and start again. Model the type of person I'd love for her to be. I don't know how I'll manage all of this when I feel like my world has collapsed, but I've got to try.

I can't be like my own mother. I just can't.

I'm worried about Zane. He's all over the map with his emotions. Screaming out Carter's name at the restaurant. Dead silence ever since we got home. I've never seen him this broken. Well, except for the day we found Carter in the park all those years ago. It's almost like something snapped.

Keep yourself together, Fee.

"Zaney, we should go to bed. It's nearly midnight." I find him in the media room, sprawled out on the couch wearing nothing but a pair of jeans. Watching a video of Limelight performing at Lollapalooza in the nineties.

He doesn't say anything. Just stares at the screen. I sit next to him. Run my nails along his scalp. Massage his head a bit while I look at the screen. Back in the day, Limelight was unlike anything anyone had ever seen.

They put the Seattle music scene on the world map. It's easy to see why. Carter's magnificent. Shirtless. Long, curly hair flowing in the breeze during his solo. He's electrifying.

On stage, Zane's exactly like his father. Same mannerisms. Same expressions. Same stage presence. It's a little eerie.

"I was probably eight or nine when he played this show," Zane mutters. "You can tell he's high as a kite. Look at his eyes."

Definitely. When the camera zooms into Carter's face you can see his pupils are like pinpricks. Sweat on his upper lip. Despite his insane musicianship, he looks like a zombie. "Yeah. You're right."

"I saw the news. According to them, Ty's on drugs again. They're making up all sorts of shit about what happened. Just wait until they find out the truth about … Carter." Zane's voice breaks. "Tell me … the guys, everyone … they know about him. Ty—don't they?"

"Well, while I was figuring out the restaurant, everyone cleaned up The Mission. Ronni and Alex straightened up the dressing room." I make little circles around his temple with my thumb. "They found the paper with the DNA results. I walked in on them talking about it, so I just told them. Seemed stupid not to."

He tilts his head up. His brown eyes are deep pools of devastation. "I should have stayed with you, Fee. I'm sorry I lost my shit. You needed me."

I did. Instead, you chose the father who always seems to let you down. Again.

I don't say that, though. I lie.

"Don't apologize, baby. You had to be with Carter. We all rallied. My staff. Connor, Ronni, Alex, and Jace. I couldn't have gotten through it without them." I smooth his wild hair from his forehead. Give him a little smile. Think about how hard I cried last night. How stupid I was to let my facade down. How embarrassed I am for exposing my weaknesses.

Stop it. That's not what happened.

Zane gets a faraway look in his eyes. "He was like a wild animal, Fee."

"Tell me what happened in that room. Connor and Jace weren't there." I don't feel capable of absorbing any information. I'm on the edge myself. But, for my Zaney, I'll listen.

Zane sits up and faces me. Recounts in great detail the entire conversation up through Ty opening the paternity results. Nothing about it seems particularly violence-inducing though.

"I don't get what happened, Zane. Why did it get so violent?" All I can think about is how selfish Ty was.

Impulsive. Did he not realize that his timing was about as bad as it could get?

"I don't even know, Fee." Zane wrings his hands. "Ty got this look in his eyes... like he lost all semblance of reality. He charged Carter without warning. Accused him of knowing all along and lying about it. Hs just started pummeling him. No, he beat the ever-loving shit out of him. Blind rage. I tried to pull Ty off, but he railed at me too. I had to use Krav Maga to stop him ... I wanted to kill him. I could have ..."

I cover his hands with mine. "No, you wouldn't have. Never, Zaney."

"All I could see was Carter on the ground at the park, Fee. I didn't even remember what happened next. Until suddenly, I was at the hospital. Bits and pieces are starting to come back, but I left you there at Gus. I fucking left you ..."

Suddenly I understand. I'm ashamed that I ever doubted his intentions. He's the one person I can always count on, and yet I always find a way to question. God. He was traumatized. I'm a horrible, horrible partner. I always think the worst, and he's always putting me first.

I try to look away because I'm so ashamed, but Zane pulls my face to his. Kisses me like his life depends on it.

In that moment I decide that he can take whatever he needs from me. I owe him that much, so I grab his face and kiss him back. He bites my lip. I dig the tips of my nails into his shoulder, leaving red half-moon marks. Our mouths are almost all the way open as we try to swallow each other whole. He flips around and grips my upper arms. Pushes me back against the cushions.

I stare him dead in the eye. Nod. Give him permission without saying a word.

He fists my T-shirt at the collar and rips it down the middle. Cups my bare breasts and squeezes. Bends down and grazes each of my nipples with his teeth. Bites them. Licks them. Pinches them so hard, I wince.

It hurts so fucking good.

I unbuckle and unzip his pants. His cock springs free. I jack him hard. Fast. Squeeze his tip until it's deep purplish red.

"Fuck yeah," Zane growls as he shoves his hand down my joggers and pinches my clit. "Harder. Beat me off harder."

Our mouths crash together again. Biting. Swallowing. Consuming.

He yanks my pants down. With both hands, he palms and cups my belly. Squishes it. Kneads it. I try to move, but he shakes his head. "Do you know how much this body fucking turns me on? Do you know how mad it makes me when you won't let me love it? I love you so fucking much, Fiona. It scares me."

"Zane ..." I tense up, but he moves behind me. Grips my wrists in one hand. Yanks my leg over his elbow so I'm spread open, jiggly parts exposed. My belly rolls are on display. I can't hide from him.

Somehow, I don't want to. Hide. I mean, what's the point? I'm fat. He seems to be into it. Might as well come.

He rams into me. Again. Again. The couch jolts each time. He releases his grip on my wrists. Bands his arms around my middle. Pinches and rubs my clit. One hand tugs and squeezes my breasts. His hips swivel and rock and screw his cock into me. I'm on the edge of an unprecedented explosion.

Then suddenly, he withdraws. Flips me over. Smooths his hands along my face. "Oh, Fee. I don't want to fuck you in anger. I want you to *see* that you're *everything* to me."

He presses his head against my forehead. His eyes bore into mine. His lips graze mine lightly when he enters me again. This time, it's slow. So slow. He's barely moving at all. Sliding in and out of my wetness. Never losing eye contact.

I notice the dark flecks of black in his brown eyes. His lashes always make him look like he rims his eyes with liner, but it's natural. Dramatic, just like him. I grip his wrists when he moves my head to receive his sweet kisses. He flicks his tongue against mine.

When his cock is buried as far as it will go, he stops. "Do you feel me, Fee?"

"Yes." I realize tears stream out of my eyes.

"Nothing else matters in this world but us. Not the band. Not the restaurant. Nothing. This." He swivels his hips pushing himself even further inside me. "This is home. Why do we need anything else?" His eyes search mine for answers. He's crying too.

I lock my legs around his thighs to hold him in place. "We don't, baby."

"Do you trust me?" His eyes beg me to say yes.

I nod vigorously. I'll do anything to make him believe it.

Mid-thrust, he blinks at me. Abruptly pulls out. Stands. His cock, wet with my juices, bobs against his taut abs. "Let's go." He clicks the television off. Grabs my hand and leads me to the elevator. We rarely use it. In fact, I can't remember ever setting foot inside after we moved in.

He presses the button but doesn't say anything. We stand there naked. Waiting.

It's all I can do not to cover myself. Instead, I force myself to stand there while his eyes scan my body. I'm so exposed. I shouldn't still feel embarrassed about my body with Zane. But sometimes I do. I have such a love-hate relationship with myself, though I hope I hide it most of the time. Somehow, I'm beginning to think I don't … which is just—gah.

Mortifying.

When the door opens, Zane gestures for me to get in. The cab has floor-to-ceiling mirrored walls on all sides. There's definitely no hiding in here. I turn to flee, but Zane blocks my way. "Just trust me. I want to show you something."

Something knocks loose in my chest. "Zane …" I plead as the doors close behind us.

"It will be okay." He taps a code into the control box and the motor shuts off. "Place your palms on the back wall and no matter what, do not shut your eyes."

My heart is thudding, but I do as he says.

"Once and for all, can you please tell me what about this gorgeous, sexy body you find repulsive." He stands behind me and traces his fingers along my neckline and drags them down to cup my heavy breasts. He looks at me and tilts his head, waiting.

"My nipples are too big. My tits are huge and saggy. I can't wear cute tops," I squeak as he thumbs my nipples into hard points.

Unlike earlier, Zane fondles my breasts like they're fine china. His cock is wedged between my ass cheeks. "Do you believe that I've made myself come a million times just visualizing these beauties since I was thirteen years old? Five years before I'd ever seen them? Oh, how I dreamed about your tits. I knew your nipples would look like ripe berries." He flicks each of them. "Holy fuck, they were delicious. Better than I imagined. And look. When I cup them like this ..." He squishes them together in his palms. "... they spill out. I want to bury my face in them. I fucking worship your tits."

He presses his cheek to mine. Trails his fingers along the underside of my arms. "What else?"

"My arms have no definition, they're just there." I shake them and watch the slight jiggle. "See?"

Zane encircles my wrists and brings each arm up above my head, keeping my hands pressed against the glass. "Do you see these little indents?" He traces the defined lines along the side of each arm, which I've never noticed. "Whenever you ride me and you're about to come, sometimes when you fully let go you'll throw your arms above your head. I want to run my tongue along this muscle."

So he does. I grind my ass against his cock. Hoping he'll slip inside me. I'm so fucking wet. I nearly get lost when he grabs my belly with both hands. "Why do you always try to hide your stomach from me?"

I squeeze my eyes shut.

"Look at me, Fee." Zane smooths his palms across my entire midsection. "Tell me why you hate your beautiful curves that I love so much."

"Ever since I had Mia, I can't get rid of the pooch. It just hangs there. I'm getting fatter. It's so embarrassing." Desire turns to shame. I try to pull free.

He holds fast to my wrists and brings them down so our hands are clasped across my stomach. "Did you hear what I said earlier about how much I love your curves?"

"Yes." I bite my lip.

"Would I lie to you?" He kisses my shoulder.

I sag back against him, evade the question. "No. You'd never hurt me. Not intentionally."

"It's not the same thing." He tilts his head. Brings my hand to his hard, throbbing cock. "I'm telling you that I love your lush body. I want you. You're like a Botticelli vixen. No—a million times more beautiful. I fucking love you."

It's too much. I pull away from him. Stand in the corner of the elevator covering myself with my hands. "I know what you're trying to do, Zaney. It doesn't change the fact that I have a hard time seeing myself the way you see me. I'm self-conscious. Your body is like an Italian marble statute. I read the comments on LTZ's social media. Everyone thinks I'm ..."

"Fiona. No. Stop it. This morning I saw you looking at the "hotfee" hashtag. Not everyone thinks anything, and none of those people are relevant in your life."

I sniff. Tears pool in my eyes. It sucks being a woman. Everyone has something to say. It's so confusing.

"Fee, let me love you. All of you. Let me in. Let me back in like it used to be with us," Zane pleads. "Remember, you and I are the only people in this world who matter. I love every part of you. I always have."

Desperate to gain some equilibrium, to stuff my insecurities deep inside, I step toward him. Grip his cock. Stroke. "Will you fuck me, baby?" My thumb flicks over his crown. "Make me come. I need it."

"Not right now. Fucking you isn't the best part of loving you." He removes my hand, steps to the keypad and punches in the code. The elevator lurches up. His face is awash in misery. I have no idea what's just happened. I know he's never turned me down before. Ever.

When the doors open into our bedroom he heads straight into the bathroom. Brushes his teeth. His boner has deflated. His entire demeanor has too.

"I don't know what I did... Just tell me. I'm sorry. I'll do anything." I cup his shoulder.

He sighs. "No, I'm the one who's sorry, Fee. I shouldn't have done that to you. I didn't mean to make you uncomfortable. I just thought ... maybe ..."

I stare at him in the mirror, trying to understand. "Please."

"Okay. I'm just going to say something to get it off my chest. I've *always* believed you love all parts of me. The good. The bad. The ugly. It's what got me through all the years we were separated. All of the times Carter never showed up. It got me through this entire fucking year when my band brothers abandoned me. From the beginning of time, you've always had my back. You're the one person in this life who gets me. I'm lucky. Blessed." Zane's voice is agitated, but not angry. He strides toward our bed and climbs in.

I follow him and crawl under the covers. Face him. "I do love every part of you."

"I know, but *you* somehow don't believe I love you with equal ferocity. And it *hurts*." Zane looks like he's in agony. "I've always seen myself through your eyes, even when I've been ashamed of myself. Or felt less than. When I was bullied in grade school. When your mom used to call me all of those horrible names. In high school when I lost my virginity to someone else. When I messed up our love hack. Even when we worked on rebuilding our relationship after Mia was born. Knowing you loved me anyway—even if you were mad at me—got me through."

I shake my head. "I don't understand, baby. I don't ..."

"Until you believe you are loved identically by me, Fee, how can you let me fully in? From the time your mom separated us when we were fourteen, you've held a part of yourself back. I've thought a lot about it. It's why you invented that stupid love hack before culinary school. Reinstated it before I left on tour ..."

I can't help but interrupt. I'm so incredibly crushed. "I *don't* hold myself back with you. Never."

"Seriously? You told me you were with a football player. I was so fucking sad when I never heard from you, I gave up my virginity to some stupid chick in the band room. Do you realize that set this entire Corey Johnson bullshit in motion? You did it again before I left on tour. You told me to be with other women. I had no intention of being with anyone else. You acted like you wanted to be with other guys, and I was okay with it. Because I loved you. It's so fucked up. *I convinced myself I was okay if it made you happy.* Do you know how this shit eats at me? I. Wasn't. Fucking. Okay." Zane punches the pillow.

It eats at me too, but I don't say a word. All I can do is motion for him to continue.

"Look, I'm sorry for bringing up old shit. All of that's in the past. It is. I'd hoped after the custody shit got resolved we'd get back to fourteen-year-old Zane and Fee. Best friends who loved and believed in each other unconditionally. We're not there, though." Zane flops on his back. "Ty's meltdown put things into perspective. I just can't lie to myself. I want all of you. I'm so tired of pretending things are fine when they're fucked ..."

Now, I'm pissed. I shove his shoulder. "So, let me get this straight. Just because I'm self-conscious about my weight means you think I'm holding myself back? Somehow my own insecurity is dredging up old history? That's some serious bullshit. I'm offended that—"

"*No*! You aren't listening. It has nothing to do with your fucking weight." He rolls back over to his side and taps my forehead. "It has to do with your head. You are my wet dream. I don't ever want to put my dick into anyone else for the rest of my life. Because I fucking worship you. I worship your fucking body. I worship your mind. It isn't about sex, Fee. It's about trust. *You. Still. Don't. Fucking. Trust. Me.*"

I'm stunned silent. "That's not true."

"It is," he says softly. Sadly. Devastatingly.

Then he turns back over. Scoots to the edge of the bed. Pulls the covers over his head.

My world collapses for the second time in two days.

If he's right ...

He is.

How long will it be until he leaves? Just like my mother said he would.

Chapter Twenty-Four

A Couple of Weeks After Fee's Overdose

THE GUILT IS KILLING me.

Am I the right man for Fiona? Are we really each other's halves?

Are we just codependent?

Maybe, Fee's my addiction.

These thoughts whirl around my brain on a loop. It's been that way for three solid days. How the fuck did we get back here? I guess I shouldn't be surprised. My entire life has come to a head.

Ty's in a mental health facility in Arizona, with Zoey by his side. He won't be out for months.

Jace nearly lost Alex when she had another miscarriage.

Connor was implicated in the craziest scandal I've ever heard of, now he and Ronni are mired in more legal shit.

My band's still broken up.

Gus and the Mission are closed.

Carter's recovering.

Faye hasn't bothered to respond to my text telling her what happened to Fiona.

Fee and I are still holding on by a string. Despite my own shortcomings, I will never be the one who gives up on us. I'll fight for her until the end. I hope she'll continue to fight for us too. Time will tell.

My phone buzzes. It's Iris Adler of The Seasons Change. I cancelled my plans to jam with them at their kick-off show in LA. I let it go to voicemail. Nothing's more important than this appointment. I'll call her back later. Apologize to the band. My focus and attention is right here. Right now.

I'm in the waiting room at Fiona's therapist's office. She finally agreed to go to counseling after her overdose. Individual sessions for now. I'll join her soon for couples counseling. Mia has her own therapist, we didn't want to make any mistakes with our daughter. Not when we both know all too well how the trauma of finding a parent can fuck with your mind …

Yeah. History motherfucking repeated itself with me and Fee. We're not letting it happen with Mia.

"Mr. Rocks, would you mind joining us in Dr. Calder's office?" A nurse pops her head out the waiting room door.

My blood pressure spikes. "Uh, sure."

I follow her back down a soothing gray-and-peach hallway into her therapist's office. It looks a lot like the place I went as a kid. Degrees hang on the wall next to huge bookcases filled with medical journals. A big wooden desk. Five oversized cream chairs are set up in a circle near the windows overlooking the city.

"Welcome, Zane." Dr. Calder gestures to a chair next to Fee. She still looks tired. Her sad blue eyes gaze up at me. I know she's ashamed. I know the events of the past month haven't helped her self-esteem. It's going to be a long road.

I sit. Lean back. Spread my legs. Drum my fingers on the armrest. I'm nervous. Moony. Trying to hide it, though. For Fee's sake.

"Fiona and I have been discussing some treatment plans, and we've come up with an idea that we thought we'd run past you. See if you're on board." She's an older woman, in her late fifties or early sixties. Not exactly grandmotherly. Cool great-auntie better describes her. She's dressed in a smart navy suit, her silver hair in a chin-length bob.

I glance up at Fee. Back at Dr. Calder. "Okay. I'd love to hear."

"Zane, Fiona and I have done hard work around her Xanax relapse. All things considered, there might be an interesting option to maximize healing. Fiona, would you like to articulate?" Dr. Calder steeples her fingers, giving Fee her full attention.

"Zane, I love you. I love our life together. We are building something we've dreamed about forever." Fee reaches over and clasps my hand, which I take as a positive sign. "It's important for me to develop new coping skills to deal with our childhood trauma. I—um—haven't gone to therapy my whole life the way you have, but it's clear my issues with Faye have caused some deep insecurities..." She breathes in and out. "My behavior and decision making isn't coming from a true place. I can't stop thinking about what you said to me that night...in the, uh, elevator." Her eyes flick to Dr. Calder, which means her therapist knows about what I did to her that night. "I don't trust you because I don't trust myself. I'm sorry I took Xanax when you took Mia to Baltimore. It seemed like my only option and my overdose caused so much pain to the two people in the world who matter most to me. I'm not going to sugarcoat it, I need some deeper help."

I wring my hands in agony. "I've apologized to you a million times, Fee. I'm so sorry that I made you feel so bad. It's my fault..."

"Hold on Zane." Dr. Calder holds up her palm. "There's a plan we want to run past you. I made a phone call today. As you know, your brother, Ty, is in Arizona undergoing treatment. I spoke with his team. I'd like to suggest you and Fiona join him in Arizona to undergo individual and family therapy. In a safe and structured setting, Fee will have the individual treatment she needs. You and Fee can work through some of this baggage. An integrated approach could be a positive experience for all of you."

"I talked to Zoey, she's on board. Ty too." Fiona pulls my wrist to her mouth and kisses it. "I want to ask Carter and Lianne to go. Maybe even Faye if she'd be open to it. We all need to do this for Mia, babe. Stop the cycle. I'm committed to change how my negative emotions and thoughts about myself affect you both. It's not fair for you to shoulder the burdens in our relationship."

"In my opinion, there are so many layers to your family dysfunction." Dr. Calder addresses both of us. "You and Fiona are both victims and survivors. As I understand it, the events of the past few decades have been catastrophic in many respects. Our goal is to bring the family into recovery to form new paths and stop generational repetitive cycles."

Fee reaches down to her purse on the floor and hands me a brochure. "We wouldn't live at the facility because Mia will come with us. Dr. Calder suggested we look into a one- or two-week sleep-away camp so we can do some intensive work while she's having a fun experience. Outside of that, we'd be in regular outpatient therapy sessions."

So much of this sounds familiar. It's been years since Al-Anon. I know that kids of addicts are high risk. They're statistically likely to engage in destructive behavior ranging from problems at school, to becoming too high-functioning, to mental health issues. There's no question this is the right answer. "I'll do it. Of course I will."

In the car on the way home, Fee seems genuinely relaxed. I don't say much until we're on the West Seattle Bridge. Mia's at home with Olga, so I want to have this conversation before we arrive.

"Is it okay to talk about it?" I turn my head to find her watching me.

She puts her hand on my thigh. "Let's take a walk?"

"Alki's busy..." My band might be broken up, but I'm still famous and we don't have security with us today.

"Yeah, I know. Just around the neighborhood. We'll be okay there." She smiles. "I'm trying to get in my steps."

I park at the house and take her hand as we slip through the side gate. We walk a few blocks before we get to Hamilton Viewpoint Park, a secluded little area overlooking downtown Seattle in our neighborhood.

She looks out at the city. A warm breeze catches a lock of her pink hair. I reach out and tuck it behind her ear. Ever since the day after Ty's mental break—when I essentially humiliated my wife in our elevator—I've had a constant gnawing feeling eating away at my insides. The knowledge that I did irreparable damage to Fee. Broke her trust in me by essentially accusing her of not trusting me.

I haven't known how to come back from it.

I ran away to Baltimore. With our daughter. Left her to cope alone.

"We have some work to do." She speaks into the air, not directly to me.

I put my arm tentatively around her. "I'm never going to forgive myself, Fee. What I did to you. It's my fault."

"What?" She looks at me quizzically. "Me taking too big a dose of Xanax is somehow your fault? How do you come to that conclusion? Aren't you the guy who spent his childhood learning that you are not the issue?"

She has a point, but I do bear some responsibility. "I humiliated you. You were devastated in that elevator."

"Look. It wasn't the best execution. Or the best timing. But, we've always been experimental with sex. That wasn't the issue." She tilts her head back against my chest. "The thing is, I know you love me no matter what. I guess I haven't figured out how to love myself. I've been in crisis mode for so many years, I don't even know how to act normally."

I kiss the top of her head. "I left you alone. I took Mia with me when I flew across the country just to play music. I ran away from my problems. It wasn't cool, babe."

"I could have come."

"Yeah." I let out a long breath. "That's not the point, though."

She turns in my arms. Brings her hands to the sides of my head. Combs through my hair with her fingers. "You know, when I was in my session a couple of days ago, Dr. Calder and I talked all about Mia. How finding me like that was going to affect her. When she gave me a list of possible reactions she might exhibit, the concept of role reversal hit me like a ton of bricks."

"I don't understand." I stare into the pools of her eyes. Wise beyond her years. It's always been that way.

"Mia is exhibiting behavior where she says and does little things to make me 'feel better.' She's used those exact words. I think she's still little enough that she doesn't know about the custody shit. Or about the Xanax, per se. But, she knows something's off with me and probably has her entire life. I'm sad. Stressed. All these things." She smooths my hair. "So, she's sassy and funny, and yeah—it's a lot like me when I was a kid. But also, it's a defense mechanism reaction to her environment. Just like my behavior was in reaction to mine."

I want to tell her she's off-base, but what she says rings true. "Sure, okay ..."

"Mia should never feel emotionally responsible for her mother." Fee states this definitively. "Just like I shouldn't have felt responsible for my mom. The difference is my mom essentially has spent her life telling me I *was* responsible for her well-being. That's our dynamic. When I break that cycle, she lashes out. Or leaves. I haven't heard from her. It's made me realize, I've got to course correct before it's too late. I would die before I did that to Mia. Or any kids we'll have."

I lean down and kiss her. Because she's talking about our future kids. "I love you. You'll never be like Faye."

"You need to work on it too. So do I with you." Fee twirls one of my curls with her finger. "We need help to figure out how to break some of our patterns."

"I don't ..." I protest.

"Yeah, you do. Not always, but you often feel responsible for my well-being. " She squints at me. "As Dr. Calder explained it to me, it's normal for adults in a relationship to want to help their partner and provide emotional support. That night in the elevator, you felt responsible to make me love my body the way you love it. We had a whole conversation about my inability to love you ..."

I shake my head. "Fee, it's different ..."

"No, it's not. You felt responsible to come find me when Faye moved me to Bellingham. You forced a relationship with Carter to get to me." She tilts her head. "Not that I'm complaining, it was a sweet and beautiful gesture. I'm grateful for you, Zaney."

"I would do anything for you, babe." I scan her eyes. Looking for acceptance. Understanding.

She loops her arms around my neck. Pulls my head to hers. "It's an observation, not an accusation. Because, as you well know, I have my own bullshit ways of manipulating things to fit my own internal narrative. I want to fully trust you again. It's not your fault. We're the product of what happened to us as kids. Somewhere deep inside me, I've always worried you'd leave me. So, I push you to fulfill my fear and then I get mad at you. There are so many examples. Just like you said. I lied to you about dating football players. The love hack. When I made you move out during the custody battle. Using Xanax to manage my anxiety, instead of dealing with my shit."

"You're oversimplifying." I press my lips to hers again. "But I get what you're saying."

"I am. But ... when we add in all of these complicated layers. Faye. Carter and Lianne, and whatever the hell's going on there. You and Carter. Now Ty and Carter ... you have a brother, Zane. He's your family. We have a daughter. He's having a son. Let's go to Arizona and do the work." She closes her eyes and sighs. "I'm ready."

I squeeze her as tightly as I can without hurting her.

Looks like we've got to make some calls.

As scary as it all seems to dig into this shit, we'll be doing it together.

Who knows what miracles might happen.

Chapter Twenty-Five

One Month Later

ARIZONA IS OPPRESSIVELY HOT in September, who the hell could live here year round? Not me, that's for damn positive.

This year, though, it's the best place I could hope for.

Our rental in Desert Mountain is in a private, gated community on six acres with stunning views of the mountains. We have six en-suite bedrooms and a casita. A huge modern pool. Amenities we could only begin to dream up. Aside from the heat, it's the perfect place for healing.

To compensate, us Northwesterners keep the AC turned up as high as it will go. The misters are working double-time on the patio. All in all, it's comfortable for our family.

Me and Zane. Mia. Olga. Zoey. Carter and Lianne. We've been here for four weeks with three to go. Ty is living at the facility, mainly because he's doing extra work to learn how to cope with the severe trauma he endured as a child. It's his story to tell, but learning some of the details has been devastating. Particularly for Carter and Zoey, but it's part of our family history.

No one is shying away from anything. It's hard, emotional work.

Well, except for Faye. She isn't here. I received a horrible, ranting voice mail raging at me for even inviting her. It's something I'm learning to cope with. She's not ready or willing, I can't force her. I'd love to have a wonderful relationship with my mother, but it takes two of us. What's been freeing is realizing I don't need to feel guilty for distancing myself from people—or behavior—that isn't healthy for me.

"Are you awake?" Zane spoons me from behind. Humps my ass playfully, though his dick is hard as a pole.

I reach back and grip his girth. "Depends on if you're using this for good or for evil."

"Always evil. Ride me." He angles his lips up to my earlobe and tugs it with his teeth. "Climb on, let me see your tits bounce a little."

I turn over and press Zane's back to the mattress. Sling my leg over his hip to straddle him. Grip his cock and tap it against my clit. Slide it between my pussy lips. "Like this?"

He watches me. "Yeah. That's a sexy start." He clutches my hips to keep me steady as I play.

I stroke him from root to tip with both hands, painstakingly slow passes. Experiment with pressure while I watch Zane's face to see what gives him the most gratification. Generally, he loves all of it so I continue for a bit, enjoying the feel of his thick cock in my palms. The quiver of his stomach muscles. The tautness of his dark-brown nipples.

He's beautiful.

Precum leaks and his hips begin moving rapidly, I lift up on my knees and angle him to my opening. Slowly take him inside my body. "Ahhh ..." We both sigh when he's fully seated.

"You're so beautiful." He runs his hands over my thighs as I grind against him. I watch him caress my hips as I roll them. His fingers travel up my waist. Along my stomach and torso. "I love you, Fee."

We both look up at the ceiling mirror. It's one of the reasons we picked this room, along with the fact it's away from the rest of the bedrooms. Part of my own therapy is to learn to love my body. At any stage it's in. To see how much enjoyment it gives me—and Zane.

A big revelation of therapy is when I stopped believing I was sexually desirable to Zane. It wasn't when we were fourteen, it happened after I got pregnant. Not because of my weight fluctuations—although that's a burden me and many women carry, Zoey and Ronni included. It was the deep guilt. Mia should be Zane's child. For years, I've taken on the entire responsibility for the demise of our relationship.

Zane called me out in the elevator. I didn't trust him. Not fully. And certainly not the way he trusted me to love him despite the mistakes he made in our relationship and felt guilty about. Like taking advantage of the love hack. And losing his virginity to someone other than me.

Part of my therapy is watching myself make love to my husband. For at least an hour every day, usually when we wake up. We vary positions and activities, but we are slow. Deliberate. Focused on being present. It's essentially tantric.

I'm learning to *see* how my body moves with his. *Feel* the sensuality we create. *Understand* how much Zane loves me. All of me. Completely. Thoroughly.

Forever.

"Come back, Fee." Zane reaches up to gently stroke my cheek. "Look at us."

I blink to focus on our merged bodies in the mirror. Shit, clearly I'm a work in progress but prescribed fucking is the most awesome way to heal. He smiles when I watch his thumb circle my clit. Bends his knees so I can lie back for a better view of his cock lodged inside me. "There you are."

"Yeah. I'm here." I splay my hands on his chest. Bend slightly so my tits are trapped between my upper arms. Zane's fingers pinch my nipples until they're tight. I circle my hips in a figure eight, stopping when he's at the perfect angle in my body to hit my G-spot. "Ahhhh. God. I love you, Zane."

I lean down and we kiss. He takes control, thrusting up into me, lazily but forcefully. Reaching between us, he uses his thumbs to spread my lips apart so my clit rubs against his pubic bone. Presses the small of my back so my undulations allow extra stimulation to my little nub. We know each other's bodies so well. When we come, it's from deep within our souls.

Zane and I are two halves of the same body. Merging together in a timeless connection we've had since birth. Our hearts and souls are fused together for all eternity.

I'll never take what we have for granted. Ever again.

"I fucking love when you let go," he whispers into my hair.

I cage his head between my arms. Touch my lips to his. Trace the seam with my tongue until he lets me in. We savor each other. He's still buried inside me, which is where he belongs. Always. I murmur against his mouth in between kisses. "I'm finding my way back to myself. Know this, I'm never letting you go, Zaney. I'll fight for us. Always."

"I know, Fee. I've always known that, baby." He rolls us over. Pulls out. Kneels between my legs and jacks his cock, which is soaked from our combined release. He's fully erect in seconds. "Mia's with my mom, I want to stay in bed and fuck you all morning."

"Yes, please." I run my hand down my stomach to my clit. Rub it in circles, recalling the brazen way I showed him how I masturbated in the park when we were eighteen.

His eyes fall to half-mast. He strokes faster then squeezes the tip of his dick while he watches me. "Yeah. Fuck, baby." My fingers trail lower. I rub myself, then insert two fingers inside. Bring them to his lips. He licks. "Sweet. Delicious."

Zane leans back on his haunches. Presses his palms against my inner thighs to spread me open. Buries his face in my pussy. Lapping us up. Drinking us in. As I dig my heels into the mattress, he slips a couple of fingers inside me and strokes until I'm writhing. Crying out. Coming.

He wriggles the tip of his tongue against my clit, sending a flurry of little aftershocks through my body. He sucks it hard. My hands fist the sheets. My stomach tightens and releases. "God, Zaney. Oh God."

"I am a sex god," he says as he kisses his way up my body. Taking time to suck on each nipple and then latch on to the spot behind my neck that always keeps me aroused. "We're not done."

I'm about to protest, when Zane rolls out of bed and drags an oversized chair to the mirror, positioning it sideways. "Come here. Lean over and rest your arms here." He points to the wide, flat armrest cushions.

"Were you planning this?" I giggle nervously. I'm going to do what he asks, but we are going to be next to the mirror. Like, right next to it.

He just beckons me with his finger. His cock is still flush against his muscled stomach. Hair flows past his shoulders. He's the most gorgeous man on the planet. His brown eyes are hungry. For me. Only for me. "I want to fuck you from behind. So bad."

I swing my legs over the bed, look in the mirror. My belly pooches over into a little roll. My breasts are not small or perky, they're substantial and sag a bit. My thighs are thick. My upper arms jiggle when I shift position.

Also, my jawline is sharp, my blue eyes sparkle, my skin is soft and creamy, my nipples are porn-star tight, my pink hair flows around my shoulder.

My face is soft and dreamy. Not only do I look like I've been properly fucked, but I also look like I've been loved. Thoroughly. Deeply. Reverentially.

By the man who's waiting to show me again how much.

I go to Zane, who kisses me and tenderly positions me the way he wants. I lean over so my cheek rests against the flat armrest and watch my husband guide his cock inside me. Grip my hips and thrust. The cords on his neck pulse. His biceps ripple. His thighs are strong. He rams into me hard and fast, crying out each time.

"You're my fucking wet dream, Fee. Look at your-self." He stares at where we're joined through the mirror. "I never get tired of this. I belong inside you. Any way you'll let me in."

I wriggle my hips against him. "Get me pregnant."

"What?" He stops moving but remains buried inside me.

"I'll go off the pill. Let's start trying." I catch his eye in the mirror. "I'm serious."

Zane withdraws and pulls me up. Wraps his arms around me. "What about Gus? Aren't you going to be busy?"

"Yes." I lean back against him. "But, I have an idea to run past you. Your cock is a little distracting, though. Can we finish the fucking and I'll tell you later?"

He spins me around and yanks my leg up and under his arm. Impales me and backs me against the wall of mirrors. "Trust me?"

"Yes," I say without hesitation.

His free hand skims down the inner thigh of my standing leg. "I'm lifting you up."

"Wait." My eyes go wide. "You won't ..."

"I will." He cants his hips. Presses his lips to my neck. "One. Two... Three." He hoists me up and is now so deep inside me my eyes roll back into my head. "Hold on to my shoulders, lean against the mirror. Let me do the work. Just feel."

So, I do. I feel weightless as he grinds into me. The angle is incredible. I'm floating. "I've got you, Fee," he whispers. "I'll always have you. Just feel me inside you."

We lock eyes. He squeezes my ass, hard. Screws his hips so I'm pinned to the mirrored wall. I lock my legs around his lower back and truly let go. He bounces me on his cock. He's never, ever been deeper and I can't even ...

"Ohmygod," I cry when I go over. "Ohmygod."

"Fee ... I ..." Zane's face is a grimace when he rams into me a final time. "Oh ... Oh ... Holy fuck ..."

He gently lets my legs down one by one, which feel like jelly. My heart, on the other hand, feels stronger than it ever has.

I trust him. On so many levels.

Zane continues to show me that my self-doubts are in my head.

Chapter Twenty-Six

A Week or so Later

I'VE BEEN GOING TO therapy for most of my life.

It kept me well-adjusted, I thought. I was lucky to have my mom. My grandparents. Stability. Coping skills. Foresight, even. After all, I'm the one who instigated Ty's initial foray into therapy years ago when he was out of control with the substance abuse and sex.

When Fee suggested joining Ty in Arizona and bringing Carter and Lianne with us, I was on board, but figured I'd be along for the ride while he and my dad finally figured their shit out.

Not. Even. Close.

Turns out, I'm an integral part of these big, huge, complicated relationships. Not only that, but I've been harboring so much resentment against my family. I've covered up my feelings to keep the peace. Ignored things, willfully, instead of talking them out.

No more. Therapy has been intense. Me and Carter. Me and my mom. The three of us. Me and Ty. Me, Ty, and Carter. Me, Ty, Carter, and Lianne.

And, of course, me and Fee.

The amount of work we've accomplished is astounding, though. Intensive family therapy is hopefully giving us skills to cope with the extraordinarily complicated web of our lives. Our trauma. Not just while we're here, but in the future.

I'll be honest, though, I have a little bit of a therapy hangover today. It's common, so our medical team says. I think we've all gone through it. Today's just my turn.

I'm standing at the breakfast bar eating a slice of toast when my mom comes in from her bedroom. "Good morning, my sweet boy." She kisses me on the cheek.

"I want you to know it's okay." I grip her shoulder. "To love him."

She stares at me puzzled. "I know."

"Do you?" I take another bite. Chew.

"I don't need your permission, Zane." She runs her fingers through the ends of her strawberry-blonde hair to untangle it. "I'm a grown woman."

I finish my toast and put the plate in the dishwasher. "Maybe not. You want my approval though. It's why the two of you have been keeping your relationship secret from me all these years."

"Not entirely. I didn't want you to know until I'd worked it out for myself. Plus, it wasn't your business." She places a coffee pod in the machine and leans against the counter, waiting.

"Aha." I hold my finger up.

She takes a sip from the coffee when it's done. "You didn't know about most of the men in my life, Zane. I had boyfriends. Even when you were younger, and I've had them since. Obviously, no one that's made the cut or you would have known."

My mouth must have dropped open because my mom laughs heartily.

"Who?" I slap my palm on the counter.

"It doesn't matter. When Carter and I started, whatever it was back then, I was always honest with him. I needed to find out who I was as an adult. I was so young when I got pregnant with you. So in love with your dad, to my demise in many ways." She crosses her elegant arms over her body. "It was important for me to learn who I was. As a woman. Not as a dancer. Not as Carter's ex. Not as your mom. All of me. When I was your age, I had a twelve-year-old kid. Surely, you can appreciate that perspective now? Especially after all of this work we've been doing."

"And he was okay with all of that?" I can't imagine being okay with Fee ...

Shit. The love hack. Holy shit. That was her purpose back then. God. She told me the exact same thing when she left for culinary school. This history repeating shit is all topsy turvy. I need a fucking break.

Mom watches me. "Something must have clicked...I can see your brain whirring."

I just shake my head.

"Well, in answer to your question, he told me to take my time. That he'd wait. So I did. Am still doing." She shrugs.

I take a minute to process. "He loves you so much. I don't think he's been with anyone else..."

"He hasn't." She places her palms on the counter. Stretches her back.

My mother, always doing some sort of ballet somethingorother. "Well, I always thought you'd end up with some rich, refined guy."

She laughs. "Wow. Okay."

"It's still almost impossible for me to picture you and Carter as a couple." I shake my head.

"And yet, he's the one I love. Have always loved." This catches me off guard because she's never said that to me directly. I overheard her conversations with my grandparents when I was young. Back when we lived with them. The sentiment never seemed like it was positive.

Carter's voice startles us. "I don't want to interrupt."

"I told Zane I love you." Lianne reaches for him. He takes her hand but looks at me with trepidation.

"So, be together." I shrug. "I'm fine with it. I'm sick of hanging on to old bullshit."

They stare at me like I'm a naughty kid. I guess, maybe, I'm acting like it.

"What's going on in here." Fee joins us, her pink hair piled in a knot on her head. Her face is still flushed. I made her come about half a dozen times this morning while she watched herself ride my face. I swear to God, this mirror sex is a game changer. I'm having them installed in strategic locations in our bedroom as a surprise for Fee when we go back home to Seattle.

"Carter and Lianne are officially back in love." I sling my arm around her shoulder. "Discuss."

My dad brings my mom's hand to his lips. "It's not up for discussion. What we do and when we do it is our business."

"Well, the three of us have a session today." Lianne speaks softly. "It's our business. Our story. It's long past time to hash it out so we can all move on."

I pinch my nose with my thumb and forefinger. I decide I need a solid three-hour block to shred. Alone. I keep my Gibson downstairs in the game room, but maybe I'll hole up in the garage later. Just the thought of playing music makes me relax a bit.

"Morning." Zoey shuffles into the kitchen, her belly protruding heavily. "I see the gang's all here. Where's Meems?"

Fee pulls out a chair at the table for her to sit. "Olga took her to horse camp this morning. We thought it would be best for her to be away for the final ten days of our sessions. We still have a lot of hard shit to cover."

"Yeah. Well, we don't need to put that much stress on ourselves. It's not like we're going to be miraculously cured. Ty and I are committing to a long-term therapy plan so he can manage his anxiety." Zoey drums her fingers on the table with one hand. She cradles her bump with the other. "But, now that we're getting closer to Ty's release date, there's something I'd like to run past you all." She looks at me. "You haven't talked to Jace and Connor about us all being here, have you?"

"Uh, no." I look at Fee. Back at Zoey. "Obviously, I've checked in on them because of the personal shit they're dealing with, but it didn't seem like the right time to out ourselves until we all figured everything out."

"Yeah...I'm glad. I still haven't heard back from Alex, Jace is probably pissed at me for not being there. I would have been, it's just ..." Zoey's face falls a bit.

My mom pours her a glass of water. "You're doing the right thing by being here with your husband, Z. She'll understand when she knows more. Physical health and mental health can both be life-threatening situations."

"I agree," Fee assures her. "You guys have been besties forever."

"I hope so." She taps her lip with her finger. "I was thinking. Should we come up with a plan to tell the rest of us what's been going on when we get back to Seattle? As you know, Ty wants to apologize to the guys for what happened. Whether or not we want to go deeper—that's obviously up to you."

Crazily when Zoey says Ty's name, her belly visibly jerks. Her eyes dart to Carter. She waves him over. She places Carter's palm on her belly. His face lights up. "He's moving." It's kind of sweet. My dad is so excited to be a grandfather again. Zoey's going out of her way to include him. Like letting him feel his grandson moving inside her.

My mom must think it's adorable too. I catch her making moony eyes at Carter.

Fee rolls her eyes at me. "So, let's get back on track. When we're back in Seattle—"

"Hold up. We have a family session later this afternoon." Carter flicks his eyes from Zoey's belly to Fee. "Let's bring it up then. See what Ty wants to do. Maybe get some suggestions on how best to let Jace and Connor know about all of this."

"And Alex and Ronni," Zoey points out.

"Well, yeah. Before we do any of this, we need to know if Ty even wants to be in the band anymore." I can't help but vocalize my biggest fear.

Carter leans back in his chair. "Of course he does."

"So you say. Even if that's true, what if Connor and Jace don't want to be in the band? Do I even have a fucking band?" I cross my arms over my chest. Pout. If I'm honest, as much as it's helping, I'm overdosing on the therapy.

Well, all but the morning sex therapy.

Fee wraps her arms around my middle. Looks up at me. Says quietly, "Zaney. Let's take it up later."

"Fine. Always later." I pull away from my wife and head toward our room. "I'm going to take a shower."

I'm standing under the spray in the double-sized shower when Fee joins me in the bathroom. My eyes are shut and I'm not even facing the door, but I can feel her presence. A couple of minutes go by before the glass door opens and she joins me.

Fiona grips my arms. Runs her hands down my biceps and forearms. Takes both hands in hers. "Talk to me."

"I'm not even certain what's got me so upset," I confess.

"Let me wash you." Fee releases my hands and picks up the honey-lavender-scented body wash that came with the rental. She squirts some out and begins to massage it into my shoulders. Back. Arms. Butt. Moving around my body, she lathers up my chest. Stomach. Upper legs.

She sits on the bench and pulls me toward her. My cock stiffly juts out against her cheek.

I grip her face and guide her mouth against the underside of my shaft. Her tongue darts out and licks my pulsing vein. Fee presses her palms against my inner thighs to spread my stance, giving her extra room. As she licks and suckles, she soaps up my balls, taint, and ass before focusing back on my cock.

"Give me the wand." Fee's blue eyes gaze up at me and she holds out her hand. I give her the skinny apparatus and turn on the water. She lovingly rinses off my bits, massaging and caressing.

I massage her scalp with the tips of my fingers as she cleans me. Marveling in how uninhibited she is in this moment. Sitting on the bench with her legs on either side of mine. Her curvy body on full, glorious display, Fee's not trying to hide herself. Her only focus is giving me pleasure.

I kneel, but she protests, "No, Zane. I'm taking care of you today."

Fiona guides my cock back in her mouth and cups my balls with her free hand, slipping her finger back and forth along my gooch as she plays. All of the sensations are so intense, within seconds I can't help but shout when I explode down her throat. I'm slumped over her, my hands grip her shoulders for support as she sucks me dry.

When I manage to pull myself together, I sit on the bench and watch as she washes herself. Soaps up her body. Shampoos her hair. Her eyes never leave mine. "You're so fucking hot." I reach up and tap her nipple.

"I am." She rinses herself. "And I'm all yours. Forever."

"Thank God." I stand and kiss her sweet, sassy mouth, which tastes of me.

Fee hands me a towel when we finish our shower. "You know, for all of the therapy you've done over the years, you're forgetting it's okay to take care of yourself. We've spent weeks dissecting so much shit from Ty's abuse to Carter's history to my own B.S. with my mom. It's time for some of this to be about you. You don't always have to put on a happy face, baby. Getting your own needs met is part of our family's healing."

I think about this as we dry off.

Remember that I, too, am a work in progress.

We all are. It's not like my life is going to be magically fixed when we leave Arizona. Not with my folks. Not with the band. Not even with Fee.

What's comforting, though?

Maybe, just maybe, this is the beginning of something better than I could have ever dreamed of.

Chapter Twenty-Seven

A Month Later

To say I'm not looking forward to tomorrow is an understatement.

It will be the first time we see Ty and Zoey—and Carter and Lianne—since Zane and I took Mia out of camp and left Arizona a week early.

Our last family therapy session turned into, well, quite a blowout. Zane got in Carter's face. Ty defended Carter, so Zane said some hurtful things. Zoey defended Ty. I got in her face and defended Zane. Lianne tried to play peacemaker, but Ty—with good reason—got upset about Zoey and the baby's health.

I tried to apologize, but we all decided it was best for us to go home.

The six of us are due for a follow-up session when Ty and Zoey get back to Seattle, which I'm equally looking forward to and dreading. The guys have said their worst. Now we can pick up the pieces.

Hopefully.

Before any of this happened, Zane and I offered to use our house as a gathering place for Ty's big apology. With tension unresolved as of yet, it's going to be super uncomfortable, but I'm a woman of my word. Tomorrow, the entire LTZ family will come by in the afternoon. The chips will fall where they may.

A couple days after Zane and I got home, I decided to rip the bandage off and confront my mom. As much as she's hurt me, she's my mother. I offered to give our relationship one final chance before I throw in the towel. She agreed to work with me and my therapist to try to establish new boundaries.

We've been to a few sessions. For now, she seems committed. She's apologized to me. To Zane. Claims to want to fix things. Hesitantly, I've agreed to let Mia spend two hours with her tomorrow afternoon during the meeting with Ty, however, I'm sending Olga too. I trust our nanny implicitly. She'll know if and when she needs to get Mia out of there.

The doorbell rings. Mia bounds down the stairs. "The twins are here!"

"Hold up, Meems. Let me get it." She stands behind me when I open the door for Ronni and her little sons. I pick up the closest boy. "Get your ass in here. Aren't you two of the most handsome boys?"

"Can the twins play in my room?" My adorable daughter looks up at me from under her bangs. She's the double of Zane. Jesus.

I can see Ronnie's uncomfortable, so I use the age-old mothering tactic of diversion. "Meems, how about we put up the baby gate in the kitchen? The three of you can hang out in the sitting room where we set up the Play-Doh and racetrack. You can put on a movie too if you want. Then Aunt Ronni and I can be in the kitchen in case you need us."

Ten minutes later, the kids are settled and wine is poured. Ronni and I sit at my kitchen island to catch up a bit. She fills me in on the latest with her and Connor's shocking scandal. Her lawsuit. Their new house. I catch her up on the latest with my restaurant. The Xanax disaster. Therapy.

Before I know it, a couple hours have passed and we've gone deep on so many subjects. Our friendship is so natural. We're two women who have a lot in common, but don't trust easily. She's becoming such a close friend, I'm looking forward to spending time with her now that she's relocated to the Seattle area on a permanent basis.

We clink our glasses. "To surviving."

"To overcoming misogyny." She fans herself, smirking.

"Fuck the patriarchy." I slap my hand on the counter. "You did the world a service taking that asshole down. And that nanny too."

Olga has the night off since she's taking Mia to Mom's tomorrow, so we constantly check on the kids. Mia's got the boys handled, though. She adores Tristan and Torin. When I see her with them, it makes me long to give her some siblings. Zane wants kids so badly. So do I.

"She'll be a great babysitter when we're all on the road," I toss out to Ronni. Zane is at Connor's tonight with Jace, giving them a little preview of tomorrow's potential shit show. "If the boys can get their shit together, that is."

Ronni studies me. I can tell she's treading lightly. I guess my attempt at neutrality hasn't masked my lingering anger at Ty—and Zoey, who hasn't returned any of my texts since we left Arizona. "Hopefully the three of them will get their game plan together. Tomorrow's a big day. Connor's convinced Ty's going to quit."

"God, I'm trying not to be a bitch. It's just that Zane has suffered so much." I can't divulge too much about the planned meeting. Before he left for Connor's house, Zane and I agreed to honor Ty and Zoey's wishes to let them deliver the news. So, I divert with a little dose of truth. "I know Carter's bullshit is not Ty's fault. I'm disappointed in Zoey. I thought we'd become close. It hurts she hasn't returned my texts."

It's hard to tell If Ronni picks up on my evasiveness. "She's not been in touch with me either. Or Alex. I'm keeping an open mind. I understand needing a break. Connor mentioned Zane saw Ty—oh, God. Tell me if I'm prying."

God. Ronni has proven to be trustworthy. I simply can't hold back. "No, it's fine. Yeah, Zane's been in a couple sessions with Ty and Carter. They're trying to work things out. Zane's in a bit of a regression when it comes to his dad. He's trying desperately not to be resentful, but their history is very—um—challenged."

"Because of Carter's addiction issues?" Ronni is concerned, not judgy.

"Yeah, that comes into play. It's about abandonment, though. I mean, he and I were six—about Mia's age—when we saw Carter overdose in the park. That night at The Mission? Serious flashbacks for me when I saw Carter unconscious in the ambulance. I shut down."

I think about the big blow up during our session. We all have our own perspectives. "Anyway, when Lianne and Zane moved to Denver, I saw more of Carter than Zane did for years. He's working through it. Well, we all are. At least, I hope we are."

"Will you reopen Gus soon?" Ronni brings up the million-dollar question.

"Oh. Yeah..." I'm still unsure about the exact details. "Maybe. I'm not going to count my chickens. Let's get through tomorrow and see if we're going to be band widows."

"Well, I hope you do. I also hope you'll be on the road with us so we can hang out." Ronni shows me some pictures on her phone. "Did you get a bus customized? Ours will be ready by March. We're psyched to tour as a family."

"I haven't had time. Wow. This is super fancy, Ronni. Well done." I'm pleasantly surprised at the cool design. I've always thought these custom buses were a waste of money, considering the odds of all of us women touring for months on end with the guys are slim. On the other hand, this bus is phenomenal. Like a mini-house. Maybe it would be worth it... "Are you on board with going on the road with the band though? I mean, don't you have a ton of projects in the works?"

Ronni sips her wine, then speaks thoughtfully. "When we were filming the show in Vancouver before all of the lawsuit madness, I was miserable knowing that Connor got to spend all day with our sons while I worked. After what we've been through this year, I realized I needed a break. A huge, huge break. This Kircher bullshit has taken its toll. The videos put me over the edge. The band stuff hasn't helped. On the glass is half-full side, it's also forced me to take stock of my life. It's funny. I'm seriously questioning whether this industry fulfills me."

"Well, I don't know if I want to take Mia out on the road." I'm glad to have another wife to talk this out with. "She loves her school. Her friends. Plus, I've not had my chance yet. All of you ladies have amazing careers. I want to live my own dream."

"You deserve that, Fee." Ronnie's raises her glass.

"Although ... God, look at them." I gaze down at the kids, who are watching a show. Mia's cuddling both boys. I love this more than words could ever say.

Ronni swoons. "See? That's what I want my boys to have. Family. We're all family."

"Yeah." Realization dawns and makes me trepidatious for all that still lies ahead. "We are."

Ronni clasps my shoulder. "Fee, are you okay? Tell me the truth."

Her question hits me in a soft spot. "I don't ... know." I look up to the ceiling. As if the answer is in the air. "Ronni, I'm going to confide in you. I've been wallowing. I'm still angry. I'm trying to be rainbows and puppies, but I worked so hard on Gus. I'm bitter. It's hard not to be resentful. I want to follow my dreams, but I truthfully don't know if I have the energy to do it all again. Or if it's worth the investment of time. Money. Zane and I spent a small fortune on the renovations for the club. My restaurant ..."

It's too much. Overwhelming. I can't stop the waterworks. Ronni's there for me. I sob against her shoulder. "I'm sorry, I think I just needed to vent."

"Don't apologize for having feelings. Better out than in." Ronni pats my back soothingly.

"I can't seem to stop crying. Or eating. I hate myself for it. I hide. Zane's the one whose band imploded. He's the one who has the family drama. Up until recently, he's the one whose wife won't give him a baby because, well ... my selfishness. My Zaney is the one who should be sobbing, and he's spending all his time comforting me."

I'm not losing my shit. Not like before. It's just ... therapy brings up so many confusing feelings. Emotions. Just when I feel I've worked through something, I'm punched in the gut with a wave of—gah. Stuff that's hard to process.

I thought I'd put it behind me.

Talking about shit over and over again doesn't solve everything like the magic Xanax pills used to—but I can't, and won't, ever go down that road again. I'll never allow Mia to find me like...God.

Never. Again.

It's just that since we've been back and out of our Arizona bubble, I've felt a bit down. Zane assures me it's normal, but still ...

Ronni's kind. "Why do women always take on so much?"

"Says the woman who brought down the slimiest men in Hollywood. Not once, but twice." I drum my fingers on the counter. She's so strong. Incredible. I would love to be like her.

"Ah, well. Maybe so, but I'd argue all of us LTZ women are overachievers. We're badasses." Ronni shakes out her hair and gives me a pout to make me laugh. Then she gets serious. "If you want my advice, maybe don't put too much strain on yourself. We're all behind you, so try to enjoy your downtime. Gus will reopen when you're ready. I'll go back to work when I'm ready. So will Alex. And Zoey. I do hope the guys can get their own shit together, though."

God, it feels wonderful to have such a friend. Someone I can trust. "What do you think they're talking about?"

Ronni shrugs and checks her phone, which just lit up. "I'm just glad they're talking. Their future essentially hinges on seeing Ty tomorrow."

Isn't that the truth?

"Jeez, Fee. Zane's going to be home soon, he left an hour ago. I should probably get going."

We gather up the twins, who are sound asleep on the couch with Mia. She promptly falls back asleep. I walk Ronni to the door. "You guys should get here a little earlier than Jace and Alex. If you can, that is." I lean in the doorway holding Tristan while Ronni loads Torin in the car seat.

"Sure. We'll leave early." Ronni buckles Tristan in next to his brother. "By the way, thank you for tonight."

I can't help but smile. "I'm glad you guys moved to the area."

"Me too." She waves from the driver's seat. "I love having a BFF."

I'm floored. It's official.

For the first time in my life, I have a bestie.

Chapter Twenty-Eight

The Same Evening - Connor's House

THE LAST TIME CONNOR, Jace, and I were together, we were at Gus.

The morning after, well ...

Only three short months ago, but it might as well be a lifetime.

Two years ago, we were contemplating taking a year off. Ty was back together with Zoey. Connor and Ronni were secretly married and pregnant. Alex and Jace faced a paternity scandal. Fee and I were fighting for custody of Mia.

Up until that point, our bond was unbreakable. Despite our challenges. No matter what, we had each other's backs. We were each other's family.

When we all settled down, I knew we'd have new priorities and life events. It never occurred to me we'd find ourselves at odds. Never. When the guys made rumblings about taking a break, I didn't need it but I never thought LTZ would find ourselves here. Never.

Nearly two years have gone by.

Uncertainty gnaws at my insides. What if tonight is the end?

I'll be devastated.

It takes longer to get to Connor's than I planned. By the time I pull up the narrow, paved road to his new mansion on Lake Washington, I'm a wreck. Not only did I got lost on my way over, I must have passed his unmarked driveway at least six times. I'm lucky I saw Jace's truck and followed him in.

"Holy shit." I take in my surroundings. I thought my house was a bit over the top, but this place looks like a fucking hotel. I've never been in this bougie neighborhood before. A lot of tech people live here. Not many rockstars, is my guess. The house itself looms up like one of the sleek places Fee and I rented in Asia on LTZ's last tour.

Please let that not be LTZ's last tour.

Jace is waiting by his beat-up truck. He just smirks at my expression of awe. Considering his dad is a tech legend and his folks' house isn't too far away, it occurs to me he's not quite as surprised as I am at the opulence of Connor's abode. I follow up the walkway where he knocks on the steel front door, which seems a million feet tall. A middle-aged woman wearing a gray dress answers. "Mr. Deveraux, Mr. Rocks please follow me."

Now, even Jace is taken aback. I mean, c'mon. Connor and Ronni have a motherfucking butler? I can't help but waggle my eyes at him when the woman escorts us past a wall of glass flanked by ginormous steel fireplaces on either side of a sitting area that looks like, well, a fancy hotel.

"There you are." Connor is waiting for us in the doorway of a kitchen that rivals the one at my house.

Fee made me promise to scope it out, so I take a mental picture. It's less "chef's kitchen" and more designer, but still high end. I run my fingers along the twelve-burner stove. "I can't show this kitchen to Fee, Connor. I hope you realize we'll never visit you, or she's going to want to gut ours and start over."

He laughs. Connor seems strangely at ease here. Lord of the manor and all that shit. Out of all of us, I'd have pegged Connor to be the most grounded and the least likely to spend his money on mansions and jets. Then again, Ronni is at least as famous—if not more—than all of us and he lived in her swanky Malibu mansion for years.

Ah, who the fuck cares. If he's happy, I'm happy. My house is fucking spectacular too.

We follow him to a room facing the lake, which is sort of like a man cave without the cavey feel. On one side, he has a fully stocked bar. The opposite wall is an enclosed-glass, temperature-controlled cabinet with easily five hundred bottles of wine.

"Obviously, since Ty's not here, the three of us can enjoy a nice, smooth vintage Midleton." Connor pours out three glasses of amber whiskey. We toast and sit down in three of the four oversized, cushiony chairs facing the lake. The empty chair stands out to me. Ty should be sitting there.

"Fuck, Connor. What is this place?" I'm babbling, not feeling settled without knowing where their heads are at—especially Jace's. "It's spectacular. Unexpected."

He leans back in his chair. "Ronni loves being by the water. After everything that happened this year, we needed to know we had a safe sanctuary. It was crazy expensive, but with her Netflix deal renewed? Let's just say it made the decision easier. Plus, the schools are great. It's private and guarded—one of our security detail answered the door. Lots of kids in the neighborhood for the boys to grow up with. And, it has all the bells and whistles, so it does."

His explanation makes perfect sense. Part of me is relieved the woman who answered the door wasn't an actual butler. I recline back and notice Jace fidgeting next to me.

"I suppose we need to get our game plan for tomorrow." He rubs his hands together. "Are we willing to listen to what Ty's going to say? Do you think he wants to get the band back together? After all, it's his world, we're all just bystanders."

"Will you stop, Jace." I can't help but snap at him. I know he's been distracted with Alex, but I've had enough of his snark about Ty and the band. I'm not interested in any of us tearing each other down.

"Stop what?" He's genuinely surprised by my tone.

Connor backs me up. "Sayin' the feckin' band's broken up. Making light of Ty's situation."

"Uh, Ty quit the band. LTZ can't go on without Ty." Jace leans forward. "I thought we were discussing the audience Sir Ty requested."

Even though Ty asked me not to say anything, given his level of resentment, I can't keep them in the dark. "There's more to it than that, my brothers. So, uh. Ehm. Heads up. Ty hasn't been in rehab. He's been in intense counseling."

"What?" they say in unison.

I swirl my whiskey without drinking any and try to figure out a way to be as transparent as possible with my band brothers without breaking my promise to Ty. "Carter's been down in Arizona with him. He's in a program for some trauma he's been dealing with since he was a kid. I've had some sessions with them about the paternity thing."

"Fuck, man. I know you've been going through your own shit. How are you coming to terms with it?" Jace's tension relaxes a hair, making me less anxious.

I want to let these guys in so badly. It's hard not to be able to tell the entire story, but I have to wait until tomorrow when we'll all be together. "It's confusing. Carter's all in on being Ty's father. It brings up some old baggage for me. I'm planning on spending time with Ty when he gets back, although Fee is still raw about the entire situation."

I guess my perspective has an effect. No one speaks. I've stunned them silent.

"How's Alex doing?" After a while, Connor redirects a question to Jace. "We've tried to give you some space so she can recover."

He purses his lips. His eyebrow twitches as he thinks about the question. "She's surprisingly well-adjusted. I'm the one who's a big mess. When the woman you love is hurt, it's literally the worst thing in the world. I hope none of you ever experience it."

"Yeah." Connor leans over and fixes his gaze on Jace. "Although all our ladies have had a fair share of shit in their lives, the only one of us who's been through something like that is Ty. When Zoey was nearly killed by that taxi."

Jace recoils, astounded. "Wait, how is that my fucking fault? Do you guys have something to say to me? Do you think that I'm the asshole here?"

"I'm going to be honest with you." Connor speaks to our drummer like a sage elder statesman. Considering the strange video scandal he just put behind him, it's almost like he's over all of the drama too. He's just done. "In retrospect, you got too involved in LTZ's media stuff, Jace, and we were all too stupid to see it. Or put an end to it." He then points at me. "Ty had a lot of baggage. We all knew that. For the past decade, you made it your personal mission to fix things when he acted out."

He scoffs. "Connor, if I hadn't—"

Connor holds up a hand. "I know. Look, I buried my head in the sand, too. It's no secret I was annoyed with him for many years. The thing is, when Ronni was fake dating him, she got to know him on a deep level. We both did. She always suspected he'd been traumatized somehow because she recognized the haunted look in his eyes. Ty is our family. It doesn't take a rocket scientist to know that he was triggered that day. We're older and wiser now. It's time for some changes that all of us need to make." He pauses and points at both of us. "We also need to remember, above all else, the four of us are brothers."

I'm nearly overwhelmed with gratitude. Connor articulates my feelings exactly. If we could all just get ourselves on the same page ...

Jace, however, doesn't look convinced. Not at all.

So, I've got to take a shot. "Jace, you always jumped in and just handled shit for us. And we let you. You never took time for yourself. Never prioritized your relationship with Alex." I pound my heart with my fist. "Take it from me, I hate that you felt you had to hide your love for her from Ty. It's fucked up that you put her on a backburner for so long." He glances up at me in surprise. "Look, there's not a doubt in my mind that's where your resentment comes from. Especially after what Alex has just gone through—what you both have gone through."

Jace grips the arms of the chair. He's uncomfortable being the focus. It's not his thing. He grits out, "Uh, isn't this about Ty?"

"No, it's about all of us." Connor sums it up perfectly.

My adrenaline spikes a bit because I feel like we're at a serious crossroads. We're either going to give the band a try again or break up. I know what I want. It's time to lay my cards out.

I can't just sit here though, so I get up and look out the window. "Fee's planning on reopening Gus when she's mentally ready again after taking time off to regroup. Luckily, her staff is still on board and ready for a redo." "I turn back toward my band-brothers and stretch out my arms, almost pleading. "I never wanted a break. The time I've had away from all of you has been tough for me. I went and jammed with friends and whatever, but for me Less Than Zero is who I am." I have to take a deep breath in order to continue. "What happened at The Mission was nuts. *Devastating*. We were minutes away from making magic happen again. I miss us. I miss making music with you all. I want us to reunite."

"I want the band back together too." Connor joins me. Bro-hugs me.

Both of us stand across from Jace, who's wide-eyed and not remotely convinced. Or maybe, just maybe, he's scared too. "Well, what if Ty doesn't? Isn't all of our fate in his hands? Again?"

"Don't let your past cloud your judgement." I try to be gentle, but he doesn't know the whole story. "Remember, Jace. You and Ty were close. For years. As far as I can tell, it's only been the past year or so that you've had this attitude about him. What the fuck, man?"

"Look, I'll try to be cool. I just want to know what we're dealing with. I don't have it in me to go through any shit with him again this year. Or ever, truth be told." Jace doesn't give in much, which is disconcerting.

So, it's up to me to push him over to our side. I plead, desperately, "I'm all in on LTZ. Connor?" He nods. "So, yeah. I'm ninety-nine percent Ty wants to continue. Before we all see him tomorrow, what do you want? Jace, you're just as important to LTZ as Ty is. Do you want LTZ to continue or are you done?"

"I don't know." He throws his hands up, not angry. Mostly exasperated. "I've just come through hell. I find myself wanting to be with Alex every minute of the day. I don't think you guys realize how close I was to losing her. She's still recovering, you know."

"Fair enough." Connor raises his glass. "Think about it. Hear what Ty has to say. We all have to be in, or it's not happening."

Clearly, Connor has more patience than me. I set my undrunk glass of whiskey on the table. "I've poured my heart out to you guys. I try to take the high road. I try to be supportive of all of you. Don't forget, Fee and I have lost millions of dollars on our businesses because of this mess. Not to mention my family is in fucking shambles and we're trying to pick up the pieces. Fiona and I have suffered through our own struggles and we have never let them affect LTZ or any of you. What I'm trying to say here is LTZ is a once-in-a-lifetime thing. Most people never get to experience what we have, which is magic. You don't fucking throw away magic."

I make a move toward the door. I'm tired of Jace's excuses. I'd rather have him quit than string us along.

Behind me, I hear Connor admonish Jace, "Go talk to him before he leaves."

"Zane, wait..." I'm in the foyer when Jace grabs my arm. "Look, I'm sorry. None of this is your fault. I know you're dealing with a lot."

"You have no fucking idea." I point at him.

Connor joins us. "Tell us what's up, my brother."

"I'll tell you, but I need you both to be honest with me too. No more of this dancing-around bullshit. We lived in each other's pockets for years. There were no secrets. Nothing was off-limits. Ty has his story to tell—that's what tomorrow's all about. Tonight, can we please be real?" I pinch the bridge of my nose. "We don't have to be here all night, but maybe take an hour and get back to basics?"

Jace nods. "Yeah. Yeah. I can do that."

So we do. Connor, Jace, and I hash through what we want.

What we expect.

How we can find a path forward. Under new terms. New expectations.

Now, all we need is for Ty to get on board.

Maybe we can salvage LTZ after all.

Chapter Twenty-Nine

The Next Day - Ty is Home

THE DAY HAS FINALLY arrived.

My band's fate is about to be decided.

On the shores of Lake Washington, at the Mc-Gloughlin's house, Connor, Jace, and I unloaded a decade's worth of shit and realized all of us want—and need—LTZ. If we rewrite some rules. Unlike when we started out, we have our families to consider. Wives, girlfriends, children.

Our lives are bigger. Richer. Fuller.

Hence, the source of Jace's hesitation. He and Alex haven't fully discussed the realities of LTZ getting back together. They've been focused on her health for a long time. Notoriously closed-lipped, both of them made it difficult for anyone to realize how bad things were. Ty and Zoey knew more than we did, though. Which makes sense why Jace resented their inability to be there for Alex during her time of need.

Jace's anger was rooted in the years they felt they had to hide their relationship. To protect Ty and Zoey. He was pissed he missed out on years with Alex. When Connor pointed out that Ty and Zoey would have never wanted them to be apart if they were truly ready for a committed relationship, Jace reluctantly acknowledged that his blame was likely misplaced.

He even laughed when I reminded him their relationship—hookups, whatever—was the worst-kept secret ever.

Getting real with my band-brothers reminds me we're all doing the best we can. My bandmates. Our partners. Our families.

Sometimes a little grace goes a long way.

Which is why Fee and I invited Carter and my mom to come over early this morning for breakfast. Neither of us wanted the baggage from our time in Arizona—or from childhood—to bleed into today's meeting. With Mia at

Faye's house, there was freedom to speak freely. Fee and I apologized for leaving so abruptly. Promised to have open hearts.

Moving forward, the four of us agreed to remember the past, and focus on the future.

Our discussion ended when Connor, Ronni, Jace, and Alex arrived a couple hours later. Carter was able to visit with us for a bit before leaving to pick up Zoey. She left Arizona a week prior to Ty's release on doctor's orders, so she's only blocks away. Together, they're meeting Ty at the private air strip at Boeing Field, where his jet is due to land any minute now.

As we wait, I'm aware of the animated conversations going on all around me, but I'm not overly engaged. The energy is charged. Uncertain. I, for one, am nervous.

Yet...hopeful.

Moments later, when the doorbell rings and I lead Ty, Zoey, and Carter into the conservatory, I suddenly feel like I'm floating above my body.

Ty walks in looking magnificent. Healthy. Confident. Authentic. The sorrow behind his eyes has been replaced with acceptance. Love. He's present. Not hiding off somewhere in his mind.

He captivates the room with his story. Explains his childhood and how that's affected him. His diagnosis. His behavior. All around me, tears flow. As for me, I've never heard him detail his own story this way. How he's managed to survive all these years is beyond me. I'm so proud this man, whom I've always considered to be a brother, is my actual brother.

When he's finished, Ty takes a deep breath and deliberately looks at Jace, me, and Connor. "I'll shut up now, but before I do, I'm sorry. I said horrible things to all of you. Things I truly didn't mean. I can't expect any of you to understand. This information is, well … It's a lot. I just need you all to know while I'm never going to be cured, I've done everything in my power to learn how to manage my CPTSD. I understand if you don't want anything to do with me. If the band is truly broken up. I hope that isn't the case, because I was so fucking excited to start things up again. No matter what happens, all of you are my family. I hope you'll find it in your hearts to forgive me. To learn more. To talk to me. I'm an open book. I'm not hiding anymore. And I'm not going to let what happened fucking define me anymore."

Ronni sobs openly, runs to Ty. "I *understand*, Ty. I'm sorry you felt so alone for so long. You're a good man, sweetheart. You deserve happiness. I'm here for you. Connor too."

I think her sentiment is echoed by all of us, as evidenced by the whispers and buzzing between the couples. Jace and Alex leave shortly after he's done, followed by Ty and Zoey, leaving just the six of us.

Fee stands next to where I'm sitting. Her expression is hard to read. I know we were both hoping that Ty and Zoey would stay.

Ronni notices. She crosses the room to embrace my wife. "Are you okay? That was a lot."

"I'm fine." She wiggles her fingers at me so I take her hand and pull her down into my lap. Cradle her head and whisper how much I love her in her ear. Give her a little head snuggle. Breathe her in until she's calm.

I realize we're in our own world when Connor joins us and asks Ronni, "Should we go?"

"No, Connor. Ronni. Please stay. Let's talk this out for a bit." My mom surprises all of us by speaking up. For most of the day, she's kept mum.

Ronni looks up at Connor. "Yes, I'd like that."

"Aye. We'll stay," he says as he kisses her lips.

I jump up and motion to the kitchen. "Fee always has delicious stuff in the fridge. Let's go eat."

"I have some soup I can heat up. Artisan bread." Fee swipes the tears from her eyes. "I'd like us to have some time to decompress after all of that."

I help Fiona pull together a bit of food surrounded by my mom, dad, Connor, and Ronni. As we eat, I'm shocked to learn about Connor and Ronni getting busy in our practice space at Carter's house. Apparently, my mom caught them as they were leaving.

"So are we back together or what?" We're in such a fantastic mood, I can't hold back a minute longer. I *have* to know what Connor thinks about how today went.

Connor sputters over his soup. Ronni thwacks him on the back. "Were you in the same room as me?"

"Uh, yeah. Ty's back in. Jace is in too. Alex wasn't feeling well, that was obvious." I can't help but throw up my hands. Did I misread what just happened?

Fee shoots me a look. "Don't be ignorant, babe. It's unbecoming. Alex was struggling because Zoey's about ready to pop. She's suffered an enormous loss. Jace isn't going to be touring anytime soon."

"Maybe we should just ask." I'm not going to leave things to speculation. I'm just not.

Carter pipes up. "Do you need some time, Zane—"

"No." I cut him off before slurping up a spoonful of soup. After our talk this morning, I'm pissed he's butting into my band's business. I'll let him know how I feel, just not with Connor and Ronni here.

The air in the room gets crunchy. Goddammit. Can I not catch a fucking break?

"Do you all mind if I go pick up Mia?" Fee, who's leaning against the counter, says. "She's at my mom's. I didn't want her to hear any of this. We haven't told her about Ty yet. But, it's time for her to come home."

I hold up my hand. "Can we please have a conversation about this, Fee? I'm trying to wrap my head around what happened today. We need to talk it out."

"Fee, you know I'm mortified. I'm so sorry," Carter interjects as he gets up from his seat and tries to hug her.

She's having none of it and reopens the gaping wound I thought we stitched up this morning. "You should be. I can't help but have sympathy for Ty. The way he grew up. You're equally responsible, Carter, for what he endured. You know that, right?"

"Now, Fee..." Mom tries to intervene.

Fiona turns around so fast it makes my head spin. "No. Don't make excuses for him, Lianne. You're so confusing. You push Carter away. You—"

"Wait." Connor, who has been sitting there the entire time, witnessing our family meltdown, speaks up. "Ronni and I are going to leave. This is family business."

Jesus. It's like the shit show that will never end.

Ronni and Connor pick up their stuff and are out the door like their asses are on fire, leaving the four of us on our own. Again.

Carter cries. Like really, really cries. Something I've never seen in my entire life. Fee looks at me and squeezes her eyes shut, visibly mortified at her own outburst. I pull her into my arms and kiss her head. Somehow comforted by the idea that my world might be in flux, but she and I will always have each other.

She's fought for me every day of her life. Just like I've fought for her. Now it's time to let the world around us settle, and we'll deal with it. Together.

Everyone else can fight their own battles as far as I'm concerned.

Out of the corner of my eye, I see my mom take Carter's hand and bring it to her lips. She sits next to him and brings his head to her chest, where he sobs. Her fingers thread through his hair. Stroke his shoulder. I can see her whisper to him, though I can't hear what she says.

Eventually she looks up, directly at me. "Zane. Carter is your father. He loves you. He's done his best. In my opinion, he's done more than make up for the years he wasn't there for you and then some. This man loves with his entire heart." She kisses his temple. "Even when he makes mistakes, it's never malicious. Never ill-intended. Maybe we should give the two of you some space until our emotions have all settled down. I am not going to put Carter in a position where his health is at risk. Not for one more minute. I nearly lost him. Life is too fucking short."

Mic drop.

Fee and I can only stare slack-jawed as Lianne helps Carter up and ushers him out the front door. She kisses my cheek on the way out and caresses Fee's arm. Then they're gone.

As the car disappears down the drive, Fee looks over at me. Understanding passes between us. We managed to forget a lot of things we worked on in Arizona. It sucks.

Fee continues to keep her talons sharpened so she's ready to deliver a fatal slash at any perceived slight. I'm the opposite. I file my talons down so I don't inadvertently hurt—or drive away—the people I love. Equally destructive, just different..

Fiona is my other half and I'm hers. Flip sides of the coin in many ways.

Now, we have a choice to make. Each of us.

We can hold on for grim death to the past.

Or ... let go.

So we can, at last, both be whole.

Chapter Thirty

Six Weeks Later

I WIPE THE SWEAT off my forehead.

Justice raises his fists in the air. Petra, Daire, and Emilie are doing a choreographed dance routine to the delight of the staff. Wolf stands to the side sullenly. Every now and then he glances at Jetta, who is lip-synching into a wooden spoon.

Tonight's song? *Kick It* by Less Than Zero.

Put it into overdrive

Now I'm just tryin' to stay

alive

And kick it, kick it

I'm just trying to stay alive

And keep my heart open wide

And kick it, kick it

Me, Zoey, and Ronni grab wooden spoons and join Jetta. The four of us shimmy around the dining room and belt out one of LTZ's biggest hits at the top of our lungs. Interact with our back-up dancers, much to the amusement of Ty, Connor, and Zane, who stand to the side, watching the whole spectacle.

When the song is over, Jetta shuts off the music. The guys join us and we're all treated to panty-melting kisses from our respective partners. The staff pretend to fan themselves until I shoo them off to clean up from dinner service.

Gus opens in the new year, all seatings but a few I've held back are sold out for twelve weeks.

Tonight, it was just the six of us plus Carter and Lianne. A mini-celebration and a soft-opening kind of evening. Ty and Zoey have been married for an entire year. Little Oliver was born about a month ago, it's their first night out.

Not that their son is far away. Olga is watching all the kids next door in the green room at The Mission while the adults celebrate. We converted it into a temporary playroom.

"Oooh. Let me get a picture of the three of you." Zoey waves Carter over to where Ty and Zane stand. It takes her at least five tries to get a serious photo between the eye rolls, faux boogies, and general boys-being-boys behavior of three adult rockstar men.

When things settle down, the guys hang out in the lounge area while the ladies visit at the U-shaped dining table.

"You've pulled it off, Fee." Ronni holds up her teacup. We all toast with caffeine-free herbal tea. Zoey's breast-feeding. Ronni and I are avoiding alcohol. Officially, we're each attempting to add members to our respective families. We're both over thirty, and I'm still considered higher risk due to my previous preeclampsia complications, so we've given up the wine in solidarity.

Zoey holds her cup with both palms and blows on the steam. "I wish Alex and Jace could be here."

"I do too." I lean back and watch my team clean the mess up from dinner. "I think they would have liked it."

"When they get back from Italy, it will be nice for the boys to reconnect. I think Jace and Ty need to have a serious conversation, though." Zoey's eyes flick over to Ty, who's joking around with Connor.

"It will be fine. I just know it." Ronni nods. "We'll bring everyone out to the ranch to get Santa pics with the horses, and voila. All will be well. Those horses make everything better."

Every now and then, Justice, Petra, Daire, or Wolf pop over to speak to me. Ask a question. Check in about how the food is. We're a well-oiled machine from all of the work we put in earlier this year.

Ronni nudges Zoey. They stare at me with cheesy grins. Zoey motions for me to speak.

"What?" I shrug. Roll my eyes up into my head. "Why are you looking at me that way?"

"Uh, did I hear you got a phone call?" Ronni gives me an exaggerated wink.

Zane. Fucking Zane. God, how I love him. "Yeah, looks like I'll be nominated as an 'Emerging Chef' at the James Beard Foundation."

"For a 'chef who displays exceptional talent, character, and leadership ability, and who is likely to make a significant impact in years to come, while contributing positively to their broader community,'" Ronni reads from the website.

Zoey shakes her head. "Congratulations, that's so amazing, Fee."

"Thank you. It's definitely a start." I'll admit, the potential accolade feels so validating. I can't help but preen a bit.

The day Ty got home, Zane and I had a serious talk about our future. Realizing Lianne had a valid point about life being too short, we decided to leave the past behind us. Not bury it. Not avoid it. Not even forget it. Just leave it where it belonged. In a place that wouldn't affect our happiness going forward. We've done the work. We have the tools if and when things get hard.

It's time to live our lives.

Zane, with the blessing of his bandmates, fired Katherine and hired Isis Management, who will take over first thing next year. Zane, Ty, and Connor are planning to present Jace with a proposal for future touring when he gets home. Essentially, LTZ won't tour for more than three months at a time, with special exceptions for awards shows, certain festivals, and industry appearances. They're going to work the bands' schedule around the kids' school. My favorite part is each family is getting a custom tour bus so we have our own private space. Finally, all writing and recording of new material will be in Seattle.

At The Mission, we hired a general manager, booking agent, marketing manager. Opening night is New Year's Eve and we're already scheduled well into next year. So far, so good. When we posted the jobs, the crème-de-la-crème of Seattle came running. Apparently, it's a fucking honor to work one of Seattle's only remaining venues dedicated to live music. Especially one that pays high wages, healthcare and retirement, and believes in plenty of PTO.

As for Gus, I called up my team and told them I was ready to reopen. By the next week, my staff was back in Seattle and I presented them with my proposal: a partnership. I'm keeping fifty-one percent of Gus, Wolf keeps his ten percent. The rest is divided between Justice, Petra, Daire and Jetta. Daire and Jetta are responsible for the front of the house. The chefs will rotate oversight of the back-of-the-house on a quarterly basis, taking supporting roles the rest of the year with one entire quarter off.

"Let's go check on the kids." Zoey looks longingly at the wall that separates Gus from The Mission.

"Oh, you are so cute." Ronni side hugs her. "New mommy brain. I swear to God, I'd stare at my boys for hours wondering how such perfect humans came out of my body."

"Uh, because I'm their dad?" Connor's big hands come to rest on her shoulders. He stands behind her. She looks up at him and smiles.

Zane scoots next to me, hanging off the edge of the seat. "Should we take Mia home? It's nearly ten."

"Doesn't matter to us, we'll be up on and off all night." Ty kisses Zoey's head then holds his hand out to her. She takes it and he helps her up.

She motions to her boobs. "Uh, it matters to me. I was trying to be discreet, but if I don't get to Ollie soon..." She makes an exploding sound and corresponding gesture.

"Seems like it's time to go." I laugh. "Thank you all for coming tonight."

"Should this be a once-a-month thing?" Zane offers. "I mean, once Alex and Jace get back."

He's so fucking adorable. And happy. Just like he deserves to be.

"Abso-fucking-lutely." Ty hooks his arm around Zane's neck. Connor just grins.

Ronni and Zoey look to me. "Are you alright with that, Fee?"

"Whose idea did you think it was? Family dinner once a month seems doable to me." I slide my arm around Zane's waist. Lean my head on his neck.

It's funny the difference a year makes. Or a month, even.

Zane and I made a pact to live in the moment. To stop wasting energy on mourning things we wanted that were beyond our control.

We let go of our past ...

Time suddenly stood still.

Fear. Hate. Anger. Hopelessness. Resentment.

Released.

The floodgates of possibility opened up.

And now, here we are, with our friends who are family, living our best life.

Together.

It's not just Zane and I who are timeless.

It's the people we care about too.

Chapter Thirty-One

New Year's Day

CONNOR, JACE, AND I sit at the island in Ty and Zoey's kitchen while our women check out a bedroom they recently converted into a playroom.

In the distance, we can hear squeals of approval and laughter, which means it must be spectacular.

Ty is at the stove making brunch for the whole gang while we relive New Year's Eve, which turned out to be epic.

"Jace, have you pulled up the article yet?" I tug on his arm.

He's rapidly clicking through links on an email our new management company sent us this morning. "Yeah, yeah, just give me a sec ... Oh, here it is. Do you want me to read it?"

"Yeah." Connor, Ty, and I shout in unison.

"Fuck, give me a second." Jace pulls out his reading glasses from his shirt pocket. Puts them on. "Okay, here we go ..."

A glorious return, nearly two-years in the making.

It was apparent Less Than Zero were ready for this delayed and overdue homecoming show. It goes without saying, their performance at the opening of Seattle's Mission nightclub was, hands down, one of their best ever.

LTZ's music is inherently catchy, poignant and impassioned. Lead singer, Tyson Rainier's lyrics are emotional and cathartic, his stage presence almost mythical. Last night didn't disappoint. Rainier was a live wire, full of pure energy and raw passion, making every single member of the audience feel like he was singing directly to them.

Witnessing savant guitarist Zane Rocks' mastery of his instrument is something every music lover in the universe needs to experience. During his extended guitar solo, one might swear that the tips of his fingers had caught fire.

Bassist Connor McGloughlin and Drummer Jace Deveraux are often referred to as the heart of the band. Their technical proficiency and musicianship are not always lauded in the same way journalists speak of Rainier and Rocks, but it's clear that both are necessary elements of the LTZ magic.

Leading up to the show, the crowd was uneasy. The elephant in the room, of course, was Rainier's epic meltdown last summer, which led to a rumored breakup of the band and a long rehab stay for LTZ's troubled lead singer.

I'll admit, it was surreal watching LTZ perform like nothing had happened for most of the show. In fact, the vibe was effortless. The guys have always come across as best friends, their support of each other is legendary.

Every single one of them clearly loved each second of their long-awaited reunion show.

Although new music is promised in the new year, LTZ stuck to the basics. Playing all of the songs that jumpstarted their career for the first third of the show, segueing seamlessly into the entire Z album, and ending with their later hits.

Noticeably absent was their hit single, Strike, from the Phantom Uprising movie, helmed by disgraced director Don Kircher, likely because McGloughlin's wife is television star Ronni Miller, who notoriously exposed him for numerous transgressions in Hollywood.

Nevertheless, witnessing a band as iconic as LTZ sincerely enjoying themselves enhanced what was already a euphoric musical experience for their fans—an extended moment of pure joy with not one, not two, not three, but four encores.

Nearly four solid hours of awesomeness. There's no other way to say it.

Which brings me to the most surprising moment of the night, a revelation LTZ decided to share with its hometown crowd.

At the end of the fourth encore, all four guys took their bow and brought out legendary Limelight guitarist, Carter Pope. Anyone with a pulse knows that Pope is Zane Rocks' father and is a frequent guest musician at LTZ shows.

During the show, however, Ty addressed the crowd and apologized for the incident last summer. Zane joined him and together they introduced Carter as their father. Which means, folks, that Zane and Ty are not just band brothers—they are real brothers.

A jaw-dropping moment that has set the music world abuzz. If you were one of the lucky few in the crowd who experienced that brief but meaningful moment of vulnerability, know that you're now a part of the most iconic moment in Seattle rock history.

LTZ will release new music this spring followed by a brief eight-week US tour this summer followed by three weeks in Europe.

"That's fucking awesome." I'm stoked. Playing together after everything we've overcome made it, quite possibly, one of my favorite shows ever.

Fee leads the women in from the converted playroom. "What's awesome?"

"Read this." Jace hands her his tablet, still looking like a rockstar professor in his readers.

The ladies all gather around to read the article, jostling for position good-naturedly. Every now and then, we hear an ooh or ahh or squeak of approval. The four of us watch them like lovestruck fools. Probably because we are.

Lovestruck fools, that is.

"This is the sweetest article ever, baby." Zoey slithers up to Ty, who's tending to the bacon frying on the flat grill. "Mythical...yeah," she sighs.

Ronni guffaws, nearly spitting out her orange juice. "Uh, we all know what you're really referring to, miss Zoey."

"Not that you'd know about that thing, my love." Connor's arched eyebrow and gruff pout at his wife has us all in stitches.

Of course I take it too far. "It runs in the family." I grab my crotch and wink at Fiona. "Inherited trait and all..."

A chorus of disgusted groans ensues.

"What? Am I wrong?" I pout, just a little. To make Fee laugh.

She grabs my jaw and leans in close. "Yes. Your cock is super huge, Zaney. So, so big. Massive. There. Now your entire family knows." She presses her lips to mine.

"Uh, what's all of this about?" Carter's face is beet red. Lianne looks like she wants to fall through a trap door in the floor.

"Nothing," we all say in unison. Too loudly.

Ty motions to the empty seats at the counter. "Have a seat."

We spend all afternoon hanging out, basking in the glory of being together after our epic reunion. Which, for me, was better than I could have ever hoped for. Considering all this year has in store for us as couples and as a band, events happened as they should have. We've all learned and grown and are in a better place now.

I look forward to every single day I get to spend with my band, their wives and my mom and dad.

And, of course, Fee.

⸻

A couple hours later, Fee, Mia, and I are bundled up in winter coats making the short trek back home. Gus's opening went off without a hitch, Fee popped in a couple times, but Justice ran the show so she could be with me at The Mission.

The little things we're doing to prioritize our relationship make all the difference in the world.

We hang out with Mia doing a puzzle until her bedtime, grateful we have a week before she goes back to school. With the holidays, my dad's proposal, Gus's opening and our show, she's been with Olga too often without us. We plan to spend the entire week doing family stuff. Cherishing our little girl the way she deserves.

"Want me to tuck you in, Meems?" I ruffle her hair as the three of us head upstairs.

She cocks her head. "I'm eight, don't you think I'm too old?"

"Uh, no. I loved it when my mom tucked me in. I think I was at least thirteen before I was too old," I lie, mainly because I want to stretch out my stories with her for as long as she'll let me. While I love the young lady Mia is becoming, I also want to freeze her in time.

"Okay. We're a little behind on *The Flea and the Fly*, as you know." She flips her hair and disappears into her closet, returning two minutes later in her jammies.

I spend the next hour creating the next installment of our story until she drifts off to sleep. I kiss her sweet forehead and shut off the light on her nightstand and leave her to have sweet dreams.

Fee's in bed reading when I cross the long hall into our room. "Hey, sexy cock man." She purses her lips, teasing me about earlier today.

"What? I do have a big cock. Why should Ty get all the mythology?" I cup my junk and shake it.

"I might need to have a look." Fee licks her lips. "Or, a taste."

My clothes are off in ten seconds. I dive bomb the bed and cage a surprised Fee with my arms. "I'm up for that."

"Oh, I feel you." She wriggles against my boner, which I grind against her heat.

I nuzzle her cheek with my nose. Press my forehead to hers. Hover my lips above hers before our mouths fuse together. We don't stop kissing, even as I rip her panties off and draw her little tank top up above her breasts.

"You're luscious." I lick her nipple. Suck it into a hard point. "Delicious." I nibble on her earlobe and press my fingers inside her.

She hums in appreciation, her eyes are half-mast. But, she watches me when I worship her beautiful body. Always. Just as I love to watch her when she explores mine.

I press up to kneel between her legs. Using both thumbs, I spread her lips apart, revealing her swollen clit. I tap it and swirl with my index finger. Her stomach clenches. "Jesus, Zane."

"Yeah, that's me." I shake out my hair around my shoulders. Angle my hips so the underside of my cock rubs along her seam.

She arches up. "You'll be going to hell if you don't feed your huge cock into me. Now."

So I do. Inch by inch until she's squirming. Fee reaches down and rubs herself. Helpfully, I pinch her nipples while I enjoy the show of my dick getting wetter and wetter from her arousal with each thrust. Finally, when I'm at my breaking point, I lean back over and buck into her. Roll my hips. Swivel. Rock. Angle my cock to touch every single millimeter of her channel.

I don't want to waste any of my boys. One of them is going to find it's home and make us a beautiful baby. We're not stressed about it. Or reading up on any fertility shit. Fee's been off birth control for a couple of months now. We trust that our love and rabid desire to procreate will make our dreams come true.

It's no hardship fucking my wife twice a day, that's for damn certain.

Like now, when I'm balls deep inside her.

"Come for me, baby." I stroke her cheek with my palm as I circle her clit.

"Ahhh, Zaney." She grips my ass and holds me against her when she clenches around me, setting me off like a geyser.

When I'm empty, I pull out and lift her hips up over my thighs. It's our new ritual. As soon as I spill my swimmers, we keep her legs elevated for fifteen minutes or so to give them a fighting chance to be the next baby.

"What do you think?" I stroke her thighs. Belly. Hips.

She lies back, watching me. "I'm looking forward to being pregnant again. It will a better experience with you by my side. I can't wait for us to get an ultrasound together. For you to sing and play music to my bump. To bring our little baby home to Mia. It's all I've dreamed of for, well, forever."

"I love you, Fee. Forever and always." Emotion suddenly overwhelms me. I have all I've ever dreamed of, too.

Our love has endured many challenges. Ups and downs. Happy times and tragedies. In this regard, we are not unique. All I have to do is look at my band-mates and their relationships. My dad and my mom. Hell, everyone in the world, truth be told.

What makes us special is Fiona and I have loved each other from the day I was born. Our love is not just romantic, although we're romantic as hell. Our love is not just sexual, although we're sexy as hell.

I'd argue we love each other better on our worst day than most people do on their best. For us, it's not just about friendship, though Fee has always been my best friend.

Our love is a unicorn. A once-in-a-lifetime love that lives in our cells. Pumps through our blood. Fills up our heart.

And most of all, endures.

Until the end of time.

Epilogue - 6 Months Later - A New Beginning

I JUST CAN'T GET over how fucking lucky I am.

Standing with Lianne by my side. Surrounded by a group of truly wonderful friends and family. I look to my left.

Jace's folks and his sisters huddle with Alex, Andrea, and Lena. Baby Lennox is too little to be here tonight, he's back at the hotel with Becca, Jen's wife.

Connor's family stands close by. Liam and Padraig look like the rockstars they are. Seamus, Brennan, and Cillian hover by Rory. Connor's mom, Maureen chats with Ronni, who rubs her nonexistent belly. She announced her pregnancy a couple days ago, Torin and Tristan will get a new baby brother or sister next year.

Zoey and Fee stand close to me, Lianne, and Zoey's parents, Mike and Olivia. Faye isn't part of the picture again, probably for good this time. When she found out Fiona was pregnant, let's just say it didn't go well. I gaze down at my two daughters-in-law, both with newly swollen bellies of about the same size.

By the end of the year, I'll be a grandpa to four precious kids. It's still hard for me to believe, after losing over a decade to my addictions, how grateful I am to be alive. How close I came to missing all of this love.

"I think this is the song before you go on." Zoey grabs my hand, bringing me back to reality.

Zane's guitar tech, Pokey, hands me my old Strat. I strap it on and give her the thumbs up. "I'm ready."

My heart swells with pride when I watch my sons onstage. LTZ kicked off their tour four nights ago with three sold-out hometown shows at Climate Pledge Arena. Tonight is the final Seattle show before the band, in their fancy new tour buses, play thirty dates in twenty cities across the country. Their most recent album is their biggest-selling album ever, which is saying something, considering the sorry state of the music industry these days.

Ty swaggers up to the mic and rips off his Mission tee. The entire crowd loses their ever-loving minds at the sight of shirtless Ty. "Are you ready to take things up a notch?" He holds the mic out to the crowd, who scream back at him.

"Fuck that, I can't hear you." He cups his hand to his ear. "Are you ready for ..."

It's my cue, I step out on stage playing the intro to Limelight's biggest hit, Ready Set Crash. The entire stadium erupts. Zane and Ty flank me. I take full advantage of my time on stage, giving them a show. Zane plays rhythm to my lead. Connor and Jace keep a steady beat. When my extended intro begins to morph into the verse, Ty takes over.

We play five Limelight songs to close out the final encore, and then we're done. The show is over.

But life is truly just beginning.

Not just for my sons, their wives, and their band.

For me too.

I have a story to tell, and I'm just getting started.

***

Look for Kaylene's new stand alone novel The Hate Date a Grumpy Sunshine, Age-Gap, Enemies to Lovers, Billionaire Romance.

For special offers, promotions, news about LTZ and all of my
upcoming releases and all sorts of behind the scenes stuff,
please sign up for my newsletter.

Behind the Scenes

TIMELESS ENCORE EDITION

WELL, THERE YOU HAVE it. The Less Than Zero series is complete.

As a writer, I'm feeling such a huge sense of accomplishment. It started out with my idea for Endless, and creating the world of LTZ has been such a joy for me. I truly had no idea where this would take me, and in many ways I'm glad I didn't know.

Writing is a lot like therapy.

Zane and Fiona come very easily to me. Their history. Their dynamic. Their dialogue. It's all so fluid. Of all the books I've written so far, TE took the least time and was the most "complete" before editing. Maybe I'm getting better at this, or maybe it's just that I connect with these two. Either way, I loved everything about writing this book.

Zane is easily the most complicated character out of the band, in my humble opinion. I'm glad he finally got to express himself and move on from his past. I love his relationship with Mia, so, so much. And, how he loves Fee. So unconditionally. It's so frustrating to him when Fee can't trust what he sees in her. But, he's never angry with her. He "sees" her.

Don't we all really just want to be seen?

Fiona's struggles may have surprised you. It's interesting because she's the most personal character to me. I relate to her in a couple of different ways.

First, I've always struggled with my weight and body image. In fact, I can't think of a time when I didn't. Part of that is because I'm a woman that did not grow up in a time where body-shaming was frowned upon. My first memory of being chastised for my size (and at the time, I was TEENY) was when my uncle called me "lard butt."

It became my nickname. In front of my entire family. Can you imagine? It continued until I was in my late twenties when I told him that he couldn't call me that anymore. To which he replied, "wow, you're so *sensitive*."

Fuck yeah I was. And am. It's hurtful!

Needless to say, I've avoided him ever since with great success.

When I was fourteen or fifteen, a friend had a party with a psychic or tarot card reader or something. I can't remember the exact details, except for one. When it came time to do my "reading" she said something like, "you'll struggle with weight your entire life." At the time, I was maybe 90 pounds soaking wet and on drill team. Talk about negative self-talk to put into someone's head. I've never forgotten that moment and how embarrassed I was that she'd say that in front of my friends.

The truth is, I'm short and I do like to eat. So, I've never been ultra-thin. I've never known a flat belly or thighs that don't touch. I've had lots of shitty comments lobbed at me – both loud and in whisper, as have most other women. I've been heavier than I'd like and in great shape.

Ultimately, I realized none of it matters unless you're comfortable in your own skin.

It took meeting my husband and his fierce defense of me to get me there. And hell, we love to go out to dinner. And eat good food. And drink wine. So sue me. No, don't. Just take the time to love yourself for who you are with all of your beauty and all your flaws.

Ultimately, that is what Timeless Encore is about. A love story that wraps up Zane and Fee, but also the entire band.

Each guy and gal are endearing and frustrating, just like the rest of us. They might say or do the wrong thing in one chapter but redeem themselves incredibly in the next.

I hope you loved LTZ. If you're ready for more from me, I have big plans. At least two new series within the LTZ universe and about a dozen standalones that will get released throughout the next few years. We need to check back in with Carter later this year, of course.

Thank you again for your support, it means the world. As an independent author, connecting with readers is my favorite thing.

Until next time,

Love

Acknowledgments

THIS BOOK WAS AN absolute labor of love, and I couldn't have done it without the help and support of the following awesome rock stars:

Cover Artist/Graphic Designer/Finder of Hotties: Regina Wamba

Editor: Grace Bradley

Formatting: Willow Yanarella

PR: Dani Sanchez, Wildfire Marketing

Literary Agent: Stephanie Phillips, SBR Media

Website Maven: Sherri Kiarsis, Ruby Moon Designs

My Right Hand: Willow Yanarella

YAY to KAYLENE'S KREW !!!

Beta Readers: Anna Theurer & Beth Carbutt

My Inspirations: Gareth, Sheila, Kris

Special thanks to the following authors and friends who have "lent" their characters to me for special guest appearances:

Mari Carr: Sky Mitchell and Teagan Collins appear in Ruby Tuesday: Rock Star Romance (Wild Irish Book 2); Hunter Maxwell and Ailis Mitchell appear in Wild Desire: Rock Star Friends to Lovers (Wilder Irish Book 2).

Wynne Roman: Ajia Stone and Bree Gallagher appear in Wycked Crush (Wycked Obsession Book 1); Zayne Prescott and Grace Alexander appear in Wycked Redemption (Wycked Obsession Book 2).Cari Quinn & Taryn Elliott: Deacon McCoy and Harper Pruitt appear in Rocked (Lost in Oblivion Book 1); Juliet Reece and Tristan Eves appear in Triple Trouble A Rockstar Romance (Found in Oblivion Book 2) and Finding Forever: A Rockstar Romance (Found in Oblivion Book 7).

Cari Quinn & Taryn Elliott: Deacon McCoy and Harper Pruitt appear in Rocked (Lost in Oblivion Book 1); Juliet Reece and Tristan Eves appear in Triple Trouble A Rockstar Romance (Found in Oblivion Book 2) and Finding Forever: A Rockstar Romance (Found in Oblivion Book 7).

L.M. Dalgleish: Tex McLain appears in Fractured Dreams: A Fractured Rock Star Romance; Connor Byrne appears in Fractured Hearts: A Fractured Rock Star Romance

Julia Wolf: Iris Adler appears in Falling in Reverse A Rock Star Romance (The Seasons Change)

Dedication

Without my husband and his golf hobby, the Less Than Zero series wouldn't exist. Thank you, G, for encouraging me to write and for continuing to support me throughout this crazy journey, I love you.

About the Author

KAYLENE WINTER IS AN best-selling author of steamy, contemporary romance.

Each character-driven novel is filled with snappy dialogue, pop-culture references and enough steam to make you fan yourself. Kaylene weaves authenticity, emotion and angst into a turbulent rollercoaster ride of love, passion and soul-searing romance always ending with a delicious HEA.

Kaylene lives in Seattle with her amazing Irish husband and her Pomsky, Phalen. She loves creating art of all kinds.

Other Titles